I0627255

Praise for *Shadowland*

At last, the much anticipated second book in the trilogy about life, murder, and mystery on Lake Vermillion in northern Minnesota. Author Engstrom brilliantly follows the lives of her characters in two different time eras and brings it all to a fateful, stunning finish. It was a treat to pick up on the lives of Carl and Elsa, stars of *The Fox*, book one in the trilogy, and meet new characters with backstories that will keep you turning pages. The writing is so beautiful you will feel, touch and smell every bit of the lives of these fascinating characters.

~~Lynn Garthwaite, author of *Starless Midnight*

Shadowland is a haunting, beautifully written mystery that lingers long after the final page. From the moment a skull surfaces in Lake Vermilion, Karen Engstrom draws us into a layered story of secrets, memory, and quiet resilience. With evocative prose and a deep sense of place, she bridges past and present to deliver a suspenseful, emotionally rich tale that's as intimate as it is chilling.

~~John Gaspard, author of the Eli Marks Mystery Series

Beautifully written, with compelling characters and a suspense-filled plot.

~~Brian Lutterman, author of *Incel* and the Pen Wilkinson series

In *Shadowland*, Karen Engstrom returns the reader to the Northwoods where Carl and Elsa are spending another summer at their remote cabin near the Canadian border. Engstrom deftly weaves a tapestry of place, time, and circumstance, allowing the reader to be fully-immersed in the story. When Elsa reels in a human skull from the depths of tranquil Lake Vermilion, they are plunged into a captivating mystery of lost love, revenge, and organized crime stretching back to Prohibition's darkest secrets. Shadowland is truly a slice of compelling history and suspense that will hold you spellbound until the final page.

~~Rob Jung, best-selling author of *The Reaper*

Shadowland, Karen Engstrom's sequel to *The Fox*, reunites readers with the Carl and Elsa Swanson family and Lake Vermillion in northern Minnesota. The Swansons hope their return trip will afford them time to relax and enjoy lake activities. Instead, the unnerving discovery of a human skull alters those plans. The subsequent and complex investigation brings to light an illegal bootlegging operation and murder from decades before. Enstrom intertwines noteworthy historical facts, several storylines, complex human relationships, and intrigue in her multi-faceted book. Another winner!"

~~Christine Husom, Author of the Winnebago County Mysteries and Snow Globe Shop Mysteries.

Karen Engstrom's *Shadowland* is the second installment of a trilogy, beginning with *The Fox*. We are back together again with Carl and Elsa up north, at Lake Vermillion. Karen carries the characters masterfully, and has plotted out a fantastic historical mystery. Can't wait for number three!

~~Jessie Chandler, Author of the Shay O'Hanlon Caper Series

Shadowland

Karen Engstrom

СКУНС

ACKNOWLEDGMENTS

For me, a story is usually sparked by something simple, like an old newspaper article tucked in an even older book or a photo found in a box of family memorabilia. In this case, Shadowland was based on both — an article and a photo unrelated to each other except for being about the same lake. Fertile ground for the challenge of tying the two together in a story. Thank you, Dad, for never throwing anything interesting away and for tossing the junk.

Most of this novel takes place on two lakes, one of which I am very familiar with. A trip to the other seemed necessary to learn more about it. The nice people at Prothero's Post Resort in Angle Inlet, Minnesota, and at River Air in Kenora, Ontario, were so helpful in making it come to life for me.

Sincere appreciation goes to Michael MacBride of Salty Books Publishing for all the amazing things he does to get a book across the finish line. Thanks to my family for their love and support. And the winner of the big door prize is Bill Allan, my partner, for his endless patience, encouragement, and wonderfully helpful penchant for finding my mistakes.

I have read and enjoyed thousands of books over my lifetime, and it's amazing to me that now I am creating books for others to enjoy. Thank you for reading *Shadowland.*

Hälsa dem därhemma. Hälsa far och mor.

Hälsa gröna hagen. Hälsa lille bror.

Om jag hade vingar, flöge jag med dig!

Svala, flyg mot hemmet. Hälsa ifrån mig!

~ Refrain to Hälsa Dem Därhemma (Greet Them at Home) a popular song among Swedish immigrants. Music by Edith Worsing and lyrics by Ludvig Brandstrup, 1922.

Elbow Lake
Bass, Crappie, and Northern Pike
Moose
Bear
Me too!
Swan Lake
LINGER LONGER CAMPS
Black Creek
Black Lake
Black Bay
RILEY'S LODGE
Norwegian Bay
RUTHERFORD'S CHAP'S LODGE
PEHRSON LODGE
MUSKEGO LODGE
MAY'S PLACE
Niles Bay
VERMILION LODGE
Beaver
Vermilion Dam
GRANDVIEW
TREASURE ISLANES
Hunting
Cultivated farm lands
COOK
Frazer Bay
Little Fork River
Modern resorts, cabins and summer homes dot the shores of Lake Vermilion.
BEAUTIFUL Lake VERMILION
The historical information is believed to be accurate.
Copyright 1936 W.A. Fisher Co., Virginia, Minnesota
Farm Lands
Winding Roads! Drive carefully
Early Indians were permitted as many wives as they pleased.
Good roads all the way

Game Reserve
Long Lake
Bootleg Lake
Little Sioux River
Old Indian and trappers route to Lac La Croix.
Crab Lake
Pine Creek
Western Lake
Pine Lake
Trout Lake
Wolf Lake
Wolf Bay
MORCOM INN
HILLCREST LODGE
GLENWOOD LODGE
Bear Creek
Mud Creek
Bear Lake
Bass Lake
Pine Island
MOCCASIN POINT LODGE
ISLE O'PINES RESORT
DAISY BAY STORE
TABINS CAMP
BIRCHPOINT INN
VERMILION BEACH
BAY VIEW INN
BIRCHWOOD
Lost Lake
EVERETT BAY RESORT
Big Bay
Ely Island
Armstrong Bay
Armstrong R.
Jasper Peak
SOUDAN
D., M. & I. R. Ry.
East Two River
Brook Trout Fishing
TOWER
ARONSON BOAT LIVERY
PIKE BAY RESORT
THE "Y"

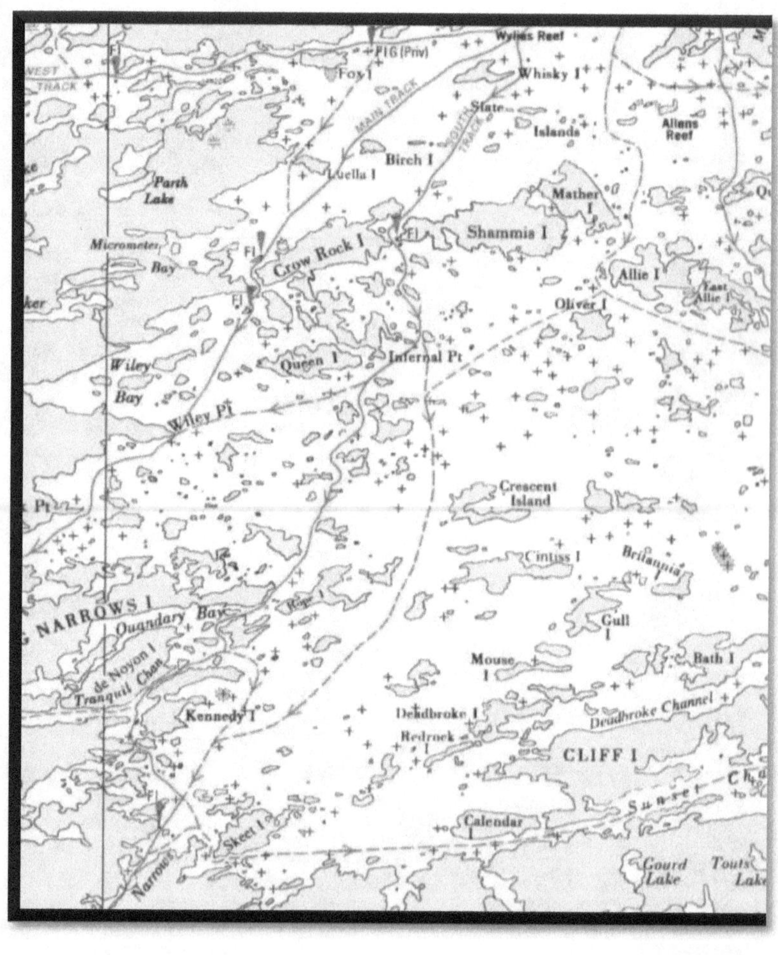

Wylias Reef
FIG (Priv)
Fox I
Whisky I
WEST TRACK
MAIN TRACK
SOUTH TRACK
Slate
Allans Reef
Islands
Birch I
Luella I
Parth Lake
Mather I
Shammis I
Micrometer Bay
Crow Rock I
Fl
Allie I
East Allie I
Fl
Oliver I
Fl
Wiley Bay
Queen I
Infernal Pt
Wiley Pt
Crescent Island
Pt
Cintiss I
Britannia
NARROWS I
Rye I
Gull
Ouandary Bay
Mouse I
Bath I
de Noyon I
Tranquil Chan
Deadbroke Channel
Kennedy I
Deadbroke I
CLIFF I
Redrock I
Sunset Chan
Fl
Calendar
Skeet I
Gourd Lake
Touts Lake
Narrows

Lake of the Woods
Northern Portion

The Discovery

1950 LAKE VERMILION

CHAPTER 1

The garden always looks so vibrant in early summer, Jane thought. The greens were so bright, and there wasn't a faded flower or dead leaf in sight. She had enjoyed the same thought about her other garden, some six hundred miles to the south just a month before. Of course, the spring garden at their home on Castlewood Terrace in Chicago was much more diverse, with formal beds of tulips, hyacinths, daffodils, and crocuses tastefully spread between old-growth lilacs and peonies heavy with blossoms. The smell of spring flowers was one of her favorite things about the garden. She missed seeing the mid- and late-summer flowers, being at the lake all summer. Nesbitt, the gardener, did the work at the Bradleys' primary residence in Chicago.

Up here at Lake Vermilion, though, there was no gardener, or cook, or maid for that matter, but Jane didn't mind. She liked working with the flowers, weeding, and keeping the casual beds looking their best. Each year before coming up north, she consulted Nesbitt about techniques and things to try with the plants she tended on the island. He always packed a box or two of clippings, seeds, chemicals to use as pesticides, one or two of the latest popular tools, and, of course, a new pair of work gloves. He also sent with her small plants he had started in the glass greenhouse attached to the side of the carriage house of the rectory.

She laid her small cultivator down at the edge of the flower bed, took off her gardening gloves, and set them neatly on top of the wood-handled tool. Her long-sleeve gardening shirt was unbuttoned and flapped gently in the wind against her thin frame. She walked over to an ornate bench made from cast iron, placed strategically for a view of both the flowers and the lake. From the high point of the island, the view was spectacular. She rested her hand on the back of the bench to look over the garden, then brushed a few leaves off the seat before she sat down. She breathed deeply and took it all in – the freshness of the lake air, the fragrance of pine and flowers, and the musky dirt of the garden soil. It was a beautiful day, sunny with lots of fluffy white clouds. A gentle wind from the southwest gave the lake a textured look like a wrinkled blue silk scarf pulled from the pocket of a magician's suit of forest green.

Across the water, she noticed the open boat with a man and a woman fishing and a small child standing at the side of the boat. Her breath caught with unwanted envy when she saw the man lean forward to the woman and kiss her. She looked away. Her thoughts wandered as she took in the expanse of water and sky and the deep green forest, turning back now and again to watch the couple continue their fishing. Her attention happened to be on them when the woman seemed to reel in a fish. Jane smiled in silent congratulation that the woman had been the one to make the catch. They seemed particularly interested in the fish, and then suddenly put their rods down and took off. She watched the boat as it retreated toward Moccasin Point. When it was out of sight, she sighed and turned her attention back to her immediate surroundings.

Jane glanced around. There were no house guests right now, but she wanted to make sure she wouldn't be disturbed by her husband. She took an envelope out of her thin jacket pocket and looked at it. It was unsealed, so she just lifted the flap. She stared down into the space holding the single sheet of paper, thinking that at some point she must burn it as the writer had suggested. But, she still couldn't make herself do that for some reason she didn't fully understand.

She sighed again and took out the paper and unfolded it, setting the envelope on the bench beside her, tucking the edge of it under her leg so it wouldn't blow away. There were no tears anymore when she read the words. For the first few years, the tears came with big sobs, and she had to refrain from reading it unless she was going to be alone for some time. The first time her husband asked her why she was sad, she was surprised that he had even noticed her tears. After that, she was more careful. Then there were the years when she no longer sobbed, but the tears fell silently.

She read it now with dry eyes for the thousandth time.

My darling,

If I were a firefly, I would flicker in front of your footsteps to light your way through the dark night to my arms.

If I were a wren, I would warble and sing to guide you to my side.

If I were a fox, I would appear in your sight, and lure you through the woods to my embrace.

If I were a butterfly, I would flit from blossom to blossom enticing you to come to me.

If I could take on other forms, no matter what form I took, I would guide you to my arms and my love.

We should be together always, not just in the shadows. Oh, how I wish we could be together in the daylight. Our souls are meant to be together through all the days and all the nights of our lives. Meet me tomorrow night. The moon is waning so I will not be seen on the water. I can be at the small cove by midnight. I'll wait for you there with beating heart. If they knew of our love, I know they would find a way to end us. Please be careful. Burn this after you read it. Know in your heart how much I love you. You have no need for a piece of paper telling you so. Please burn this letter — and any you might have kept for sentimental reasons - so no harm can ever come to you because of my loving words. I couldn't bear that thought.

All my love, until we meet. Robert

Twenty years ago, this summer, she had retrieved it from the secret place where they would leave notes to each other. There had been no tears the first time she read it or the other times during that day when she slipped away to feast on its words in anticipation of the meeting she and her lover would have that night.

She had waited at the rendezvous, but he never showed. Initially, the tears that came the next day were of anger and hurt. As the days passed, the tears were filled with concern and worry. And finally, they were tears of loss and utter sadness.

One Sunday some years ago, while she sat in the front row of the People's Church listening to her husband preach to an enthralled congregation, she had an epiphany. It made her smile, now that she had thought of it as such. Epiphany was such a biblical word, and she didn't have a shred of religion in her. Perhaps it was the surroundings of the simple but beautiful place of worship that had evoked the word. Regardless, the thought she had had that morning changed everything for her; thus, it was an epiphany.

What she realized was the real meaning of her tears and how shallow they had become. They were a sham of lost love. She had loved him, yes, and she had shed initial tears of pain, yes, but the epiphany was that she suddenly realized all the tears since those tears of real pain and disappointment of his betrayal were just tears of self-pity. After the pain had passed and she recognized he was never coming back, she felt sorry for herself and for her pathetic fate – abandoned by her lover, destined to tend to her aging and loveless husband, childless and lonely. The thought that she was crying out of self-pity made her so angry. She was not one for self-pity. She shifted abruptly in her seat, bumping the person next to her on the pew. The woman gave her a puzzled look, as if to ask her if she was all right. Jane faked a smile and nodded with a set jaw and turned back to face the pulpit where her husband was going on and on about finding one's true worth in the eyes of God and being true to one's inner core of morality given to us by God. The irony did not escape her, and she vowed never to cry another tear of self-pity.

After the epiphany, she was tempted to destroy that last letter as she had all the others. Still, she could not bring herself to do it, despite the complicated pain it carried in its very existence.

Lately, the letter had become something of a talisman for contemplation, and she often read it to begin a lengthy and conscious thought process about her life and the choices she had made and about good and evil, love and respect, loyalty and endurance, and, more recently, about freedom and pain.

Oh, for a chance to do it all again - differently this time, she thought.

Without meaning to, she whispered out loud, "Where are you now, my love?"

CHAPTER 2

It had been a long winter, and Carl and Elsa were looking forward to summer at the cabin. The car trip from Chicago to Lake Vermilion in Northern Minnesota had taken much longer than usual. Katy, who was only eighteen months old and newly potty trained, was the reason for so many stops. They only made good time when she was stretched out on the back seat, sleeping, the plaid car blanket covering her. Highway 41 through Wisconsin took them through so many towns familiar to Carl, places he and Elsa had stopped to eat or get gas, or places Carl had gone with friends to fish long before he and Elsa met.

But now their destination was much further north, almost to the Canadian border. As he drove, Carl mused that the best thing he had ever done, other than proposing to Elsa, was to buy the property on Lake Vermilion. It was as much like the home he left back in Sweden as he could ever imagine any place ever being. But then he knew that time can bend memories to make a contented person happier. The sweet memories he had of his childhood home in Sweden were based on the love of his family and painted the harsh reality of everyday life back then with a rosy haze. He had a profound understanding of his good fortune during the extremes of sickness, poverty, and war. He glanced at his wife and child now and again with a full heart.

It was very late in the evening when they arrived at the dirt road, marked only by a few mailboxes, which took them a quarter mile back into the woods to the cabin on Daisy Bay. Katy was asleep, so they left her in the car until they had unloaded everything. Elsa had just finished making the crib, tucked behind a cloth screen in the corner of the main room, as Carl carried the toddler in from the car. He kissed her on the forehead and tucked her in.

"I'm bushed," said Elsa, pulling off her cardigan. "I'll put the food away and do the rest in the morning."

Carl just nodded with a smile and headed outside to walk down to the dock with Bruno, the big lab-mix dog. The sky was darkening from the east, but there was still the flame of vibrant color to the west for which the lake was named. He breathed in and held his breath as he sat on the bench he had built at the edge of the dock. There was no view of the sunset because the small bay faced due south, but still, the lake itself appeared to be on fire with color. Bruno sat down next to Carl with an umph and leaned heavily against his people's leg. The two sat in silence until the color was gone, then, after a quick stop to take care of business for the night, they returned to the cabin.

Bruno circled his bed on the floor near the cast iron stove and lay down with a thump. The small, hammered brass table lamp in the tiny bedroom was the only light on. When Carl climbed in next to Elsa, he thought, "It doesn't get any better than this." He could tell she was already asleep, so he got comfortable and gave the back of her neck a soft kiss.

The following two days passed quickly as they settled in for the summer. There were so many chores to do when 'opening' the cabin. One was to lower the boat from its sling which held it in the rafters of the boat house during the winter months. When they finally got the boat in the water, Carl and Elsa Swanson were both excited to be out on the lake. Carl had prepared the rods with trolling lures the night before, so they were ready to go in the morning. Over breakfast, they discussed where to fish and decided on Frazer Bay even though it was farther than their usual fishing spots.

Lake Vermilion, with its twelve hundred miles of shoreline and hundreds of islands, is one of the most complicated bodies of water in Minnesota. Daisy Bay and Frazer Bay were linked by the narrow section of water. Because their motor was small for the heavy wooden boat, the trip in the 17-foot open fishing boat took them almost an hour.

They slowed down as they entered the strait, Mocassin Point Lodge stood on a small grassy area off to the left where the road ended in a boat launch. They rounded the rocky, narrow point of land, which was the eastern point of Frazer Bay, and turned sharply to the west, hugging the shoreline. The huge mass of granite rising out of the water, topped with stately pines, looked like most of the shoreline of the big lake – picturesque Northwoods beauty.

Katy, in her gray corduroy overalls and pink gingham shirt, napped most of the way on Elsa's lap, the noise of the outboard motor humming a lullaby. Her little red kapok life jacket was soft like a pillow between them. Elsa Swanson loved riding in the boat and preferred facing forward to have the wind in her face, but when Katy was on her lap, she sat facing the back to protect Katy. Watching her husband, one hand on his knee, the other on the handle of the Evinrude, squinting against the wind, she thought again how fortunate they were. Carl had returned unharmed from the war, their painting business was prosperous enough to allow them to have summers at the cabin, and after nine years of marriage, they had a beautiful child. She looked down at the sweet little girl and smiled as she pulled her closer. Life's good, she thought.

Bruno snoozed too, sprawled on the life jackets on the bottom of the boat between the two forward seats, his big black lab body stretched out comfortably. When Carl slowed the Evinrude to a crawl, Bruno sat up and stretched. He sniffed the air, hopped over the next seat to be close to his people, and checked out the toddler who also awoke when the boat slowed down. He was, after all, in charge of Katy's safety and well-being, so he sniffed her head to toe, which made her giggle sleepily. Satisfied everything was as it should be, he lay back down, although he kept his eyes open, just in case.

Elsa set Katy down between the seats on a folded quilt, took a couple of wooden blocks from her bag, and gave them to the little girl to play with. Carl rolled up the sleeves of his plaid flannel shirt, untangled the rods, and handed Elsa hers. They dropped their fishing lines and began to troll along the shore for walleye. Half an hour went by. It was quiet except for the thrumming noise of the motor. Elsa had a nibble or two, but nothing serious. Carl wasn't even that lucky.

"Oh, honey. Don't look so disappointed. It's such a beautiful day. A perfect June day. You know the walleye like it better when it's a little overcast," said Elsa.

"Oh, I didn't know I was that obvious," he said. "Okay. Who says we have to catch something every time we're out fishing, anyway?"

After a minute, he continued, "So I think we should move over to the reefs in Black Duck Bay and try our luck over there."

They reeled in their lures and laid the poles across the seat next to each other, careful to have the lures away from both the dog and the baby. Katy was still sitting on the floor, and Elsa pulled her tight up against her legs as Carl cranked the motor's throttle handle. They drove further west, where there were reefs that promised to hold the fish they'd have for dinner.

Carl again slowed to trolling speed just outside the red and white markers, which bobbed in the waves, warning of the potential disaster waiting beneath the surface for any boater who ignored them. Katy pulled herself up on tiptoe and hung on to the gunwale to see down into the water. She made gurgling sounds that made her parents laugh. Carl leaned the distance between the seats and gave Elsa a kiss.

"I think she's calling the fish," he said. "Here fishy, fishy, fishy! Here fishy, fishy, fishy," he called in a high-pitched, funny voice.

Katy squealed happily and flung herself at her dad. Carl returned her hug and sat her on his lap with one arm around her as he steered the outboard motor with the other.

"You go ahead and drop your line. I have better things to do," he said to Elsa. He tickled his daughter as he held her on his lap, and she giggled some more.

"Okay. I'll show you I can be the one to catch dinner," said Elsa with a smirk.

She lowered her line into the water. As they trolled the reef, they chatted about things they planned for the summer, what they expected to get done during their vacation at the cabin, and if there would be a good crop of blueberries. They talked about their visit the day before to Tower, the small town where they bought groceries and supplies, about who they saw and about how nothing ever seemed to change, year after year.

"Say, aren't we somewhere near where that man who started the public library in Tower has his island?" asked Elsa, "I really love that quaint little library. Next year, I want to bring up a bunch of books from home to donate."

"Yeah, you're right. We are near his place. Preston Bradley is his name and he owns that island right over there. Black Duck Island."

"Just think. A whole island all to himself!"

"We should drop in on them sometime. He's invited us, you know."

"What do you mean 'invited us'? I didn't know we'd been invited anywhere," said Elsa with a huff.

"Remember? Yes, I told you. Eric and I painted his home on Castlewood Terrace in Chicago a year or so ago. We got talking, you know, and I mentioned we had a place on Lake Vermilion. Of course, I already knew about his place, but I pretended I didn't know. I was interested to see what kind of man he is. Turns out he's quite humble. Just said he had a cabin on the world's most beautiful lake. He's been coming up here since 1916. He said that we should stop by any time. I've bumped into him several times since then 'cause we got to paint the Sunday school building, too. And he's repeated his invitation. His wife, Jane, is quite nice. Kind of quiet and reserved. She's a lot younger than he is though, but they both seem like swell people."

"Okay, then, maybe we should stop by there sometime. There are so many islands, which one is it exactly?"

"It's that island right there to the west," said Carl, pointing in that direction. But Elsa was looking at her rod.

"Oh, no!" Elsa exclaimed. "I think I'm stuck!"

"Don't worry," said Carl, standing Katy between his knees. He reached back and put the motor in reverse for a moment.

Elsa released tension on the line to prevent it from breaking as Carl turned the boat around to drag the line behind the culprit rocks that had snagged her lure.

"Don't pull on it. Let it loose," he commanded urgently, staring at the taut line. He hated to lose a nice lure. It was a matter of pride that he seldom got stuck himself and hadn't lost a lure to the rocks in several years. But he tried to be patient with his less experienced wife.

"I know. I know," she replied, a bit peeved. It wasn't the first time she'd been stuck, after all.

She fed the line out as Carl guided the boat in a large circle around the minuscule point on the surface where her line entered the water. They both stared at the spot as if concentrating on it would release the lure.

"Okay, now give it a jerk," Carl said, when they had reached a certain point.

Elsa held the rod upright and snapped it a few times, trying to extricate the lure. The line whipped through the air, allowing the lure to drop, hopefully to find free passage to the surface. No luck. Carl maneuvered the boat so it was directly in line with their initial approach, which logically was the best place to try to pull the lure free - it went into the snare from that direction, so it should come out that same way. He held Katy snuggly between his knees, and she stood quietly, sensing the tension between her parents.

"Try again," he said.

Elsa whipped her pole gently a few times. Still no luck.

"Jerk it harder," he said, "but not so hard you'll set it permanently in the rocks."

"Okay. Okay. I'm trying," she said as she gave her rod a sharp snap backward over her head.

Suddenly, her pole relaxed, and the line loosened a bit.

"Did you break the line?"

"I don't know. I don't think so. I think the lure came loose," she said.

She started reeling in the line, feeling some resistance. The line was still taut and bent the pole slightly.

"Something's on the line," she said, "It's loose but heavy. Not a fish. I can tell that. It's a dead weight. Not swimming around or pulling."

"Must be a branch," said Carl, "judging by the bend of the pole. There're no weeds out here."

As the end of the line came close to the boat, they saw a round piece of wood, like a burl, attached to the hook. Elsa continued to reel it in and, as it approached the side of the boat, she lifted her rod and swung the object over the side of the boat, grabbing the line with one hand as she did so. She lowered it into the space where Bruno was lying. Annoyed at being disturbed, he sat up and snuffled. He nosed the object and woofed his objection at the intrusion.

"Careful, Bruno. Watch out for the hooks," said Carl.

Elsa had leaned forward, complaining about the water that the object had splashed on her gabardine pants as it had landed next to Bruno and picked it up. She started to remove the lure's hook when her face turned pale. Katy had been squealing in delight at her mom's entertaining gyrations with the pole and the swinging object, but she went quiet when she sensed the change in her mother's expression. Something was wrong.

"Honey, I don't think we can have this for dinner, and it's definitely not a piece of wood," she said.

"What is it?" Carl asked as he concentrated on steering away from the reef.

Without hesitation, she rubbed at the thin layer of greenish algae, confirming her suspicion. "It's a human skull," she said.

Carl shifted the motor into neutral.

They both sat still, stunned. Without realizing they were thinking the same thing, they remembered the body they had found in the lake the summer before last.

Elsa set the skull down on the pile of life jackets. She wiped her hands on her pants – long, hard strokes against the gabardine to rid herself of the slime and the memories.

"I can't imag…"

"What are the chanc…"

They both spoke at the same time and stopped mid-sentence, staring at each other. No words were needed for the understanding they had. The trauma of finding their friend, Ike Isaacson, lying face down in the shallow water off Gull Island was something they didn't talk about often, but the shock and grief they each felt were transparent to the other. Carl let go of the motor handle and reached for Elsa's hand. After a moment, Elsa reached for the baby. Katy went to her mom and started to fuss. Elsa reached into her bag and gave the child a zwieback to occupy her.

"What should we do?" asked Elsa.

"Last time, I stayed with the body while you went for help. We can't do that here, though," said Carl, "but somehow we have to be able to show where we found it."

"Let's both concentrate on where we are in relationship to the shore and the markers. We'll be pretty close at least when we come back," said Elsa.

"How far have we drifted since you pulled it out of the water?" asked Carl.

"Not far. I'd say it was right over there," Elsa said, pointing about ten feet away.

"Okay. I've got an idea," said Carl, "I'm not sure this will work but it's worth a shot. The anchor rope isn't very long, you know. We only use it to anchor close to shore. But maybe this will work."

He reached into his tackle box for his knife and used it to cut the lure off his fishing line. He tossed the lure into the tackle box. He tied the fishing line to the end of the anchor rope in the convoluted double loop knot he always used to fasten lures to the line.

"Hold the pole while I lower the anchor," he said to Elsa. He put the motor in gear and positioned the boat close to where he thought Elsa's lure had hooked the skull. He put the motor in neutral again and began to lower the anchor hand over hand down into the water. It went straight down, taking the fishing line with it. When the anchor rope was taut, he took the pole from Elsa. He whipped it back and forth to test the line. It seemed to hold.

"I sure hope this works," Carl said. "Hand me a life jacket, will you?"

Elsa reached behind her, grabbed an orange canvas life jacket by the strap, and handed it to Carl. He put the rod between his knees and held it firmly. Then he pulled a little more fishing line off the reel and tied it to the strap buckle of the life jacket. When the jacket was securely tied, he used the knife to cut the fishing line and dropped the life jacket into the water. They watched it bob gently as they drifted slowly away.

"My thought is if the lake doesn't get too rough, the fishing line should hold," said Carl. "But it's anybody's guess how long that sixty-pound test line will last if the wind picks up and the waves start yanking on the life jacket."

"Okay. So where do we go now? I'm not that familiar with this part of the lake," said Elsa.

"There's Shamrock Landing. They're new and would definitely have a phone. Or we could head toward home and stop at Moccasin Point."

"Let's just go back to Moccasin Point," suggested Elsa.

Carl nodded and started to pull away from the reef slowly. When he was sure he was clear, he sped up and took a gentle arch to the east. After twenty minutes or so, they had gone a mile and a half and headed south into the entrance of Vermilion Dells. They slowed down as they approached Moccasin Point Lodge and came to a stop at a dock near the public boat ramp.

"I think you should cover your 'catch' with something," said Carl, turning off the motor.

Elsa took a small quilt out of the baby's bag and threw it loosely over the skull, which looked like it was just a bump in the pile of life jackets.

Elsa held Katy as Carl hopped out and tied up the boat. Then she handed the child up to him and stepped onto the dock, too. They walked together up the dirt path to the main building. The dog, who had jumped out first, led the way.

"Bruno, you stay out here," said Carl when they came up to the building.

They made their way across the wide wooden porch to the front door, and, good dog that he was, Bruno stepped to the side and lay down. They entered the large community room through the screen door and, once inside, hurried through the small bar area to the office in the back. They had met the owner, Sven Nordman, several times and knew him to be a level-headed person. They knocked on the door, which stood slightly ajar.

"'Allo?" a voice called from inside.

Pushing the door open, Carl stepped in and said, "Hey, Sven. Sorry to bother you. Would you mind if we used your telephone? It's kind of urgent."

Sven looked a little concerned, but answered quickly, "A' course. Go right ahead."

Sven nodded to both Elsa and Carl as he left the room and shut the door.

Carl set Katy down, and she ran to her mother. He went around the desk, picked up the receiver, and listened. All the phones in the area were party lines shared with several neighbors. Although Carl and Elsa didn't have a phone at their cabin, they knew the protocol. It was polite to make sure the line was not being used before dialing. If you picked up the receiver and heard voices, you hung up immediately and tried again in a few minutes. If you were chatting on the phone and heard the telltale click of someone picking up their receiver, you wrapped up your conversation quickly so your neighbor could use the line.

Carl heard nothing, so he dialed '0'. After the rotating dial clicked all the way around and the operator answered, Carl asked to be connected to the Deputy Sheriff's Office in Tower. The ringing only lasted a few seconds.

"Deputy Sheriff's Office," said the voice.

"Hi. This is Carl Swanson. Is Harvey there?"

"Hi, Carl. This is Patrolman Korchenko. You sound a little upset. Is this an emergency? Can I help you?"

Carl thought for a second and replied, "Not really an emergency, but it is urgent."

"Okay. Well, the Deputy Sheriff just pulled up and should be coming in any minute. Hold on."

There were muffled sounds as Korchenko rustled the phone against papers on his desk, pushed his chair back. Carl could hear footsteps as Korchenko stepped out into the back hall.

"Harvey!" the assistant deputy called out, "Telephone!"

A few more muffled footsteps and noises, then, "Hello. This is Deputy Sheriff Pittella."

"Hi, Harvey. This is Carl Swanson. I don't really know how to say this other than straightforward," Carl paused for a beat. "We were trolling the reefs in Frazer Bay near Black Duck Island and Elsa got stuck."

Harvey chuckled despite himself. He was fond of the younger couple from Chicago. They had been stalwart and helpful through the murder investigation of Isaacson's murder the summer before last. So, he refrained from voicing the comment that was on the tip of his tongue. Instead, he waited.

"We worked at getting the lure loose and when Elsa finally

was able to pull in her line, we saw she had hooked a skull," finished Carl.

"A skull. Hah. Are you sure?" said Pittella after a long moment.

"Yes. There's no mistaking it."

"Where are you now?"

"We're at Moccasin Point Lodge using Sven's telephone."

"Do you have the item in question with you?" asked Pittella.

"Yes."

"Can you remain with the item until I get there?"

"Of course. We'll be by our boat down at the dock."

"First, tell me. Will you be able to show me where you found the item?"

"Yah, sure. We left a life jacket attached to our anchor line at the spot," said Carl.

"I should have known you'd have thought of something. Okay, then. We'll come by boat. Please wait for us where you are. Korchenko and I will be there in…" He looked at his watch before continuing, "in approximately forty-five minutes."

"Okay. We'll watch for you," said Carl.

"And tell Elsa no 'Nick and Nora' stuff, okay?"

"Yah, sure. No problem," Carl said with a laugh. "See you soon."

The black duck is a close relative of the mallard and often crossbreeds with them. They have similar calls, quacks actually, but differ significantly in their plumage from their colorful relatives. Both male and female black ducks are black with orange fleshy legs and vary only in the color of their bills. Males have yellow bills and females have dull green bills. With a wingspan of up to a meter, they are the largest of the dabbling ducks, meaning they eat primarily at or just below the water's surface. They are not endangered and are hunted similarly to the mallard and are desirable because of their size, often weighing up to 3.5 pounds. They prefer to breed along a marshy shore in dense vegetation, but often choose a tree cavity or, if available, a wooden man-made house placed near the water's edge.

1930 LAKE VERMILION

CHAPTER 3

The Bradleys had been at Black Duck Island for two weeks. Every morning, Jane would rise before her husband, make herself a cup of coffee, and take it with her down the short walk to the boathouse at the back side of the island. She would sit on the wooden bench and sip the coffee, anxious to do what she had come to do. She knew the small bay was secluded and couldn't be seen from the house, and Preston wouldn't come down the path even if he were awake. But she wanted to make sure no one was coming around the tree-lined shore, perhaps a fisherman or even Skibo stopping by unannounced as he frequently did. So, she sipped and waited a few minutes before she set the cup on the bench and made her way behind the boathouse and on along the sandy shoreline a short way to where long ago someone had hung a duck house on a cedar tree close to the water.

The American Black Duck was known to sometimes nest in the holes in trees along the shore, and several of these duck houses had been installed on Black Duck Island by the man who first built the cabin and named the island. Jane had been curious about them that first summer Preston brought her to the island. The large bird houses were in disrepair. When she asked Preston if he would have them repaired, he had brushed her suggestion away as a waste of money, and so they continued to deteriorate. She was surprised because he was a card-carrying conservationist, having been a founding member of the Izaak Walton League just a few years before.

The one she was headed to now was the closest one to the boathouse. The walk along the small sand beach was an easy one. No big waves made their way into this little bay, so her feet stayed dry. She just had to remember to wipe the sand off her shoes when she returned.

When they had first arrived two weeks prior, Jane had pried a piece of the back off and reached in and cleaned out twigs and old nesting fluff. It made a perfect place to hide messages. She had explained to Robert where the birdhouse was and how he could pull a boat up on the sand without being noticed – if he didn't use a motor.

Every day for the first two weeks, she found the birdhouse empty, but then one day, there it was.

Hello, my darling, how I've missed you. But now I am finally here and can't wait to see you. Can you get away tonight at 11 pm? I'll row over and be waiting on your dock. Until then. All my love, Robert.

She almost missed it; it was such a small piece of paper. But when she found it, all her worries melted away. The day passed slowly, and when Preston went to his room for the night at his usual nine o'clock bedtime, she could hardly sit still—two hours to wait.

She took a flashlight with her but didn't need to turn it on. There were no clouds, and despite only a quarter moon, the path was clear. Robert was waiting, and she ran into his arms. They sat on the bench and talked in low tones, happy just to be near each other for a while. Then she stood, took his hand, and led him into the boathouse where the twenty-two-foot Chris Craft was moored. In the darkness, they found the long Naugahyde seats and each other.

They met again five nights later. Robert was late, and Jane worried, pacing the dock. Coming around from the opposite side of the island, the rowboat finally appeared. When he tied up at the dock, Jane clutched him to her and said, "I was so afraid you wouldn't come. Is everything all right?"

"Of course. I wouldn't miss seeing you. But I decided to be a little more cautious in case they are watching me when I take the boat. If they see me going directly to Black Duck Island, they might put two and two together or Martinelli might mention it to Preston in passing. I don't want you involved in any way, so I decided to row toward Fectos Point instead of directly here. That's why it took longer." He held her tight and kissed her.

"I promise this will all be over soon. By the end of fall, I will be finished with my assignment and I'll be moving back home. Are you sure you won't mind living in Ohio?"

"Of course not! I want to be with you wherever. Like right in here," she laughed as she led the way into the boathouse.

Their meetings were infrequent and all the more passionate for it. The weather sometimes interfered, and Robert had to return to Chicago for ten days at the beginning of July. Even though she knew he was gone, she continued to check the duck house each morning. Her mind was occupied with where she

had come from, where she was, and the wonderful life she would
have with Robert.

Jane Addams, born in Cedarville, Illinois, in 1860, was an activist who spent her life working for equality for all, helping poor people, and promoting education. Along with her life-partner, Ellen Gates Starr, she founded Hull House in 1889, the first settlement house in the United States, in the slums of the West side of Chicago. Initially a day care in a rented section of an abandoned mansion, Hull House grew into a complex of 12 buildings featuring a hostel, a community kitchen, a gymnasium and playground, classrooms offering courses at all levels, and a boarding house for working girls. A seminary graduate, Addams spent her entire life in service effecting social change in Chicago slums. She wrote "Democracy and Social Ethics" in 1902, "Twenty Years at Hull House" in 1910, along with several other books, and received a Nobel Peace Prize in 1930.

1915 ILLINOIS

CHAPTER 4

The closest town was Hindsboro, Illinois, population 307, just a mile from the Tindall farm. The one-room schoolhouse had the traditional bell in the small turret on the roof. When it rang, it meant she and her siblings were supposed to be in the school yard. If they weren't, they finished the walk from their house in an all-out sprint. The boys always managed to get there first and smile coyly at the pretty, young schoolteacher, who would reprimand them with a few gentle words. But when the Tindall girls came rushing in a few minutes later, brushing down their skirts and smoothing their hair, Miss Harrison would assign them extra work with stern words. Still, Jane liked school.

The classroom held about twenty students, and eight of them were Tindalls. The school year revolved around the weather and the planting and harvest schedule of the local farms when all hands were needed, even small ones. Students walked to school or, if they lived several miles away, rode an old horse, usually a couple of siblings to a bareback nag saved from slaughter for that singular purpose. The horses were kept in a small, fenced area behind the schoolhouse, where they would nibble at what little grass there was and wait for their trip home. The Tindalls couldn't afford a horse.

Jane was one of the middle children in the Tindall family, but as she was about to turn fifteen in a few months and a new baby sister or brother was on the way, she would soon fall into the category her parents called "the big kids". The younger children had chores, but they were allowed to play once they finished them, and they didn't have to participate in the more serious Bible studies. The middle children had no time to play after school and were expected to read the Bible whenever they weren't busy with chores or tending the little ones. The big kids didn't attend school. Instead, they either worked the family farm, went to work on a nearby farm, or got married and struggled to make it on their own. The Tindalls' farmland had good soil, and, unlike many others, they had a good well. But God had chosen to test Eustis Tindall; at least that was his explanation for years of bad luck and poor decisions. Tindall ran his family with a strong arm and a conviction that prayer was the answer. Although few of his prayers were ever answered, he never seemed to blame his god for that.

Jane wanted to continue in school mainly because she loved to read. But no books, other than the Bible or schoolbooks, were allowed in the Tindall home. She was thankful that the teacher, who didn't particularly seem to like Jane, allowed her to stay at her desk to read during recess. She hated to put the book she was reading down when the rest of the children came back in and class started again.

She had read most of the small collection, which was kept on a high bookshelf on the back wall of the school. They were old books donated by a few local townspeople. Melville's *Moby Dick*, Louisa May Alcott's *Little Women*, Nathanial Hawthorne's *The Scarlet Letter*, and Mark Twain's *Tom Sawyer* were among her favorites. Most had been written more than fifty years before she read them, but they were new and exciting to Jane.

But the one book that changed her life was *Twenty Years at Hull House* by Jane Addams. Jane – her namesake, no less – became her hero. Jane Addams cared about poor children, immigrants without a home or direction, and, most of all, girls and women, whom she saw as oppressed. When Addams founded Hull House, she opened its doors to all people regardless of religion and fought for dignity, rights, and justice for all people. Jane couldn't understand why her father, for all his religious ways, praying and bible reading, couldn't see that all God's children were to be loved and treated equally. Jane knew now, thanks to Ms. Addams, that any one person – even a woman – could make a difference, and that gave her the courage to contemplate a future away from Hindsboro. She felt that she had found her calling. Jane became determined to go to Chicago and devote her life to working at Hull House, helping the poor and the hungry.

When the end of the school year came, Jane had to inform Miss Harrison that she wouldn't be coming back in the fall because she had to go to work. Miss Harrison, always so upright and strict, hugged Jane and asked if she'd like to take one of the books she'd read.

"Thank you so much, Miss Harrison, but I couldn't do that. There are so few books here, you should keep them all for the other students." Jane's heart was breaking because she wanted to have *Twenty Years in Hull House* for her very own, but she knew that if her father found it, he would toss it into the fire, and that she couldn't bear.

All during that long summer working on the family farm, Jane begged her father to let her contribute to the family by finding work in Hindsboro. He finally relented when a man with whom he had dealings in town mentioned one day that his wife was ill, and they needed someone to care for their two small children.

Jane slept on a cot in the pantry off the kitchen, her few belongings tucked neatly underneath it. She was allowed to go home once a month to see her family, always on a Sunday, so she could attend worship services and read the Bible with the family. The work was not hard, and she did more than she was asked, so the man and his wife appreciated her. At the end of the month, the man met with Mr. Tindall when he came into town and gave him Jane's pay as the two men had agreed. After a few months, the man asked Jane if her father gave her any of her earnings. When she shook her head, he didn't respond. But at the end of the next month, before he left to meet her father, he called Jane to the kitchen table.

"I've been very pleased with your work, Jane, and I hope you're happy here."

"Why, yes, sir. I am pleased to be here, sir."

"I am going to meet your father to give him your wages today and I have been thinking long and hard about it. I have decided that our arrangement isn't fair to you. You remind me so of my sweet wife when she was much younger, and I wouldn't want her to be treated as you are being treated. All this work and…"

"Oh, no, sir," Jane interrupted. "I am very happy here. Please don't send me back. I don't mind the work at all, sir."

The man smiled at her misunderstanding. "Oh, I won't do that, Jane. I was about to say that you deserve to keep some of your wages for yourself. My dilemma is that I realize I can't renegotiate with your father as he is a very rigid man and would have some bible verse to justify his actions, I'm sure. Not that he isn't a righteous man, to be sure.

"Nonetheless, I'm not comfortable with that, so therefore, I have decided to pay you on top of the money I give your father. It won't be much, of course, as we don't have a lot of money to start with, but I can't see you work so hard and long for only your room and board, such as it is. But I wanted to ask you if you feel your father must know about this. If so, I will tell him today. If not, I won't tell him. It is up to you."

Jane looked him straight in the eye and said, "Do you know what he will do if you tell him?"

"Yes, I think I do. He will demand that you give it to him. Which is why this is your choice. I won't tell him if you don't want me to. And I won't think less of you because of it. You deserve it, that's my opinion, because you earned it."

"Oh, thank you, sir. Please don't tell him."

After six months had passed, her employer called Jane to the kitchen table for a talk.

"I don't see any evidence that you are spending your earnings, Jane."

"No, sir. I have been saving it."

He looked at her for a long time, then said, "Jane, I have seen for myself how single-minded you can be and so I must ask something of you."

"Yes, sir?"

"If you are going to leave us, please do so with some notice beforehand. That is what you are saving for, isn't it?"

Surprised that she was so transparent, Jane blurted out, "Yes, sir. I very much want to go to Chicago, to Hull House."

"Hull House, is it? I have heard of the place. That Addams woman has raised a ruckus about women's rights and poverty for some years now. I understand they offer food and shelter to those who need it, regardless of who they are. You think you will need help when you get to Chicago, do you?"

"Oh, no, sir. I want to go to Hull House to work. To help the poor and nurse the sick. To assist Miss Addams. If she'll have me, of course." She looked down at her hands folded on her lap.

"Well, then, if that is your desire. I suggest you have a plan," he said with a smile. "My wife's health is improving, as you know, but I wouldn't want her to relapse. How about you work here until you are sixteen? That will give us both time to make arrangements. You will have a tidy little nest egg by then, too.

And, if you'd like, when the time comes, I could write you a letter of recommendation. Speaking of writing letters, you could write to Hull House ahead of time and send them the letter of recommendation. That way you'd know if you had a place when you got there."

"Oh, sir, that would be wonderful. Thank you so much."

"What shall I tell your father?"

Now it was Jane's turn to think. "I certainly can't tell him or he won't allow me to leave the farm ever again. And I won't ask you to lie, so I think the truth is the best choice. Once I've gone, when you meet him to pay him my earnings, you can tell him that I've gone to Chicago. That I up and left. Don't mention that you're helping me or he'll be vindictive. Maybe even hit you. That would be bad. He can get awfully angry and he will be angry when he hears there'll be no more money from me. I'm so sorry to ask you to be the one to tell him. But, I am so afraid of him."

"He doesn't frighten me. I'll tell him whatever comes to my mind the last time I pay him. And the devil take care."

The last Sunday before Jane left for Chicago, she visited the Tindall farm as usual. Other than the extra plate at the table and voice at prayer time, the family, as usual, barely noticed she was there. She paid her mother extra attention, though, and stayed near her most of the day. Once, her mother stopped to look at her with a questioning look. Nothing was said, but when their eyes met, Jane was sure her mother knew that she planned to leave. They exchanged long hugs at the end of the day. Jane never saw her again.

The following Wednesday, her employer drove Jane to Arcola, six miles to the west, and dropped her at the Illinois Central train station. He hugged her for a long moment, held her by the shoulders, and wished her a happy and fulfilling life. Jane never saw him again, either, but thought of him often when she had doubts about herself. He was a stranger who cared more for her than her own father did. She would be forever grateful.

* * *

The train was so loud as it came into the station that she couldn't stop herself from covering her ears. It screamed past, each car causing a rhythmical throb in her chest. It seemed to go on forever, but once it passed, she quickly lowered her hands, embarrassed. But that hadn't been her train. It had been the Panama Limited, a sleek Pullman car express racing from New

Orleans to Chicago, which passed through twice a week. The station master had told her all about it when she bought her ticket to Chicago. He had said she was in for a treat. When she asked him why, he said she was going to see the fabulous Panama Limited, named in honor of the opening of the Panama Canal. She hadn't felt particularly privileged, but she had been impressed with the speed and noise.

She waited another hour before the Illinois Central local passenger train made its scheduled stop. She clutched the ticket in her hand, reticent to give it up to the conductor as she boarded the train, subconsciously afraid the ticket would be useless, and she'd have to return home. The trip took over ten hours. It stopped at every town with a grain elevator on the one-hundred-and-seventy-mile trip. Two of the stops along the way were extended so passengers could purchase meals inside the station. Jane skipped the lunch offerings, but by the time of the evening meal stop, she was so hungry that she used some of her precious savings to purchase some sustenance.

When the train finally reached Grand Central Station, it was almost midnight. Jane had little to carry, only a small stylish clutch the lady of the house had given her and a carpetbag she bought to carry her few possessions. She was swept up in the crowd and carried along the platform and into the huge marble hall of the station.

Suddenly, she realized two things - that her jaw had dropped and her hands were clutched tightly on her bags. She stepped to the side of the moving crowd and took a breath. Excitement filled her. 'I'm here! I'm finally here!' she thought. She composed herself and went to find the person sent from Hull House to meet her. He was an older man holding a sign with her name on it. She couldn't believe the weeks of writing letters had worked. She was glad she hadn't wasted her time on prayer.

The man, who said his name was Charlie, led her outside to a waiting car. Jane was exhausted when she finally lay down, miles and miles from the only two places she had ever slept. Her tiny room was on the third floor of Hull House. It held a single bed, a small dresser, and a tiny bedside table. When the excitement of arriving at her dreamed-of future faded for the night, she finally fell asleep.

The next few months passed quickly. She barely took note of her seventeenth birthday. Jane worked long days cooking meals, washing linens, tending small children, and helping wherever she was needed. She met and talked with Jane Addams several times each week during her daily routines. Inspired by the wisdom and counsel of Miss Addams and feeling good about herself, she decided she would seek out a church where she could again worship without the pressure, guilt, and fear that she felt from her father.

One afternoon, sitting with her mentor in the yard behind Hull House during a short break from work, she asked Miss Addams where she worshipped.

"I don't worship in the traditional sense of the word. I seek out the company of others who can accept the fact that I love all people and abhor their suffering without the worldly trappings of the more formal traditional religions."

"So, you don't go to church?"

"Oh, of course, I go to the People's Church whenever I can. Reverend Bradley and I have long been on the side of equality and justice for women and the oppressed. He's a great warrior for civil liberty. Would you like to go with me on Sunday?"

* * *

He wasn't what she had expected. Certainly not warrior-like. Already balding, Bradley was short and round. But his presence on the pulpit was grand. His voice was captivating. His message rang true to all that she knew in her heart to be important. His smile was beatific. She sat through that first Sunday's ministering with silent excitement. Here she was, Jane Tindall, from Hindsboro, Illinois, sitting next to the famous Jane Addams listening to the equally renowned Reverend Doctor Preston Bradley.

After the sermon, as the congregation was filing out of the imposing Presbyterian cathedral, Miss Addams took the opportunity to introduce Jane Tindall to Reverend Bradley. As they shook hands, the Reverend covered her right hand with his left and held it there, meeting her eye, he said, "You are so welcome here, in our church, and in our hearts."

Jane felt so honored she couldn't respond and just smiled as she and Miss Addams moved away. Little did she realize how smitten the Reverend had become at that first handshake.

It wasn't long before Jane started volunteering at the People's Church. She began teaching Sunday School and found that she enjoyed teaching the children. This surprised her because she hadn't enjoyed the company of her younger siblings. There had been so much strife in her family household that she hadn't really seen those tender children in the same light she saw children now.

Each Sunday, when she listened to Reverend Bradley's sermon, she swore he was speaking directly to her. His words struck home in so many ways that she always came away feeling part of something bigger and more important than herself. And she sought that out more and more because at Hull House, a situation was developing that made her uncomfortable.

Hull House offered hostel quarters to newly arrived immigrants for short periods while they looked for work and a permanent place to live. One of these was a young man who barely spoke English and had made advances to her. She kept her distance and brushed him off as much as possible. He was smooth and confident and somehow made her feel repulsed and excited at the same time. She had no experience with flirting or sexual innuendo. She had no idea how to respond.

One afternoon, the young man cornered her in the back hall of the cafeteria when she was hanging up her coat, having just come in from the produce market. He gently pushed her against the wall where her coat was hanging, and they fell together, lips and bodies pressed together. She was gasping for breath when he took her by the hand up the back stairs to an empty storeroom.

The young man moved on the next day, and she never heard from him again. The weeks passed, and she knew enough from watching her mother's situation to know that what she was feeling meant she was pregnant. She hadn't resisted enough. That's what she kept telling herself. She was bad and deserving of this inevitability. She covered her nausea and despair as best she could and kept up her routine. She couldn't bear the thought that she had failed Miss Addams and avoided seeing her whenever possible.

Late one Sunday afternoon, while she was tidying up the classroom after the last Sunday School group had left, she was feeling sick to her stomach and even more upset with herself. The door opened, and Reverend Bradley came in and sat at one of the tiny desks. Her first impulse was to giggle at how impossible it was that his girth would fit in the child's chair, but she quickly realized he had come with a purpose.

"Why, hello, Reverend Bradley. How nice to see you," she stammered.

"My dear, Jane. I hope you don't mind me stopping by."

"Of course not. What can I do for you?" Her mind was reeling, and so was her stomach. She was beginning to panic that she would have to bolt for the restroom, but she gritted her teeth and stayed still.

"Jane, I am an observant person. And a compassionate one," he said with a simple gesture of his hands. "I have no judgement about people's personal situations and yet I am acutely aware of them. I have noticed that you are not the same cheerful person you were when you first came to Chicago. I am concerned about you. Is there anything you'd like to talk about?"

As her tears fell, she poured out her dilemma and shame in words that tumbled from her lips like they were desperate to escape. He made some semblance of them. How she hadn't resisted hard enough. How she let everyone down who had been so kind to her. How she feared rejection if she told Miss Addams. Her fear of the future alone with a baby she felt unprepared to care for. Her fear of her own feelings. Her mistrust of herself.

He listened, leaning across the little table toward where she sat, and patted her shaking hands. The tears of humiliation fell, relieving some of her complicated emotions. When she was done and spent, he leaned back and said, "Our belief, here at the People's Church, is that every person must have the right to choose their own path. It is my belief that a child should be brought into the world with intent and love. You must come to your own decision. You must decide what is it you truly want? Come to me if and when you decide you need my help. Whether you decide to become a mother at your tender age. Whether you decide to give the baby up for adoption. Or whether you decide to have a safe medical procedure. We will be here for you no matter what you decide."

The next few weeks were a blur. She met with the sympathetic doctor that the Reverend recommended. She covered her brief absence from Hull House with a plausible story, and life continued. She cried herself to sleep at night with shame and emotions she didn't understand. But during the day, she managed to maintain her routine. Time passed, and her wounds healed.

After a few months, the Reverend Bradley began to stop by to see her more and more frequently, often asking her to dine with him. They went on walks and talked about all manner of things, philosophical and mundane. A year later, they were married in a modest ceremony. She was nineteen. He was thirty-eight.

Preston often spoke about his summer place on Lake Vermilion, but it wasn't until they were married that she traveled there with him. She shared his love of the place and found that when they were there, they related to one another as a couple, whereas in Chicago, their lives were pressed with separate obligations and formalities. She ran the vicarage and the many church programs and, of course, the Sunday School. He ministered to a large congregation and was active in many levels of local affairs and politics, always at the forefront of controversial issues facing the community. His radio broadcasts were nationally renowned. With so many responsibilities for each of them, they seldom dined or went to bed at the same time.

At the lake, however, they slept in or rose early, but always together. They talked or enjoyed each other's company in silence as they read. There were lots of visitors and casual entertaining, and, on rare occasions, Preston chipped in to help. At the lake, Jane was at least content, her broken heart hidden like a crack in a wall covered by many coats of paint. And so, the years passed.

Bidding for the 1933 World's Fair started in 1923 and was awarded to the city of Chicago. In 1928, a nonprofit corporation named A Century of Progress was organized to plan, build, and host the Fair. The city's wealthy and powerful were anxious to participate and contribute. A Century of Progress International Exposition, also known as the Chicago World's Fair, was built with private funds on newly created land made by filling in the Lake Michigan shoreline. To accommodate the short time frame in which it all had to be built, almost all the structures were made of plywood and newly developed man-made materials like Sheetrock and Masonite. Unlike the Columbian Exposition, known as "The White City" in 1893, these exhibits were painted in many colors, and the Fair was nicknamed "Rainbow City." While the Fair had many exhibits of natural and anthropological interest, its main theme was modern and featured a futuristic look at innovations that would change the daily lives of people everywhere. Over 25 million people attended during the six months it was open. Within a year of its closing, only a few buildings remained.

Prohibition had begun in 1920, and the changes in business, both legal and illegal, had become institutionalized. Petty crime, graft, bribes, bootlegging, smuggling, and under-the-table sale and consumption of alcohol *were part of everyday life. The Mafia had its tendrils in all levels of business and looked forward to reaping huge economic rewards during the World's Fair. In 1931, Al Capone was convicted of tax evasion and sent to prison. Politicians had hoped to use the Fair to force crime out and create a new, wholesome reputation for the city, but Al Capone's successors adapted to the challenge. The mayor and city officials, true to form, caved to the pressure of the underworld and doled out permits and licenses to whomever offered concomitant rewards in the form of bribes. While there were innumerable controversies and disagreements about how to create and run the Fair, there was one thing everyone agreed on: there was plenty of money to be made.*

1929 CHICAGO

CHAPTER 5

The Chicago World's Fair was four years away, and the city was already in high anticipation mode. There was so much to be done. So many plans to be made, bids awarded, permits and permissions to be granted, even before the work could start. The affair at the Drake was to unveil the model of the fairgrounds along with scores of large-format drawings of the exhibitions and buildings that were planned. It was a gala affair with everyone who was anyone in Chicago attending. Old money and the newly rich alike were looking to the World's Fair to pull up the Chicago economy and to make them all the richer. The political machinery was well-oiled and ready to facilitate the enormous undertaking. Politicians anticipated increased profits and power. Just as the transportation system included vast layered networks - elevated trains, subways, streetcars, connecting here and there at strategic points to accomplish their common goal, so, too, did the unique Chicago political power system. The powerful came from those who were elected, those who worked within the system above board, those who used the system illegally, and those who squeezed profit from the system through bribery and graft; many times, one and the same people. The systems these powerful people controlled all intersected at strategic points, as well. This evening at the Drake was one of them.

As the leader of the largest non-denominational church in Chicago, Reverend Preston Bradley was also known as a civic leader, public speaker, and educator. He was pleased, of course, to be invited. His friendship with a variety of elected officials, businessmen, and some not quite so above-board power brokers had guaranteed an invite. Still, his inclusion was due to the growing acknowledgement that he was a power broker in his own right. In the seven years since he started The People's Church, his reputation as a rabble-rouser for social justice had skyrocketed his fame, not only in Chicago but across the country, due in large part to his powerfully delivered radio sermons on feminist and anti-racist themes. Outwardly humble and a man of the people, Reverend Bradley enjoyed the finer things, and an affair at the Drake Hotel, rubbing elbows with the beautiful and powerful of Chicago, was exciting. Jane would, of course, accompany him, although she wasn't particularly thrilled. She went willingly, though, because she saw it as part of her job of being the Reverend's wife, and she was, if nothing else, dutiful.

There was no darkness around the Drake Hotel. The streetlights were bright, the lights of hundreds of automobiles lined up to drop off their passengers all reflected on the shiny surfaces of the cars in front of them, and the grand hotel itself was aglow with giant Hollywood-style searchlights throwing swaths of silvery light every which way up and down its impressive façade and on into the infinite night sky.

Valets with long, gold-braided epaulets on the shoulders of their navy blue uniforms opened the doors of one limousine after another. Gowned and bejeweled ladies - some wives, some mistresses - stepped onto the red carpet running up the steps to the entrance to the Grand Ballroom. The men who accompanied them all had one thing in common - power of one sort or another.

The Reverend Doctor Preston Bradley, dressed in a tuxedo, and Mrs. Bradley, in an understated navy gown with simple lines, a matching cloche, and a set of pearl earrings and single strand necklace, stepped out of their Duesenberg. A uniformed attendant held the door for them to enter, and they paused at the base of the marble stairs. He offered her his elbow. Jane smiled at him as she accepted his arm and, holding her long skirt with her other hand, walked up the stairs with him. Liveried housemen ushered them into the Palm Court. In some ways, even after ten years of marriage, she was still in awe of her husband. Despite his short stature, he exuded a presence. He greeted many of the people they walked by with familiarity, and when he spoke, those around would turn to notice who was speaking. He patted her hand, still on his arm, now and then, as if to quiet her discomfort at being introduced to the rich, the famous, and the infamous. They made their way to the far side of the Grand Ballroom reception hall and took a couple of glasses of bubbly ginger ale from a passing waiter. They stood to the side and sipped from the cut crystal stemware, watching their fellow guests mingle, laughing and chatting. Several people came up to them, warmly greeting the Reverend and acknowledging Jane with smiles and nods. Cardinal George Mundelein, the Archbishop of Chicago, approached with his robed entourage in tow. He shook hands with Bradley and congratulated him on a eulogy he had given for a recently deceased Northside alderman.

"Why, thank you, Cardinal. I hadn't realized you were in attendance at that funeral."

"Oh, my gracious, no. I wasn't there, of course, but I do have excellent staff who keep me up to date on what goes on in my diocese," replied the cardinal.

He leaned in to quietly say to the Reverend, "And by the way, if you'd prefer real champagne, try the glasses on the oval trays."

"Why, thank you, again," said Bradley, "We'll be sure to do that."

"I do hope you and your lovely wife have a delightful evening," and with that said, the cardinal moved on, his entourage falling in behind him.

Bradley chuckled. "What a pompous ass," he said under his breath to Jane. "'Of course, I wasn't there.' As if I thought he'd ever step foot in a non-Catholic cemetery."

They made their way through the crowd to view the exhibits and drank champagne from the oval trays. No one spoke of the prevalence of the illegal beverages, and Jane noticed how few people took glasses from the round trays. At first, the bubbly drink tickled her nose unpleasantly and tasted very sharp. But the second glass tasted wonderful to her. The third even better.

The reception hour passed uneventfully. Everyone took the opportunity to peruse the model of the proposed fairgrounds built on a platform that took up a large portion of the center of the reception area and the fifty or so drawings displayed on easels set up around the periphery of the large room. At 8:00 pm, the dinner gong rang out, and the oak-paneled doors were opened. The guests passed through a wide hall to a beautiful ballroom, the Gold Coast Room. Tables for five hundred people had been set with masses of flowers and candelabras. There was no finer view of Lake Michigan than from the huge north-facing windows, which looked up Lake Shore Drive with luxurious residential apartments on the one side and the vast expanse of Lake Michigan on the other. Everyone's eyes were drawn to the view as they entered the room.

Preston and Jane made their way to their assigned table, where they sat with Gunnar Ericson, Colonel in the Salvation Army; Stanley Witmer, Chairman of the Board of Directors of United Charities of Chicago; Charles Simpson, Executive Director of Hull House; and their respective spouses. The Director of the Public Library System was at the next table, and Bradley greeted him warmly before he sat down. Bradley had served on the library board for several years, but he had recently stepped down.

The speeches began, and the many courses of food came and went. Jane maintained a pleasant smile, but felt so uncomfortable and out of place. After an hour and a half, as one speaker was replacing another on the dais, Jane whispered her excuses to her husband and, nodding to those closest to her, left the table. Her skirt rustled and caught on chairs as she made her way through the tight spaces between the tables. Her face flushed with embarrassment. She could hardly breathe and wasn't sure she'd have the courage to return.

The white-gloved attendant standing at attention by the ballroom door directed her to the ladies' room at the end of the hall. There another white-gloved attendant, this one a woman, opened the door for her. The opulence of the lounge area was striking, breathtaking, actually. Jane tried not to gape as she looked around. Finally, she located the toilet rooms and relieved herself. When she returned to the lounge area, several ladies were sitting on chaise lounges with their shoes off, feet up, sipping from stemless glasses. Some talked across the spaces, a few others sat close together, chatting and laughing behind cupped hands. As she walked by one older lady reclining gracefully and sipping from a dark green crystal glass, she caught a whiff of liquor she associated with her father. On a whim, Jane sat down next to her. The lady smiled and tipped her glass toward the dark-skinned attendant in a black uniform, who came over immediately.

"Justine, dear, please bring this young woman a refreshment, would you?" said the woman.

"Oh, thank you, but I couldn't," replied Jane with wide eyes.

"Nonsense. Anyone can see you're in need of such refreshment. These events can be such a bore. My name, by the way, is Mrs. William Hall, Jr. You can call me Ardis. And who, pray tell, are you?"

"I'm Jane Bradley. Mrs. Preston Bradley."

The attendant approached and set a colored glass on the cloisonné table next to Jane.

"Thank you," Jane said to the attendant. Then again, to Mrs. Hall, as she picked up the glass.

The first sip tingled her tongue but made her mouth taste bright. She smiled at Mrs. Hall, who was chatting on about who was attending the event and what they were wearing. Jane sipped and nodded pleasantly. The alcohol on top of the champagne she had drunk earlier made her want to giggle, but she refrained.

"Oh, now I remember who your husband is," said Ardis after a long drink from the refill the attendant had brought her. "He's that firebrand reverend who preaches at the big sidewalk church over on Lawrence Avenue. I've heard him on the radio once or twice. Quite impressive. Although I dare say he has made some enemies with his talk of equality and personal rights."

"Enemies? Because he speaks up for people who are downtrodden?" Jane was taken aback.

"The powers that be, my dear, they don't want the applecart upset, you know. Don't get me wrong, I do feel for all those poor hungry people you see on the streets. But I really don't believe their problems would be solved if we just gave them money, do you? I do wish there were more jobs, though, so those who want to could work. I mean, they have children and wives to feed."

"Oh, I'm quite sure you're right, Mrs. Hall, but I wouldn't know. I'm so busy in the manse most of the time," said Jane with a smile. "I really should be going. Thank you again for the refreshment." She laughed a little giddily as she stood up and said, "I really do feel refreshed."

Jane headed back to the Gold Coast Ballroom, but as she turned into the entry hallway, she noticed a door off to the right farther down which was ajar. She thought perhaps she could find a quiet place to wait out a little more of the program before she rejoined her husband.

The room was dark except for the light coming in from the outside. The searchlights didn't shine in directly, but their rotation bathed the room in reflected light like a faraway lighthouse beacon. A window was open just a crack, and a slight breeze was discernible even from the door where she hesitated. Finally, she shrugged to herself and walked in. She took her shoes off and carried them in one hand as she made her way across the plush carpet over to the window. There was a chair nearby, so she pulled it close to the window and sat down. She put her feet up on the low sill, lay her head back as far as it would go, and stretched her arms above her head.

"Mmmmm," she said as she sat up. Suddenly, she was aware that the door had been opened and closed, and someone was walking up to her from behind. She turned to see who it was. All she could see was a shadowy figure approaching.

"Beautiful, isn't it?" the man said, walking up to the window. The lights of the four- and five-story residential buildings along Lake Shore Drive were bright, fixed in place, in counterpoint to the streaming lights of the automobiles as they raced past Oak Street beach. The moon, a smiling crescent, was visible to the east over Lake Michigan.

She had never met the man, she was sure, but somehow, she wasn't afraid of being alone in this dark, empty space with him. His voice was mellow and confiding, as if they had been friends for years. She stared at his profile, showing clearly when the spotlights made their sweep of the sky, then fading into darkness as the light passed. He had sharp features accentuated by a rather long nose. A handsome, regal face, she thought.

"Why, yes, it certainly is," she replied, turning back to the view. Now, it was his turn to look at her. She felt as if they were playing a game, and, to her surprise, she knew how to play it.

"I had noticed you in the ballroom and how uncomfortable you appeared. I was struck by how lovely you are. I hope you don't mind me being so forward, but when I was coming back from an errand to the lobby for my boss, I saw you slipping in here and I followed to see if you were all right."

"You're here with your boss? You mean your wife?"

He laughed, "No, no. I don't have a wife, but I do have a very demanding boss."

"My goodness, I'd say so," she laughed. "Demanding you come to this magnificent soiree with him to enjoy caviar and cake and be bored to death. Oh, I'm sorry. Perhaps this is all your cup of tea."

"Well, not really my everyday cup of tea, no. But at any rate, I can leave now. I'm glad you seem to be fine." He turned to leave. "Oh, by the way, my name is Robert Olds. And I hope we meet again sometime."

"Oh, no. Please don't leave, Robert Olds," she said. "I'm delighted to have someone to share this glorious view with."

They chatted for ages, or perhaps it was just a few minutes. She wasn't sure exactly when she had joined him at the window. The glass felt cool on her forehead when she leaned into it to look down at the entrance of the hotel. Happy people were coming and going, dressed in their finest. The women in sequined gowns and wraps of fine furs; the men looking so handsome in their formal attire, each one fawning over the beautiful woman on his arm. When she pulled back from the window and turned, she was in his arms. She gave in willingly to his kiss. So natural. So exciting. So passionate.

And so, it began.

* * *

At first, they met in public places where they could walk and have casual conversations, the Field Museum, Grant Park, or along the lake shore. Sometimes they would shop at Marshall Fields on Michigan Avenue, the grandest of Chicago's department stores, pretending they were furnishing their home together or buying clothes for trips to faraway places.

Always careful to only appear to be old friends, they never touched or held hands in public. After a morning or afternoon together, they would part, formally shaking hands goodbye, and go their separate ways only to rendezvous in a pre-determined hotel room shortly thereafter. Their trysts were all the more passionate for their play-acting as friends in public. The Palmer House was their favorite place to meet. The stately hotel on Michigan Avenue had so many entrances and many small shops on the ground level, it was easy for them to avoid an unseemly encounter with an acquaintance or to explain it away if one did happen.

The early part of 1930 flew by for Jane. She lived from one secret meeting to the next, always careful to maintain her composure and fulfill her many responsibilities as the wife of a minister.

* * *

"Robert, look at this," Jane said as she handed him a volume of poetry by Carl Sandberg. "I just love his work."

The lovers liked to meet at Booksellers' Row on State Street. The largest bookstore in Chicago, it had long aisles lined with tall shelves and overstuffed chairs and settees placed at random to allow people to spend time with their choice of books.

"What?" exclaimed Robert, holding the hand offering him the book for a long moment as he took it from her. "You like that rough, tough, and tumble stuff he writes? I'd have taken you for a Robert Frost kind of girl. You know, thoughtful, in nature."

"Well, Sandberg shows me a side of Chicago I don't get to see. And truth be told, I hope I never have to see. But viewing despair and strength through someone else's eyes is a learning experience for me. Besides, he uses words in such powerful ways. I wish I could express myself with such power. Preston likes him too, but he prefers Countee Cullen and his liberal presentments, and yes, he's pretty powerful, too," replied Jane. "Oh, sorry. I didn't mean to talk about my husband." She took the book from Robert and put it back on the shelf.

They wandered down the next aisle and stopped to peruse the books of poetry there. Robert pulled a pocket-sized volume off the shelf and began to read the poems. "Oh, now this is so wonderful. Simpson here describes you exactly. I swear he's written each of these poems about you," he said quietly, standing next to her elbows touching while they perused the books. "It inspires me to try writing poetry, too."

She laughed and wanted to melt into his arms right then and there. He moved closer and said in a more serious tone, "But, we need to talk. Can you stay a while longer?" When she nodded, he continued, "I'll walk down to the Berghoff and get us a table at the back. Come join me there in a few minutes. Okay?"

"Okay. I'll see you soon." They touched hands before he departed.

He was twisting his napkin when she appeared, smiling at the table. The Berghoff wasn't busy in the early afternoon, and there was no one at any of the nearby tables. He looked at her with concern.

"What's wrong?" she asked as soon as the maître d' finished

pushing in her chair and left.

"I have to tell you some things. And I'm afraid they will change how things are with us," he said.

Her gay mood still lingered, so she answered, "Oh, please don't spoil our marvelous day just yet. Look, I have a present for you!"

Gently removing the bookseller's wrapping, he held the Simpson book of poetry, then opened the cover to read the inscription she had written. "To Robert, I'm yours forever and always. Love, Jane." He looked up at her and smiled, tucking the gift into his inside jacket pocket.

"I want you to be inspired and to think of me all the time, too," she said, reaching for his hand across the table.

He smiled, "That's no problem. I am and I do. But I love this and will keep it with me always. Thank you."

They shared a light meal and drank the soda pop that Berghoff's was famous for. "Now, Jane. Now, I have to tell you some things. I'm really sorry that I have to, but I do. I just can't take hiding things from you anymore."

"All right, darling. Whatever it is, we can deal with it. I mean, I know we can't go on like this forever, but we've talked about my leaving Preston, and you know I'm anxious to do that."

He took a breath and began, "My name isn't Robert Olds. I was born Robert Owen McCarthy. I work for the federal government as an undercover agent in the IRS Intelligence Unit. I'm actually an accountant by trade and have a degree from Ohio State University in accounting. I was working for a firm in Cleveland, when the IRS recruited me to come to Chicago and be infiltrated into the Mob here. They set up a backstory for me and gave me my new name. I've been working at the firm of

Martinelli and Shackley for four years now. They are a legit accounting firm with mostly normal clients, but also a few very important, shady ones. They are masters at keeping double books. That's what I'm collecting evidence about."

Jane pulled her hands off the table and into her lap and stared at him, "What does this all mean? Are you in danger? Where does this leave us?"

"I love you. And I'm so sorry I'm in this messy job that I can't get out of – just yet."

"What do you mean 'just yet'?"

"Well, there are things I can't tell you, but I can tell you that this will all be over soon, and I will be released from this assignment. Then I'll have a steady job at the IRS but no more undercover work. We can be married as soon as you get divorced. Do you think you can wait for me to be free of my obligations? There are things that I can't tell you or it would put you in danger. I'm trying very hard to keep my head down and see this thing through safely. We just have to be careful for the next few months."

"Oh, Robert! Of course, I can wait a few months." she gushed as she reached for his hands across the table.

"And I have some really good news. You know how we were not going to be able to see each other during the summer because you go up to your cabin on Lake Vermilion? Well, I just learned that I will be going up there a few times with Martinelli. He's come to rely on me and wants to keep me working closely with him while he's on vacation up there. He has an island somewhere. Let's see. I can't remember the name of it. Oh, yes. That's right. It's like money which is what all this is about. His place is called Gold Island."

Jane gasped. "That Martinelli? I don't really know them, but their island is just across the bay from Black Duck Island – that's our, I mean, Preston's island."

Over coffee, they planned how to communicate and where they could meet. When they parted ways, with a public handshake and platonic cheek kisses, they were both filled with lovers' hope.

1930 LAKE VERMILION

CHAPTER 6

It was a drizzly day, and Jane was restless. She had read everything there was to read in the cabin. Her embroidery was so boring that she wanted to throw it in the fireplace. Robert had been in Chicago for over a week, the weather had been dreary, the garden was in full bloom with nary a weed, and Preston had been out of sorts and complaining. A trip to town was what she needed, she decided.

"Dear, would you mind very much if I went into Tower to the library? I'm dying for something new to read and I can do some filing and tidying up while I'm there. The place does need some attention, don't you think?" She stood next to the armchair where Preston was jotting on a notepad, working on a future sermon.

"Of course, dear," he replied, glancing at his watch. "Skibo should be here soon. Would you mind stopping at Martilla's to see if they have any of that new drug for my dyspepsia. What's it called again," he rubbed his chin. "Oh, yes. Tums. Quite the catchy name, don't you think?"

"I certainly can do that. I'd better hurry if I'm going to catch Skibo. I'll arrange for him to pick me up at 4:00 after he's done with his route, so I'll be back in time to make dinner." She snatched up her purse and jacket and hurried down to the dock to wait for the mailboat. Skibo was more than happy to make the short diversion to drop her off at Shamrock Landing, where the Bradleys stored their car. He offered her a hand into the boat.

She tied the silk scarf she always kept in her jacket pocket tightly under her chin. A few wayward strands of hair tickled across her forehead, distracting her just like her thoughts were doing. She captured them and tucked them into the scarf. Her breath caught as she remembered Robert had tenderly done the same thing when they parted last, how she missed his smile, his touch. She hoped he would be back from Chicago soon.

She turned to the front of the boat as Skibo slowed, pulled up to the dock, and reversed the engine to come to a smooth stop, idling while the dock attendant approached. Jane accepted his hand and stepped onto the weathered planks.

"Thank you," she smiled at the young man, and turning back, she said, "Thanks, Skibo. I'll be here at 4:00 for a ride back."

On the drive to Tower, she made a plan for a pleasant, solitary afternoon with no one's needs to tend to but her own. She would stop at the beauty parlor to have her hair cut, do a little shopping at Zup's and Martilla's Drugs, and spend time at the library cleaning and catching up on whatever needed to be done there.

She parked near the Town Hall, figuring that was where she'd be spending the last part of the afternoon, and walked across and down the street to Suzie's Styles. The bell atop the door tinkled pleasantly as she entered. The hairdresser looked up from the magazine she was reading.

"Hi. Do you have time for a quick hair cut? I just need it chopped off about here." Jane gestured to just below her ears with a smile. "I'm not one for a smart style or anything. Just a quick bob."

"Sure," the young woman replied. "Have a seat."

Twenty minutes later, Jane felt lighter and refreshed from the shampoo and cut. She ran her fingers through her hair, relishing the springy curl that came naturally when her hair was short. She popped into the drugstore and spent a few minutes flipping through magazines. There was nothing she really needed, but she bought some bobby pins and some Jergens lotion. She was paying for the items when she remembered Preston's request.

"Do you have the new tummy medicine, Tums?" she asked Mrs. Martilla.

"Of course," the woman snorted her answer.

Jane stifled her laughter at the fake indignation and paid with exact change. She was tempted to have an ice cream but decided to have lunch first. Down the block at Zup's Grocery, she picked out a few things, then went to the butcher's counter in the back and asked for a bologna and Swiss cheese sandwich to eat at the library while she worked.

After dropping the bag of groceries in the car, she walked up the wide white stairs to the Town Hall and proceeded up the interior stairs to the library on the second floor. There was a lot to do, but first she laid out her small lunch on the center table, pulled up a chair, took off her jacket, and started to eat, thinking about which task to start first. Since it was the Preston Bradley Library, the management of it fell to her. She pondered for a moment how there were so few things that she did because she chose them. Her life had always been a constant flow of other people telling her, directly or indirectly, what to do. Here, just like back in Chicago at the rectory, she was constantly busy doing what others either asked or expected of her. Life with Robert would be so different.

The people who cleaned the Town Hall dusted and cleaned the floors, but they didn't touch the books or the filing system. Over the summer, it fell to her to spend a few hours now and again to keep things in order. The rest of the year, dust accumulated, and the cards went unfiled until the school librarian would solicit the help of a couple of fifth graders to help her tidy up.

Jane enjoyed the banal task of finding the checkout cards for each of the returned books, sliding them into the pockets at the front of the appropriate book, then finding their rightful place on the shelves. The system was based on honesty, so if a book was late or never came back, there really wasn't a way to track it, but the little sign-out cards seemed to be enough incentive to be honest. There was seldom a missing book, unless you counted the ones that were left with the card still in the pocket and were never returned.

Today, she had decided to do a more thorough job. She might even get to replace the sign-out cards that were completely filled with fresh blank ones, a task that hadn't been done in years. She had lots of time, she decided. She'd start by shelving the stack of returned books.

She heard the door open, but continued her reach to put the two books she was holding where they belonged. The small step stool she was standing on tipped, as someone grabbed her from behind.

"What? Stop, stop!" she sputtered, frightened and off balance, turning to see who was holding her. "Robert! What are you doing here?" She threw her arms around him to return his embrace as he lifted her away from the stool and held her off the ground to kiss her.

"You're back! How did you know I was here?

"I didn't. I had some time to kill, so I decided to see this amazing 'library' you keep talking about while I wait for my ride back to Martinelli's. Roy is supposed to pick me up at 3:00 when the train from Duluth comes in. My FBI contact in Duluth was driving up to the Cook end of the lake, so I drove with him, and he just dropped me off here. But, no, you shouldn't know that. Please forget I said that." He looked at her concerned, then kissed her again.

Jane broke from his embrace, "Darling, who cares. We're here now. I've missed you so." She walked to the door, pulled down the roller shade on the upper glass section of the door, and flipped the deadbolt. She took his hand and led him to the old chenille settee in the reading corner.

"I missed you, too," he said.

* * *

Roy pulled into the train station lot to wait for the accountant who had been staying at Gold Island on and off all summer. Mr. Martinelli seemed to think he was competent and trustworthy. Roy had other ideas. Roy also prided himself on never being late, so he arrived long before the train was due and was reading a Zane Grey paperback on a bench near the station. He glanced up as he turned the page to a new chapter and was surprised to

~61~

see Robert exiting the Town Hall from the side door. He seemed preoccupied and made his way directly across the short distance to the train station, without looking around, and then went around to the back where the train platform was.

Roy closed his book with pursed lips and a slight shake of his head. He went back to the car and sat in the driver's seat, waiting for the train to arrive. He would definitely be telling Mr. Martinelli about this.

1950 LAKE VERMILION

CHAPTER 7

Carl and Elsa, still shaken up from their grisly find, waited for the Deputy Sheriff to arrive. They hung out for a bit in the community room with its big windows overlooking the lake and the dock where their boat was tied up. They could keep an eye on Bruno there, too. The big black dog had sauntered off the porch and was stretched out on the grass under a tree. The room was all but empty except for an old couple who were reading at a table by the window in the far corner.

Katy wiggled her way to the floor and ran back and forth between her mother and father, giggling. The old couple watched over the tops of their books, smiling, remembering their little ones. Katy ran partway across the room to them but thought better of it and hurried back to cling to her mother's pant legs. Elsa offered her a zwieback and a wooden toy, and the toddler occupied herself on the floor near her parents.

Carl went to the bar in the other room and brought back two beers. They drank in silence for a bit, watching Katy play.

Each time the door opened, they came to attention, thinking it was Pittella. Finally, when they got tired of waiting inside, they went out and sat on the steps. Bruno came over and lay down near them. Katy climbed back and forth over him as if he were part of a play yard.

"The patience of that dog is astounding!" said Elsa.

"I know! He's terrific with her, isn't he?" said Carl. They sat in somber silence again as their thoughts pulled them back to Elsa's gruesome catch.

It was almost an hour before the Sheriff's Department boat arrived, the big wake overtaking the launch as it slowed to approach land. Pittella reversed the engine and, with a sharp turn of the wheel, gently pulled the side of the boat to within inches of the dock. Korchenko hopped out at the rear and secured the back rope to the brass cleat on the pier. Pittella grabbed the front rope from where it rested along the gunwale and handed it to Korchenko to tie up the front, then he too stepped onto the dock.

The Swansons came down the lawn to greet them. The men shook hands as they all said hello.

"Well," said Pittella, "Let's get right to it. What have you got to show me?"

They all went over to Carl and Elsa's boat, which was tied up to the next dock over. Carl stepped in and retrieved the skull from under the small quilt. He held it in the crook of his arm as he got back up onto the dock.

"I'm so sorry," said Carl as he handed it to Pittella, who took it with both hands and rotated it until he was looking at its face. The eye sockets appeared to be black because the inside of the skull was covered with dark green algae. A patch of bone showed at the top of the skull where Elsa had rubbed some of the algae away. The mandible was missing, and so were all of the teeth along the upper jaw.

"No mistaking it," said Pittella. "I've seen a few skulls over the years, and this one is definitely human. Let's go back to our boat."

Pittella led the way, nodding to the people as he passed them. There was a small crowd of ten or twelve people gathered around now, curious as to why the Sheriff's Department boat was there. When they got back to the other dock, he handed the skull, which he had tucked under his jacket, to Korchenko and said, "Pete, would you mind putting this in one of those big evidence bags and stowing it in the cabin."

Korchenko stepped on board and disappeared below. Pittella turned to Carl and Elsa and said, "Would you mind showing me where you found that?"

"Of course," said Carl.

"You are welcome to come or stay if that's easier for you," Pittella said to Elsa, gesturing with a nod of his head at Katy.

"I'd like to come along, thanks. She'll be fine. What about Bruno?"

"He's welcome to come. He's been aboard the cruiser before."

Sven had come down to the dock and made his way to the front of the people milling around.

"Okay, then. What's up, eh?" Sven said.

"Hi, Sven. Looks like we might have something we need to investigate over in Frazer Bay. We'd appreciate it if you'd keep an eye on Carl and Elsa's boat for a bit. Oh, and would you mind convincing anybody who might want to follow us that they shouldn't do that. We sure don't need more distractions out there."

"Sure, I can do that, Deputy," said Sven, "All of the boats tied up here right now belong to me. They come with the rental cabins. I'll just tell them they can't use them right now."

"That's great, Sven. Thanks."

Then, turning to Carl and Elsa, Pittella said, "Okay, let's get rolling. Call your dog and hop on board."

Carl whistled, and Bruno leisurely got up from his nap under the big oak, stretched from head to toe, and came trotting down the lawn. Carl got in, then helped Elsa and Katy get in.

"Come on, Bruno. Hop in." And he did.

Pittella started the big engines and smoothly pulled away from the dock in reverse. When they rounded the corner and came into Frazer Bay, he throttled back and put the engine into neutral to idle.

"Pete, will you take the wheel, please. Just keep us at an idle for a bit," Pittella said as he went to sit in the passenger area by Carl and Elsa.

"I didn't want to talk with all those people around. So, now tell me what happened," he said to them.

"Well, nothing, really. Nothing happened except I got stuck. Carl swung back around and when the line finally loosened, I reeled in the lure and the skull was attached," said Elsa.

"The lure came out easily when we got it in the boat. I'm sure you'll be able to see where it had been lodged inside the eye hole. I actually think the lure itself was wedged sideways in there. Not the hooks themselves. You know what I mean? 'Cause the lure just dropped to the back of the skull when we turned it," said Carl.

"What on earth are the odds of that?" said Pittella. "Your Red Devil just dropping through the eye socket and getting stuck in there."

"I can see that, though," said Elsa. "I was whipping the line quite a bit. You know how you have to jerk up and down real fast to try to get it dislodged? I think the lure was stuck between rocks right next to the skull and it must have jerked loose on one of my up motions, then it must have dropped vertically into the nearby eye socket hole on the next down movement. Then when I flicked the rod up again the boat had moved just enough off center so that the lure got wedged horizontally and stayed like that long enough for us to bring it to the surface. But I certainly agree, the odds of that are phenomenal."

"It's almost like it wanted you to find it," said Carl.

Elsa gave him a cross look that implied he was out of line.

"Oh, honey, you know I don't mean it like that. It's just such a coincidence that you've stumbled on three murders now," said Carl.

"Well, let's not jump to conclusions. This might not be a murder at all," said Pittella. "This could very well be skeletal remains from an accidental death. As you know, we have had more than a few unsolved disappearances over the last hundred years or so, like the case you helped solve the summer before last. Then there are accidents. People fall through the ice. Boats capsize in storms. Could be any number of accidents that happen. It's also possible the skull is all there is. It could be an illegal souvenir, for example. How it got here, though, is still a mystery. And we're just going to have to find all that out. The coroner will provide some forensic information, even if that's all we find.

"When I get back to town, I'll have the dive team from the main office in Duluth get up here. But right now, I'd like to get out to the spot you found it. Let's head out there. Carl, how about you stand up there next to Pete and show him where to go."

Carl made his way to the helm of the 1947 24-foot Chris Craft and stood facing forward next to Korchenko, his left arm outstretched, hand on the windshield. Pete slowly brought the launch up on plane heading west. Then he looked over at Carl for direction. The twin engines rumbled as they sped forward.

Just a few minutes later, Carl pointed to the reefs not far ahead, just to the east of Black Duck Island. Pete throttled back and swung wide around the north side of the markers. Carl pointed again. The floating life jacket was just a few hundred feet away. The big boat circled and came to idle upwind so that it would slowly float past the life jacket.

"It's only 12 lb. test. But it is a braided line. I think that makes it stronger. Sorry I didn't have a better way to mark the spot," said Carl.

"It seems to be working so far. Let's hope the wind doesn't pick up," said Pittella, looking around. "Well, there's not much we can see from here. There are cabins scattered around the bay, but none are really close. No point in interviewing anyone at this point. And, I don't see anything strange here in the water around the reef. The markers are where they should be, and there's no debris anywhere.

"Carl, Elsa," Pittella said, looking back and forth at them, "Is there anything else you can think of about this spot or how you pulled the item up from the bottom? Was there anything else attached to it? Perhaps something fell back in the water?"

Carl and Elsa looked at each other and shrugged, "No," they said at the same time.

Katy was trying to wiggle from Elsa's grasp, wanting her daddy. Bruno was pacing in the back of the boat.

Pittella turned to Korchenko and said, "Take us back to Moccasin Point, will you please, Pete?"

Then, turning to Elsa, he said, "We'll drop you at your boat. I'll stop by your place to talk with you again, probably tomorrow sometime, if that's okay."

"Sure. We'll stay close to home until you come by. It'll be interesting to hear about what you find out," said Elsa, raising her voice a little as the boat sped up.

Katy finally managed to escape her mother's hold and, instead of running to her father, she made a beeline for Pittella sitting on the next bench seat and flung herself at him with a squeal.

He laughed out loud in surprise and lifted her onto his knee and tickled her. Katy squealed with delight, flailing her arms and legs with exuberance.

"Oh, my. You are a sweetheart, aren't you?" he said, giving her a little hug as he set her back down.

For a minute, they all forgot the grim circumstances and reveled in the little girl's delight. Back at the dock, the Swansons quickly moved to their boat and waved as Pittella and Korchenko sped away.

Before Carl started the small outboard motor, he said to Elsa, "Do we need anything up at the store?" nodding his head in the direction of the Moccasin Point Lodge building.

"No. I think we're fine. Got milk the other day. We're okay," Elsa answered, shaking her head. "Let's go home. Somehow the lake feels a little threatening right now." She hugged Katy, who was starting to doze in her arms, as Carl powered away from the dock.

For no particular reason, he headed east around the north side of the islands, then turned south through Sylvan Dells. The channel was calm, and he squared off the approach to the narrows between the two little islands, where there was a clear passage, always careful never to cut corners when going through a channel. Carl had great respect for the damage underwater hazards could do. As they came close to Pine Island on their left, he barely noticed the dock with a wooden archway at the edge of the woods decorated with the word "Shadowland" across the top. His mind was preoccupied with visions of the algae-covered skull.

CHAPTER 8

It was early afternoon by the time Pittella and Korchenko tied up at the municipal dock at Hoodoo Point. The Deputy Sheriff's car and the patrolman's car were both parked around the back of the boathouse. Pittella had outlined his plans to Korchenko during their trip back to Tower, and when the boat was secured, they each took off in their vehicles.

Korchenko went home to get the items he'd need to spend the night on the boat: food, water, a thermos of coffee, warm clothes, a rifle, and extra batteries. When he had all the things he needed, he went back to the marina, parked, and locked the patrol car. He patted the roof as he left. He liked the big four-door Pontiac Chieftain sedan. He'd been driving it now for a year and secretly thought of it as his partner. With his pat, he was telling it that he would be back. He loaded his gear and supplies, untied the big boat, and returned to the reef where the skull was found.

Pittella drove to his office in Tower and immediately

telephoned headquarters in Duluth. He arranged for a dive team to come north. They would arrive in the early evening and stay at the Marjo Motel on the outskirts of Tower. They would bring their boat and equipment and be ready to investigate the reef site first thing the next morning. The medical examiner from Duluth would accompany the dive team because he had more experience with remains found in water than the medical examiner from Ely. The skull and any other remains they might find would be taken back to Duluth for examination. Pittella called the Marjo Motel and the Tower Hotel and reserved rooms for the men.

When Pittella had made all the arrangements he needed, he went home. There was nothing else that couldn't wait. When he got there, he hung his service weapon in its holster behind the front door as he always did. He took off his shoes and walked through the house to the kitchen. The back door was open, and he could see the yard where his and Minnie's children had played; their grandchildren were playing there now. The metal Montgomery Ward swing set creaked and squeaked, making as much noise as the children climbing and swinging on it.

"*Boozhoo, Manoominikeshins,*" he said as he approached Minnie, who was standing at the sink. He called her 'little rice bird' because, when he first met her, she was harvesting wild rice into a birch bark canoe with her uncle on a remote bay on Lake Vermilion. She was called Minnie, but her Ojibwe name was Ominotago.

"Ah, there you are," she said as he wrapped his arms around her from behind. She twisted to face him, and her face changed from happiness to concern. "What's the matter?" she asked, pulling her long hair all to one side.

They were as physically different as two people could be. He was tall, muscular, and built like a large, straight birch tree. He had short white-blonde hair, pale blue eyes, and eyebrows so light that, from a distance, people often thought he had none. He exuded a powerful presence, even more so when he was silent, which he was most of the time. The young neighborhood kids loved him, and the older ones respected him and worked hard to keep from getting caught at whatever mischief they were into because they didn't want to disappoint or anger him. Minnie was short, plump, and dark. Her blue-black hair shone like the lake on a starlit night and never kept a curl, even after being braided overnight. Her round face held eyes like obsidian, which twinkled when her grandchildren were around. She was deeply rooted in her Native culture, which brought her a sense of peace and understanding that persisted despite her years living in town with non-natives, following her marriage to Harvey Pittella.

Pittella gave the top of her head a long kiss, then sat at the kitchen table with his hands clasped together in front of him. She gave him a long look, then went to the screened door and stepped out onto the stoop. "Time to go home, kids," she called out to the children. They scrambled down from the swings and ladders and waved to their grandmother. She watched as they ran across the backyards of several houses, their shiny, long, black hair bouncing on their shoulders, and disappeared into the fourth house down. She heard the screen door slam behind them. She went back inside, sat down across from Harvey, and waited.

"You know, I really thought that my job would get easier as time went by," he said finally. He shook his head just a little bit. "How could I have even think that could be true?"

"What has happened?" she asked.

"Today, Carl and Elsa pulled a skull out of Lake Vermilion while they were fishing."

"Another old story is wanting to be told," said Minnie, shaking her head slowly. "And you have been chosen, again, to tell it."

They sat in silence for a while, then Minnie asked, "Do you have any idea who it might be?"

Pittella again shook his head. "There have been many missing persons cases over the years, but most were found lost in the woods. There have only been a few cases where the person wasn't found. There was that nine year-old girl from Iowa who drowned on Trout Lake back in 1934. We weren't allocated the resources then to search that deep water or even to keep up the search for very long. We know bodies can sink initially, but why hers never floated up during the decomposition process is the puzzle. Some fisherman should have spotted at least some scrap of clothing along the shore at some point even if her body was eaten by animals."

"Do you remember the case?" he asked after a pause.

Minnie nodded, "Of course. You were so distraught by what happened you hardly slept that whole summer."

"The thing about that case. I never really got a good feeling from the father. The mother was obviously afraid of him and did nothing but cry. The father's grief seemed shallow, and he seemed relieved at the end of every day when we had to stop searching," he said.

He leaned back in his chair before he continued, "I was sure some evidence would come out or he would crack, or the mother would. They had been camping up there for several days already when they hailed some other campers and said their canoe had tipped over while they were fishing. Personally, I think he walked for a day into the woods with the girl's body over his shoulder and buried the child somewhere she will never be found. Then he walked back and trumped up the canoe accident. They actually had a small shovel in their camping gear. He said he had it to dig a latrine, but he hadn't done that. Said he changed his mind. He could have gotten rid of the shovel too, but he didn't. Either he didn't think of it or he was cocky enough to think he was beyond suspicion."

They sat in silence again for a bit, then Harvey continued, "It's also possible that the girl never came with her parents to the Northwoods. She could be buried in her own back yard in Indiana. No one remembered seeing a nine-year-old girl in Tower with those people. Only the mother went into Zup's, and at the gas station, the father made a point to say that his wife and daughter were shopping."

"It is terrible to think of a parent hurting their child," said Minnie.

"What bothers me is there could be missing persons we don't even know about. Someone that no one reported, for instance. Or how easy it would be to cover up a disappearance if that's what someone wanted to do. And then there are cases where a logical explanation seems to explain a disappearance but isn't, in fact, the truth. Like my first unsolved missing persons case back in 1928. The fellow from Duluth who was killed by his partner. Everyone thought he had taken off with the money from their real estate scheme over on Pine Island. Took twenty years for that one to be finally solved, remember?"

"I certainly do," said Minnie, "Year before last, it was."

They sat in silence for a while, until Minnie continued, "A truth cannot be hidden forever. That your friend Ike had to lose his life to uncover it was hard for you, I know. Some justice seems so unjust."

"That's for sure," Harvey said. He chuckled, "Boy, Carl and Elsa sure helped with that case. Kind of bumbled onto things but had the clarity of mind to spot subtle inconsistencies that might have been missed. They are such nice folks and that baby of theirs is such a sweetheart."

He sighed, "You know I always loved that toddler stage. And now our grandkids are all way beyond that and there probably won't be any more."

Minnie reached over and patted his hand, "We had many good years with the little ones. Now you must use your memories to ease your longing. Perhaps we will live to see the children of our grandchildren."

Pittella smiled, then he stood and said, "I'd better get prepared for tomorrow. I'll be upstairs if you need me."

After he left, Minnie closed the back door and started dinner.

CHAPTER 9

Pittella picked up Grant Henke, the Duluth medical examiner, at the Tower Hotel, then headed back to the west end of town where the Marjo Motel was located. It was just 8:00 a.m. when they arrived. The rest of the group was waiting outside. Pittella stopped his car, got out, and shook hands with each one of the team, thanking them again for their help. As they stood around in the chill air of the early morning, Pittella gave them a quick briefing of what had transpired the previous day. Their team leader, John Larvik, an experienced diver who Pittella had worked with before when a tourist couple's canoe overturned in Big Bay, spoke next.

"We'll take all three vehicles to the marina and launch both of our boats. Deputy Pittella will ride with Miller and I in the lead boat. As I understand the situation, there will be no need to protect potential shoreline evidence because this is a fully underwater site. But we'll have to assess the underwater area before we can drop anchor. We'll idle near the site during the initial dive. Miller and Harrison will dive first." Larvik looked at Pittella and nodded.

"Patrolman Korchenko has been keeping watch over the site aboard the Sheriff's department boat during the night. The couple who discovered the skull managed to mark the spot, although we have no idea how accurate their marker is," said Pittella.

"That will be our first task. To determine as best we can, where the initial find took place," said Larvik. "Anyone need anything before we head out?"

Heads shook all around. "Well, then, Deputy, we'll follow you," said Larvik.

The trip from Hoodoo Point across Big Bay was uneventful. When they were passing Moccasin Point Lodge, Pittella motioned for Larvik to slow down. Pointing to the buildings on the western shore, Pittella explained that was where Carl and Elsa Swanson had first called him with news of their find.

"No need to stop there at this point, at any rate," finished Pittella. Larvik maintained a no-wake speed through the narrows, then went up on plane again as they came into the open water and turned west at St. Paul Island. After just a few minutes, Pittella pointed to the ChrisCraft near the markers and shouted over the motor noise.

"There's our boat."

Larvik slowed and made a wide circular approach, avoiding the markers along the reef and coming up to a waveless stop close to the Sheriff's boat from the west. Korchenko raised a hand in greeting. Pittella responded with a nod. Miller leaned over the gunwale to soften the contact between the two boats. He arranged a couple of bumpers between them and proceeded to tie the boats together.

The lake was usually calm in the morning when the weather was good. Today was no exception. The second dive boat tied up to the first one with their engine at idle. Everyone introduced themselves and looked to Larvik for direction.

"It looks like your anchor will hold all three boats at least while there's no wind," Larkin said, addressing Korchenko. "We'll do an assessment dive, then choose our anchorage depending on the wind at that point. Then we'll determine a grid pattern and begin our work. Once we're anchored separately, you'll be free to head back to town or whatever you need to do at that point. Does this work for you, Deputy?"

Pittella nodded. "We'll be fine with that. Just let us know what we can do to help."

Henke, Pittella, and Korchenko stayed on the big boat and watched the divers take turns descending into the water from the two smaller boats.

Leaning against the gunwale of the boat, Pittella turned to Korchenko, "So how did it go last night?"

"There were a couple of fishermen who came by. They went off sure enough when I told 'em to. Then after dark, must a been around midnight, the two Gillespie boys and their friend from over on Birch Point came sneaking up. I had my lights off, so they didn't much notice me, they were so full of themselves. They'd heard about the skull being found and had made up all sorts of stuff. They were going to dive down and find the dead guy's gold. They had their clothes off down to their skivvies and were about to jump in the water, when I turned on the spotlight and hit the bullhorn."

Pittella laughed, "I'll bet they peed in their pants!"

"Yah, one of them fell into the water, he got so scared. When his buddies pulled him up, I gave them all the what-for. And off home they went," said Korchenko. "Got a few hours sleep after that. No problem."

After a while, Larvik came aboard and gave them a progress report. The team started by swimming in formation along the reef, and after the third pass, one of them spotted a long bone. It was from this point that they would set up the grid pattern, he told them. Once they had the perimeter staked out and the position of the long bone recorded, they would bring it up for Dr. Henke to examine. An underwater camera was used to record the process.

The Medical Examiner moved over to the larger of the dive boats, which had an examination table and evidence storage lockers on board. He quickly confirmed the bone was a human femur and was the right size to have come from the same body that the skull had. The area was officially declared a crime scene, and the hunt for further remains was on.

Making use of the long summer's day of daylight, the dive team worked continuously, but nothing else was found. The next day, the group of divers arrived early and set to work again. Almost immediately, they found some small bones and a clavicle spread out, all in the same direction away from where the femur had been found. They focused on the sections of the grid in that direction, and at midday, they found the pelvis bones. Everyone was very excited by the discovery, but it was getting too dark to search productively. The next day, they found nothing.

At the end of that day, the group was fatigued, and Larvik called a meeting back at the Deputy Sheriff's office. Dr. Henke laid out all the bones that had been found on a table set up in

Pittella's office for everyone to see.

Larvik started the meeting, "Thanks to all your hard work, guys, we can say definitively we have a body. Dr. Henke states that with the skull, femur, pelvis and the few other smaller bones, he can state that the deceased is a male. It's my opinion that this is probably about all we'll find. So, I'd like to call it quits and move the investigation on to the next stage. Dr. Henke will take all this to his lab in Duluth and do a much more thorough examination."

"You all did a great job, and I want to thank you again for putting up with the cold water and long hours. Tomorrow, we'll leave about 9:00. Get a little extra shut-eye in the morning."

The men start to leave, talking and making plans for the next day's departure.

"Hold up a minute, please," said Pittella. He waited until he had everyone's attention. "I'd like you to reconsider. Watching you guys work has been terrific. I never saw anything quite like it. But I've been on this lake for forty years and my gut tells me things don't move too far down there on the bottom. Ice does move things around a bit but that's near the shore not in the deep water like that reef. The lake is most clear early in the morning, which is when you've found most of the bones. So I'd like to ask you to look one more day – actually just tomorrow morning. If you haven't found anything else by noon, I'll agree we should call it quits. What do you say?"

Larvik looked at his men, who nodded their agreement. "Okay, then. One more day on beautiful Lake Vermilion. Let's get some rest, guys."

CHAPTER 10

On the fourth day after finding the skull, while Katy was taking her afternoon nap, Elsa and Carl relaxed together at the painted metal table and chairs on the lakeside of the cabin so they could hear through the open window if Katy awoke. Bruno sprawled on his side in the grass nearby. They sat in silence for a bit, sipping their long neck beers and snacking on hardtack and caraway cheese. Bruno lifted his head and woofed once in the general direction of the driveway behind the cabin.

"I wonder how the identification of the skull is going," said Carl, voicing what they had both been thinking. Bruno sat up, woofed again, and took off at a trot around the side of the cabin.

A few minutes later, they heard a car door slam. Bruno came back and shoved his nose under Carl's arm just as Deputy Sheriff Pittella walked toward them.

"Hope you don't mind the intrusion," he said.

"No, of course not. You're always welcome," said Elsa. "Have a seat."

"Would you like a Blatz?" asked Carl, raising his bottle.

"No, no. Thanks. I'm on duty and anyway I can't stay long. I just thought you'd like to know what the Duluth team has found out." Pittella sat down in one of the other chairs around the table and absentmindedly picked up a piece of cheese and popped it into his mouth.

"They've identified the body, then?" asked Elsa.

"Not quite yet, but we're confident that will be forthcoming. The dive team finished their search this morning and went back to Duluth after they briefed me about what they had found. They collected quite a few bones, which the ME and some specialists will work on back at headquarters. It looks like there was only one set of remains.

"It's the jewelry that they found which will probably lead to an identification. A man's class ring from Northwestern University, class of 1925, with the initials OR engraved on the inside. They also found a gold watch which had an inscription on the back. 'All my love, J.' The two items were very close together."

"Were they near where we found the skull?" asked Elsa.

"No way to tell that, I'm afraid. You'd already moved the skull."

"Well, what about how the man died? The skull seemed to be intact, at least."

Pittella paused for just a second. "It does not look like it was an accident. That's about all they have determined at this point, except that whatever happened took place some time ago."

"How do they know it's not an accident?" asked Carl.

"Actually, I'm not sure you'd like to know the details. They are a bit disturbing." Pittella looked from Elsa to Carl and back again, hoping they wouldn't ask for more. He contemplated making up an excuse for not telling them, but he could think of none that sounded valid. After all, there was no possibility that they had committed the murder or would pass on any information to any potential suspect. And eventually, the details would come out anyway.

Elsa sat forward in her chair and said, "Of course, we want to know the details. This is real life. This happened to some family. A man was murdered and probably the people who cared about him have no idea what happened to him. His remains have been on the bottom of the lake for years. That's what you're saying, isn't it? Well, we'd like to know how he died or at least know more details."

Pittella smiled. He was continually amazed at how differently people reacted to situations. His daughter, who was about Elsa's age, would never have asked for details of a crime. She hated that he had to deal with death and bad things. She only wanted to know nice things, do nice things, think nice things. He loved her for that and did his best to protect her, but secretly he saw her as weak and felt that she would be unprepared when life dealt her even a soft blow. Elsa, on the other hand, he thought, was like a terrier on a scent. Better give her the facts, horrible as they were, or she'd never give up looking.

"There was some silt and muck on the bottom, but you must have disturbed the area when you hooked on the skull. Something shiny caught the eye of one of the divers and after that they were even more meticulous in their search. The jewelry was found within inches of two good-sized anchors attached to a mass of tangled chains. The medical examiner speculates that the man's hands and feet were bound together with the chains, or possibly ropes and chains. The chains were attached to the anchors to weigh the body down. There's no way to know if the man was dead when he went into the water. It's possible the ME will be able to determine cause of death by studying the bones. We'll know that in a few weeks."

"Why does the ME think his feet were tied with his hands?" Elsa asked.

"They also found the remnants of shoes with metal eyes that shoelaces go through. They were very near the jewelry."

Pittella sat back in the chair. "It appears the man had been bound hands and feet together, an awkward but efficient way to sink a body."

Elsa and Carl sat silently, looking at Pittella for a moment.

Finally, Elsa spoke, "That's pretty gruesome. I certainly hope the man was dead before all that happened."

"Hard to know," said Pittella, as he stood up. "But I'd better be going. Stop in to see me next time you're in Tower. I'd like to finish up the paperwork on my end and need you to sign a statement. And again, thanks for your help. Don't bother seeing me off."

They said their goodbyes there, and Carl and Elsa sat back down. He reached over and took her hand, and together they stared at the lake, thinking dark thoughts. Bruno accompanied the Deputy Sheriff to his car and sat at the end of the driveway as the big man got into his cruiser. The tires on the gravel driveway and Bruno's solitary woof told Carl and Elsa that Pittella was gone.

CHAPTER 11

The Swansons' cabin was in a small bay which Carl had named Half Bay. He had painted 'Half Bay' in big letters on the front of the boathouse for the world to see, or at least the fishermen who trolled by. The shoreline was rocks, rocks, and more rocks, as was the case with most of Lake Vermilion's shoreline. Carl was glad about that because usually a sandy shore was bordered by marsh with rushes and underwater weeds. However, the downside was that Half Bay's rocky shoreline meant there was no safe place for a small child to swim. Elsa went swimming off the dock almost every day when they were at the cabin, but now that they had Katy, her swimming routine had changed. She used to swim across the little bay and back. Never touching bottom, she would dive from the dock to start her swim and swing herself up onto it when she was done. Now she stayed by the shore where she knew the bottom well enough to be confident holding the small child. She learned where the taller flat rocks were that she could easily balance herself on, where there were small patches of silt without any rocks, and where there were sharp rocks to avoid. Katy loved being in the water, but with no sandy beach or easy way to get in, Elsa had to tread carefully over slippery stones, holding Katy, and then hold her as long as she could manage while the happy child splashed and kicked. The shore was nothing but rocks, most of them large, rough-edged, and underwater there were more slippery rocks – a dangerous place for a small child.

Carl decided to fix this with a little hard work. At a shallow point along the shore where the water was about hip-deep, Carl had built up a small ledge. Using two railroad ties held in place with long iron stakes, he filled in the spaces between the large rocks with smaller, flat ones and some dirt already sprouting grass. The effect was a place to get into the water without having to step on the slippery rocks on the shoreline, a place to sit and dangle your legs. From it, Elsa could hop down into the water while Katy stood waiting for permission to jump to her mother. They played in the water during the warmth of midday, right after lunch every day that week while Carl was off doing some chores around the place. Bruno would go back and forth between the lakeshore and wherever Carl was working, keeping an eye on everyone. Sometimes Carl would join them to cool off after some strenuous task or another. Katy would squeal with delight when he would swim with her on his back, her arms around his neck. Elsa never felt confident enough to swim with Katy, but Carl was strong and could swim with one arm, keeping his other hand on the precious cargo on his back. Katy would cling to his neck, her little body floating and bouncing along, face held up out of the water with lips pursed tight, eyes squinty, enjoying every second. Katy would squeal with delight when he made funny whale sounds by blowing hard on the surface of the water with his lips tight like Dizzy Gillespie.

Before Katy, Carl never swam for fun. As a boy in his native Sweden, he had worked after school cutting firewood, so there was never much time for swimming in the big lake, named Big Lake, which he passed every day on his way to and from school. A few times each summer when the temperature was inviting, the local boys would swim on a Sunday afternoon, but most of the time they were more interested in fishing than swimming.

In the Army, he learned to swim for stealth, with powerful, silent strokes which never broke the surface. He could swim side-stroke long distances using only one arm, leaving the other to keep his gear and rifle dry, his face and head above water. Now, he swam using the same technique with a much lighter load and for a more pleasant reason.

With the swim ledge finished, Carl had started to clear the bottom of the lake in that area so that it would be soft to stand on. He had been clearing rocks from the water all morning when he heard the bell letting him know that Elsa had lunch or dinner ready. "Come on, Bruno. Let's go have lunch," Carl said to the big dog who had been snoozing in the shade. Carl went into the boathouse where he changed, swapping his swim trunks on the same hook that had held his clothes. Bruno led the way up to the house.

"I think I'll be ready to start working on the fireplace tomorrow. I'm almost finished clearing the rocks off the bottom," said Carl between spoonfuls of soup.

"Wow, really? That's great. How's the bottom feel? Is it mucky?" asked Elsa.

"No. Not really. I'm amazed at how sandy it is."

They ended lunch with lefse rolled with butter and cinnamon sugar. As Carl started out the door, Elsa said, "Do you mind keeping Katy while I walk up to the mailbox. She's getting kind of heavy for me to carry if she gets tired. Half a mile is quite a walk for her little legs."

"Sure, honey, I can work on shore. I'll go back in the water tomorrow and finish with the rocks," Carl answered from the doorway. "Come on, Katy. Let's go down to the lake."

"Oh, wait. I think she'll need a sweater," said Elsa. She went to the bureau, came back with a bright yellow cardigan with red flower-shaped buttons, and put it on the toddler. "Go with Daddy, sweetie. And remember, be careful, don't go by the water." He reached out his hand, Katy took it, and away they went, Bruno in the lead.

First, they stopped at the shed to get some tools to work on preparing the site for the rock fireplace. He grabbed a stiff rake, a shovel, and a pry bar and stuck snippers in his pocket. Carl dug around on a shelf and found a hand trowel, which he gave to Katy. "Here, you can carry this for Daddy. Okay. All set. Let's go," he said.

The rise of land on which the cabin was built ran straight, while the lake shore curved around the little bay, creating a wide, relatively flat piece of land near water level. It was here that Carl was planning to have the picnic area and fireplace. Since last summer, he had been clearing the brush, moving larger rocks and boulders away, and filling in holes with dirt to make way for grass to grow. He wasn't trying to turn the property into a manicured suburban yard, rather he was trying to make a welcoming meadow nestled between the lake and the small hill. A place where they could have a picnic table and eat meals cooked on the large flat cast iron slab he was installing in the fireplace. A place to have lawn chairs that wouldn't tip over when you sat down to drink a beer or a cocktail in the evening. Or where you could lie on the ground and look up at the stars if you wanted to. A place where Katy could play safely. Carl knew that, unlike Sweden, Minnesota had no poisonous snakes. A bee sting was the worst thing that could happen, or so he thought. It was the perfect place to him.

The previous summer, using a draw shave he had brought from Sweden, he had hand-planed a long cedar log to have a flat surface and set it on stacks of rocks he had cemented together as supports near the water's edge to use as a bench. He set his tools against it and said, "Here, Katy. You play over here. Daddy's going to try to move that big rock over there." Bruno lay down nearby and watched his people, his head on his paws. The earth was soft around the bench, and Katy dug some up and made a pile on the bench, then topped it with leaves and patted it like she had made a loaf of bread. Carl smiled as he watched her, then he picked up the shovel and walked over to the boulder, which was in the middle of the clearing.

He dug a trench around it with the shovel to get a pry bar under it. He was tossing dirt and loose rocks to the side when Katy came right next to him and squatted to dig in the dirt with her trowel. He almost hit her with the shovel on the back swing.

"No, Katy! Look out! You're in the way!" he cried out. "You'll get hurt, honey. You've got to go play over there. Go on!" Carl said in a calmer voice, pointing to the log bench. "Go on. Go over by Bruno."

When the little girl didn't move but just looked at him with big eyes, he set the shovel down and scooped her up with a 'whoosh' and a kiss. She giggled and hung on to him as he walked over to the bench. This time, he gathered some pinecones, sticks, and small rocks and laid them out on the bench for her to play with.

"Here ya go. I should have brought better toys from the house, but these will have to do. Now, you play here for just a bit. Your mama will be back soon," he said and kissed the top of her head before he went back to the boulder.

The trench around the boulder was deep enough, and Carl was jamming the pry bar under it over and over to get it as deep as possible when Bruno started barking. For a moment, Carl thought that Elsa had returned, and Bruno was letting him know, so he looked toward the cabin. But immediately he realized it wasn't the usual bark of 'greetings', this was the dog's bark for 'danger'. Carl turned to Bruno, who was barking continuously at the lake's edge. "Bruno, what's wrong?" Then he saw it - the yellow sweater out in the water. It took only a second to realize it wasn't just the sweater floating in the shadow of an overhanging tree.

Carl raced toward the lake. At the shore, he fell forward, slamming his knees on the sharp rocks. He scrambled to get up and flung himself into the water. It only took two strokes to reach her little body floating face down, arms out loose-limbed as a rag doll. He flipped her over, holding her head up with one hand, and took powerful sidestrokes back toward the shore until he could stand and walk out of the water. This time, he was careful on the rocks. He didn't want to fall on her. She was completely limp, and her eyes were closed. *"Herre Gud. Herre Gud,"* kept running through his head.

Some combination of instinct and Army emergency training

took over. He had to get her breathing again. Without thinking, he turned her upside down, holding her by an ankle with one hand, and began to slap her on the back. When she didn't respond and with the 'oh, my god' repeating in his head, he smacked her harder and finally, after he hit her harder than he thought he should ever hit any living thing, she coughed. Then she began to cry. The 'oh, my god' continued, but now in a different tone, one of relief. He righted her and held her close, covering her head with kisses as he hurried toward the cabin. Bruno ran with them, still barking.

* * *

Elsa's heart stopped in her chest when she heard Bruno barking. She could tell something was terribly wrong. It wasn't Bruno's normal bark. She started running and had just made it to the driveway when she saw Carl coming up the hill with Katy in his arms. They met at the cabin steps.

"What happened?" Elsa cried, taking the wet bundle from Carl. He couldn't speak as he opened the door for them. They went to the sofa and sat close to each other as Elsa calmed the crying child.

"Come on, sweetie," she said when Katy had finally stopped crying. "Let's get some dry clothes on. Did you go for a swim without me?" She asked while rubbing the chubby body with a towel. Katy nodded.

"Next time, wait for Mama, okay." Katy nodded. "Okay, then. How about you look at a book for a little bit and I'll get you a cookie." She set the toddler on the floor with a Golden Book about Donald and Daisy Duck.

Carl had changed into dry clothes, too, and had put the

coffee pot on. He sat at the table, his head in his hands. He hadn't spoken yet, and when Elsa put her hand on his shoulder, he looked up, silent tears running down his face.

"You want to tell me what happened now?" she snapped. She was furious, and she knew he could tell. She didn't want to be angry at him, but she was. *He almost killed our baby. Our precious Katy. How could he have been so careless!*

He wiped his face on his sleeve, took a deep breath, and told her how he had let his guard down and that if it hadn't been for Bruno's barking – he couldn't finish the sentence.

Elsa didn't say a word. Her anger hung in the air. After a minute, she went to Katy and picked her up, "Time for your nap, little one." She took the baby behind the screen and laid her in the crib. Sitting on the stool next to the crib, she sang a lullaby and gently rubbed Katy's back until she was asleep. Elsa sat there watching her precious baby sleep for a long while. Her anger raged at the man who almost lost everything that she had wanted, everything that was so important in their lives. She swore at him under her breath. She sat with her head in her hands, crying tears of frustrated anger that eventually turned to tears of gratitude. A reluctant admission crept into her thoughts that what happened could have happened even if she were there. She had helped Carl with projects many times while Katy was momentarily unattended by both of them. She resolved to keep closer watch; this couldn't happen again.

When she finally came out from behind the screen, she saw Carl on the sofa, looking at her with red eyes and a desperate face. She sat down beside him on the sofa. They hugged long and hard. No words were needed. Their tears said everything.

"Was there any mail?" asked Carl, finally breaking the silence.

"A few things," Elsa replied, adjusting her sweater and rubbing her eyes. "Couple of bills. A letter from your friend Gunnar. And a letter from Victoria Martinelli. Remember, I told you about the little girl Katy has played with a several times back home at the playground in Lincoln Park. It was such a pleasant surprise when we found out we both had cabins on Vermilion. Victoria and I kind of hit it off even though she's a little younger than I am."

She retrieved several envelopes from the red crocheted bag she always wore crossbody over her shoulder whenever she went to the mailbox. She liked to have her hands free to pick wild strawberries along the road.

"Gunnar Ericson has retired and has a place on Lake Superior just north of Duluth. We should visit him on our way home in September. He says he'd like us to stay with him and see the big lake," said Carl, reading his friend's letter.

"That would be fun. And here's another invitation. Victoria has suggested we meet in Tower for a play date and lunch on Tuesday next week," said Elsa, holding the letter from Victoria.

"That sounds like a nice thing for you two. Bruno and I can hold down the fort," Carl replied. Bruno came over for an ear scratch when he heard his name.

CHAPTER 12

When Tuesday came, Carl carried Katy to the car and put her in the back seat with a kiss. "Have a nice time with your friend, honey."

Elsa set a small canvas bag full of books on the front passenger seat and got in to drive. Carl came to her window and kissed her goodbye.

Victoria and Angelina were waiting in the playground near the train station. The women sat on the bench and talked while the girls played in the sandbox and climbed on the smaller jungle gym. They pushed the little ones on the swings for a bit, then laid out some lunch things on the picnic table nearby.

After they had wiped little hands and faces and let the toddlers go back to the sandbox, Victoria said, "I'm so glad this worked out. Living on the island can get a little claustrophobic and compared to Chicago, it's a little lonely, too. I didn't think I'd miss television this much. I just love the Perry Como show. He's so dreamy!"

"Oh, yes, he really is. And the Ed Sullivan show is great, too. I really like the musical talents he has on there. Really new and hip. Carl likes the Video Ballroom contest on the Fred Waring Show, so we always watch that, but the music is a little old-fashioned for me," said Elsa.

"Do you let Katy watch the Howdy Doody Show? I've turned it on to see what it's like, but I haven't let Angelina watch it yet. To tell you the truth, the clowns are kind of scary."

"I agree," said Elsa, packing up the lunch things. "This was great, but before we head home, I have some books to return to the library. Would you like to come with us? I go there whenever we're in town. It's in the municipal building, that two-story white building right there."

"Sure. Can anyone take out books? I could definitely use some new reading material. There are a lot of old books at the cabin but nothing I'm interested in," said Victoria.

"Yeah, anyone can take out books. There isn't even a librarian. You just take what you want," Elsa said. "The books I want to return are in my car. Can you watch Katy for a minute while I run get them?"

A few minutes later, when Elsa returned with a bag of books, they walked up the steps of City Hall where the library was on the second floor. Deputy Sheriff Pittella was just leaving.

"Hello!" he said with a smile. "How are you, Elsa?"

He waited for the four of them on the landing at the top of the wide marble stairs. Elsa introduced him to Victoria, who had carried Angelina up the stairs. "I've met your father before, of course. He's had Gold Island since Prohibition days. But I haven't had the pleasure of meeting you before. What a cute little girl you have there," said the tall, pale man, reaching a tickle finger toward the toddler she was holding in her arms.

The little girl, dressed in pink gingham, giggled and hid her face in her mother's shoulder. He turned his attention to Katy, who let go of her mother's hand and stood directly in front of him, looking up. With a nod from Elsa, the Deputy leaned down and picked her up. She giggled too as he barely touched her tummy. He tickled her more with his eyes than his fingers. He remembered how his children hated being tickled. With a little hug, he set her down and turned back to the women.

"Are you here on official business? I was just headed out for an errand, but I can go back in if you're here to see me."

"Oh, no need," Elsa laughed. "I have some books to return, and Victoria has never been to our illustrious library before, so I thought I'd show her how special it is," said Elsa.

"Well, you ladies have a nice afternoon, then," Pittella said, making a silly face and a finger wag to the toddlers who giggled at his antics.

Elsa and Victoria said goodbye to Pittella, and Elsa led the way up the worn marble stairs to the second floor. At the top were several doors and a hallway to the back. The old-time office door with frosted glass stenciled with Library was closed, but a dim light shone through the glass upper half from the windows on the far wall. Elsa turned the knob, went in, and flipped the light switch.

"You can just walk in here?" asked Victoria, setting Angelina down.

"Sure. I take books out all the time. You just write your name on the card in the front of the book and put it in the little box over there."

They wandered along the shelves looking for titles that

interested them while the toddlers chased each other around and under the table in the center of the room, squealing and giggling.

"I can't believe they still have so much energy," said Elsa.

"I know!" said Victoria, looking around a little dismayed. "I don't see any children's books."

"Well, there really aren't many. Just that small shelf over there. The library was started by Preston Bradley. You know him, right? The pastor from Chicago with that radio ministry everybody talks about? He has the church on Lawrence Avenue. He's like the Franklin Roosevelt of preaching. Even if you don't believe what he's saying, you still have to listen to that voice reaching out to you from the radio," Elsa chuckled, imitating spellbinding with wiggling fingers.

"I don't go to that church or anything, but I do know them from here at the lake. He owns the island east of us. We run into them sometimes at the marina. I think my father knows Reverend Bradley fairly well but not to socialize with. I think it's mainly because they've been in the Chicago economic scene for so many years."

"It seems like such a small world sometimes. Carl and Eric, his partner, painted the Bradleys' home and some parts of the church, too. That's how Bradley found out we have a cabin here, too, and he told Carl we should stop by sometime. So, last week we did. Their cabin on Black Duck is really nice. And both of them were so gracious to us. I mean we're not in the same social class or anything."

"Yes, they seem really nice. When we bump into each other at the marina, Reverend Bradley is always so talkative and gushes about the weather and the lake and whatever, but she is so reserved, hardly ever says a thing. She always has sweet words for Angelina though," said Victoria, smiling at her daughter giggling on the floor between the table legs.

"She was like that with Katy, too, when we visited them recently. It's like she's missing grandkids or something. I guess they never had children. I feel bad for her if that's the case." Elsa looked at Katy. "We're so lucky! What beautiful healthy little girls we have!"

The two women finished choosing their books, filled out the cards, and put them in the file box. The few children's books they found didn't even have the check-out cards, so only took two each. Elsa turned out the light and shut the door behind them. They balanced purses, books, and little girls' hands as they made their way down the broad marble stairs. On the sidewalk, they talked as they headed back to their automobiles.

"Next summer I think I'll have to bring some books from home to donate," said Elsa.

"That's a great idea. We have lots and lots of books here, though. I'll put together a box or two to bring when we come back again," said Victoria. "I don't know if you know about my grandfather, Frank Hibbing. He was quite the powerful man up here. He even named the town after himself. He paid for the public library in Hibbing. And he funded the public-school buildings and a theater and, would you believe it, a trolley car system and paved streets. He was quite the guy," She laughed. "It's kind of disdainful to me that one man could have that much money. But at least he did some good with it. I'm sorry I never got to meet him."

"Wow. That's quite a legacy!" said Elsa. "I'm going to drop my books in the car and do a little shopping at Zup's. What about you?"

"No need for me to shop. Roy and Ethel do all that."

They parted ways at Victoria's car with a hug. The toddlers mimicked their mothers with hugs and giggles; then fussed and cried when they had to be separated.

"Let's do this again," said Victoria. "It's so good to get away for a little bit."

"Sure. Whenever you want."

"How about we meet next week at the same time? If you can't make it, no matter. Angelina will still get to play on the jungle gym."

"Okay. That sounds like a great plan. Same for me. I'll save my shopping for this time and if the weather is bad, we'll both know not to come."

"You and Carl should come out to Gold Island. Just stop by anytime. I'm only going to be up here for another few weeks, so don't wait too long. Dad and I would love to see you and meet Carl."

Elsa waved goodbye as Victoria drove away. Katy, who had calmed down in her mother's arms, waved bye-bye and blew toddler kisses to her little friend looking out the back window.

Production of iron, which began in the 15th century, required high heat, and charcoal, which burned at a higher temperature than raw wood, provided that. As the charcoal forests of England became depleted, Sweden stepped up production of charcoal for trade as well as for making its own iron. Charcoal was important for many other aspects of industry as well as for home heating until the development of coal production. In Sweden, charcoal remained an important part of the economy until the early 1900s.

The traditional way to make charcoal was to build piles of tightly packed logs standing upright and allow them to smolder at a low temperature for an extended period of time. The wood used to make charcoal was cut from nearby forests by lumbermen from local villages. After the branches were removed, the uniformly sized logs, each eight to ten feet long, were delivered to the fire camp by horse-drawn wagon. The 'kolare', or charcoal tender, would erect a cone-shaped structure by standing the logs on end in a large circle. It took skill to build it so that the mass of logs was just the right thickness to get proper air flow through the spaces between them. On the ground, the center of the structure was open, and this is where a fire would be kept burning using regular firewood. The outside of the massive cone was covered with moss, mud, and bark tailings and kept slightly moist.

The master charcoal maker would tend the center fire through arched holes he had skillfully constructed around the bottom of the structure. Night and day, he had to keep the center fire smoldering, burning but not hot enough to incinerate the logs destined to become charcoal, just hot enough to dry and char them. He also had to keep the moss moist but not too wet. After several weeks, the cone of logs would be transformed into charcoal, black as coal and just as useful as fuel.

CHAPTER 13

As usual, Katy woke them with her chirps. "Mama? Mama? Mama?" she called repeatedly from her crib.

"Okay," said Elsa to Carl, giving him a smile and a perfunctory kiss as she turned over in bed. "Your turn to get the little lumpkin."

Half-awake, Elsa heard the comfortable noises of the baby and her daddy going through their morning routine, hugs and squeals, a potty trip, and then pattering of feet to the bedside. Carl lifted her onto the bed and joined her to formally wake up Elsa with cold hands and giggles.

The day had started out chilly. The mid-June sun was out, but it hadn't brought much summer warmth yet. On days like this, Carl would start a fire in the cast iron stove at the end of the main room of the cabin while Elsa prepared breakfast in the tiny kitchen. He checked the firebox and saw there were only ashes inside, even though the draft had been shut after yesterday's fire to conserve the logs.

"C'mon, Bruno. Let's go visit the woodpile. We need some wood," said Carl. Bruno stretched, went to the door and waited with his nose to the door handle, while Carl grabbed the wood carrier from its hook near the wood stove. It was fashioned from a simple flat rectangular piece of tough canvas about as wide as the pieces of wood were long. The four corners were folded in on the narrow ends, and a loop of rope was sewn into the seams at each end to make handles. Rugged, simple, and efficient.

Outside, at the top of the small stoop, both man and dog stretched again and breathed in a lungful of early morning air. After a few head pats and a good ear scratch from Carl, Bruno lumbered down the porch steps and trotted off into the woods. Carl headed for the woodpile out back of the cabin, past the two small sheds, one of which was the outhouse, no longer needed since they had the indoor plumbing put in.

The woodpile was an unspoken source of pride for Carl. All summer, he felled trees from the vacant land across the dirt road from their cabin, cut off the branches, and hauled the lengths to the yard in a wheelbarrow. Using the same cross-cut saw, he cut them into the correct length for the small, cast-iron stove. Then he split the wood and stacked the pieces carefully, the way his grandfather had taught him. He loved the heft and feel of the split logs as he stacked them. He worked on making the wood pile bigger almost every day, even if it wasn't for very long. It satisfied a few of a man's needs to feel like a man, Carl thought, to provide the basic necessity of warmth for his family, and to use his muscles to feel strong. Next to fishing, it was one of his favorite things to do.

He laid the canvas carrier out flat on the ground and began to lay pieces of wood on it. As he reached for the highest ones on the pile, the smell of cut wood brought back memories of his childhood. His mother's father, Per Äng, had been a *kolare*, a master charcoal maker in rural northeastern Sweden, not far from where Carl was born and raised. Äng was a skilled craftsman and a respected man. Charcoal was a necessity to run the machinery for the lumber mill he worked for, and it was an additional source of revenue for the company that the entire community relied on for their livelihoods.

For weeks at a time during the summer, his grandfather would stay alone at the charcoal fire camp. He ate and slept only a few hours at a stretch in a one-room log cabin built in a large clearing deep in the forest where he tended the charcoal-making fires.

As a small boy, Carl would accompany his mother and grandmother when, once a week or so, they took food to Per Äng at the fire camp. The smell of the smoldering fire and his grandfather's happiness to see them were strong memories that came back to Carl now as he neatly loaded the canvas carrier with the cut firewood. He hummed an old tune that his grandfather used to sing, "*Violer til Mor*", on his way back to the cabin. Bruno had returned from his jaunt in the woods and took the lead back to the house.

As they ate breakfast, Elsa said, "You know, I'm not really up for fishing yet, so how about we take a boat ride and go visit someone. How about the Bradleys'? You've piqued my curiosity about the Tower Library's benefactor. Or maybe we should drop by the Martinellis'. Victoria invited us when we were in Tower together."

"Well, sure. Let's try the Bradleys' first. There's no guarantee that they'll be there this early in the summer, but it will be a nice boat ride anyway. If they're not home, we can ride over to Gold Island. It's just across the bay from Black Duck."

"Okay. I think I'll quick make up a batch of oatmeal raisin cookies to take along. How about we leave in an hour or so?"

Carl and Bruno went outside to do some guy things and get the boat ready.

In the kitchen, Elsa set Katy on the little potty chair with the decal bunny on the backrest, fastened the plastic belt around her chubby tummy, and slid the tray across the front. The toddler played with the toys her mother set on the tray as Elsa cleaned the dishes.

"All done?" Elsa asked the toddler. After removing the wooden tray from the potty chair and setting it on the table, she lifted Katy off her seat and praised the toddler for the good job. Katy laughed happily, rewarded with lots of little kisses from her mother, a clean bottom, and fresh clothes for the day.

"Come with me, Katy, you can play in the kitchen while I make some cookies, okay?" Elsa pulled back the curtain that covered the space under the kitchen counter. On the shelf, there was a wooden box that held metal measuring cups and a few wooden spoons. She took out a few items she didn't need to make the cookies and set them on the floor for Katy to play with. She also took a wooden bowl down from an upper shelf and put it on the floor, too. Katy came over and squatted next to the makeshift toys as only an eighteen-month-old can do. As her mother measured and mixed, the little girl mimicked her actions, hitting the cups together and banging the spoon in the bowl. The two chatted and sang little nursery songs as they worked, and finally, there was cookie dough to taste. Katy stood on tiptoes to see in the bowl her mother was holding down for her to dip a teaspoon in.

"Just a little bit, Katy. Not too much or you'll get a tummy ache. We have to wait until they're cooked to eat the rest."

When Carl came in, the cabin smelled of freshly baked cookies.

"How's it going in here with my two bakers?" he asked as he picked up the little girl.

"Cookies are done and packed in a tin to take along. I saved some out for us so you can have a couple if you want. They're up on the shelf there. Get Katy's coat on, will you? I'll be ready to go in a minute."

Bruno was already at the boathouse waiting for them. Carl opened the simple door with the grip and latched it to the outside wall so it wouldn't blow shut in the wind. Carl got in the boat first, and Elsa handed Katy down to him, then the bag she always brought along on boat rides. After she got in, she put the little red kapok life vest on Katy. Both Carl and Elsa released the ropes holding the boat, and together they pushed it under the front half-wall and out of the boat house, ducking as they went. Elsa held onto the dock as Carl pulled the starter rope; the motor started on the third pull. He put it in gear, Elsa pushed away from the dock, and off they went.

The Gruben family emigrated from Norway in the late 1800s, homesteaded in the Tower, Minnesota area and bought land on Lake Vermilion. One of the Gruben brothers owned most of Arrowhead Point, and built the marina, gas dock, small store, and several housekeeping cabins that perched on the solid rock of the point.

Another brother purchased most of the island where the Hotel Idlewild was located, a popular steamboat destination for vacationers who preferred amenities, dining, and dancing, which he renamed "Isle of Pines". It had been used as a hideaway for the mob when they needed to get out of Chicago for a while during prohibition. When the grand lodge fell into disrepair after World War II, the property was split into separate parcels to be sold to families who were feeling the post-war economic prosperity.

Isle of Pines is only a few hundred feet from Arrowhead Point, but the county road ends at the water's edge. The Gruben brothers got permission from the county to build and maintain the bridge which still stands today. The wooden structure was supported by three log cribs filled with rocks. The underwater structures attract certain types of fish, making it a favorite spot for still fishermen. The wood railings on the one lane bridge made walking across the bridge safer, although the spaces between the planks of the roadbed still cause more than a few twisted ankles.

CHAPTER 14

The day was lovely with big fluffy clouds hanging on a brilliant blue sky. The lake was calm, and Carl twisted the throttle handle to top speed, then reduced it a bit. It was no speedboat, but Carl liked it that way. He saw no reason to hurry once you were on the water, and besides, this was a fishing boat meant for trolling most of all.

They made their way out of Daisy Bay, weaving between the markers by School Teacher's Island. For years, Mr. and Mrs. Harrison, who owned the tiny island, had been coming up to Lake Vermilion for the summer from Duluth, where they were both schoolteachers. The island was just a huge rock sticking out of the water with a tiny white house, a boat house and dock, a couple of dozen trees, and a few scrubby bushes. On one end of the rock, where nothing but lichen grew, there was a pole that held a cat's cradle of clothesline. The old couple's laundry waved at Carl and Elsa as they motored by.

They slowed when they came up to Gruben's gas dock and

continued past the big, galvanized metal boat house filled with the boats of people who had cabins on islands or remote mainland where there were no roads.

Carl and Elsa's boat was passing slowly under the bridge when a car drove over them. The planks that made up the driving surface clattered loudly, and the log cribbing creaked under the weight of the vehicle. The sounds brought Carl back to the time when his friends Werner and Gertrude Nelson had taken him to dinner at Isle of Pines Lodge. Carl had been sitting in the back seat of Werner's new Nash Ambassador and remembered the same creaking and clattering sounds as they crossed the bridge. He knew the year was 1930 because they were taking him out to celebrate his becoming a US citizen. Carl was enjoying the pleasant memory when a flash of something disturbing crossed his mind. Carl couldn't quite remember what it was, but as he steered the boat clear of the bridge and the no-wake zone on either side, it came to him. That fleeting moment was many years ago, but somehow Carl felt unsettled by the unbeckoned memory. He impulsively wanted to stop to see Irv, hoping to dispel the unease he was feeling.

As they crossed the wide bay heading toward the narrow stretch of water that led to Frazer Bay, Carl was reminded of how interesting and unpredictable, even dangerous, Lake Vermilion was – just like some people. The waters of Daisy Bay had been calm a mere mile away, but now, on the opposite side of the bridge, the water was rough and choppy as they headed northwest. The heavy wooden boat plowed through the waves, but spray hit Elsa and Katy, making them squeal with surprise. Carl reduced speed to avoid getting them all soaked.

Pine Island, to their right, was ten miles long and even had a small lake of its own on the eastern end. They passed the reef where a man had been killed the previous summer when he ran his boat aground late one night. The small mound of rocks that protruded from the water was easily visible in calm weather during the day, but hard to see at night or when the waves obscured it. Carl noticed that someone had attached a reflector of some sort to a tall stick and had succeeded in getting it to stay upright, wedged in a pile of small rocks.

"Look, Elsa," he said, pointing out the warning device. "Someone had a good idea, eh?" he said, "It's a miracle more people haven't been killed running into those rocks."

"So much death on this beautiful lake," Elsa said sadly.

Carl slowed to a crawl and leaned forward to speak to Elsa, who had turned to see what he was doing. "Let's stop and see if Irv is up yet. I was just thinking about him."

"Sure. That'd be okay."

Halfway through the narrow strait to Frazer Bay, Carl aimed the boat toward the Pine Island shore where a long dock beckoned. When the tall timber had been logged many years before, shrub forest of poplar, pine, ash, spruce, and balsam grew in its place. But here and there, small patches of white, red, or Norwegian pine managed to take hold, perhaps seedlings from the old growth. This particular section of Pine Island was covered with dense, dark pine forest, not yet towering over a hundred feet as their predecessors had, but still tall for only being fifty or so years old. Along the shore, cedar, birch, and balsam grew, but there was no sunlight for those smaller trees under the canopy of the pines.

Looking into the conifers at the end of the dock, Carl could see nothing but darkness, even so early in the day. The white trellised archway was like a door standing open to a room with the drapes drawn and the lights off, pitch dark inside. The letters painted in dark green across the top of the arch seemed a pleasant design, but somehow weren't welcoming. "Shadowland" it read.

As Carl pulled up to the dock and jumped out, he noticed Elsa pull Katy close to her as she looked into the darkness of the woods. Instinctively protecting our child from the boat hitting the dock, or was it something else, Carl wondered. Bruno jumped out as Carl tied up and then lent a hand getting Katy out of the boat. He put his arm around Elsa's waist as they walked the length of the dock. She shivered as they stepped into the darkness.

It took a moment for their eyes to adjust once they stepped through the archway and onto the dirt path which led straight ahead through the dense trees. It was cool and surprisingly quiet. The dark was not actually dark after all, as mottled sunlight managed to make its way through the trees here and there. The pine branches cast a maze of overlapping shadows on the ground. The house loomed at the end of the long path. It wasn't a cabin as most structures on the lake were, but rather it looked like a Midwest farmhouse, totally out of place in a dense pine forest. Two stories tall, it was white and adorned with dark green shutters and a wrap-around porch. Several tall-backed rocking chairs sat side by side. The front door had a large oval beveled glass window through which they could see a staircase directly ahead.

Elsa looked over her shoulder, then turned back to the house ahead. "Strange. Why build so far back in the woods when there is a beautiful lake view just out there," she said to Carl under her breath.

A path led off to their right through the trees. At the end of it, a float plane was tied between two docks in a small bay, the nose, propeller, and one wing barely visible. Nearby was a dark green boathouse. Carl knew that many years ago, Irv's father had dredged the marshy cove, which was hidden behind a long, thin point of land running parallel to the shore. To keep the water calm during storms, he had a rock barrier built out from the opening to the cove. Access to the shallow cove required a steady hand maneuvering the plane through the gap with the wings on one side extending over the rock barrier and the land on the other. Once inside its protected harbor, there was no chance that it would be disturbed or even noticed. A passing boat couldn't see the plane or even the secluded little harbor because the rocks were a strong deterrent to exploring the shoreline.

Carl had been up in Irv's plane twice, once over Lake Vermilion and Trout Lake to the north and a second time to the east over Shagawa and Burntside Lakes near Ely, Minnesota. The flights were an hour or so long and gave an eagle's perspective of the lake-filled Northwoods. Carl hadn't even imagined how beautiful yet wild the area was from the air. Most visitors and cabin owners who had looked at maps of the area knew there were so many lakes with so many islands all across the Arrowhead Region of Minnesota. It was, after all, the Land of 10,000 Lakes. But when Carl saw it from the air, he realized how paltry man's foray into the wilderness was.

As Elsa and Carl stepped up onto the porch, they could see Irv coming down the stairs. He opened the front door with a smile.

"Hallo! It's so good to see you. Come. Come. Sit down over here and tell me, how are things?" Irv said, gesturing at the rocking chairs on the long, narrow porch. He leaned against the railing facing them.

"Ruth hasn't come up yet. Her arthritis is really bad, so her sister is visiting to help her with some things for a month or so. I'll go back to Chicago and bring her up here for the rest of the summer when all the sisterly stuff is over. I'm enjoying the solitude, truth be told." He chuckled.

"Oh, I'm so sorry to hear she isn't feeling well. But it's wonderful she has her sister," said Elsa.

They chatted about people they knew and various things that had happened since they'd last met for dinner in Chicago some months before. When the conversation turned to the Bradleys, Carl mentioned that they were on their way to Black Duck Island to say hello to Preston and his wife.

"Well, then. I didn't know you were friends with the Bradleys," said Irv.

"Well, I can't say we're friends exactly. We've never visited before. A few years back Eric and I painted the manse at the Peoples' Church and that's how I first met the Reverend and his wife. Since then, we've painted almost all of the church property. Sunday school classrooms. And the main chapel was a really big job. We needed extra high scaffolding. We had to rent that. Anyway, Preston had asked us to drop by their cabin here at the lake a couple of times," said Carl.

"I haven't met them yet and I kept hearing about what nice people they are, so I told Carl we should drop over to say hello. Today seemed like a good day," said Elsa.

"That's wonderful. You'll enjoy them. Ruth and I get

together with them a few times a year now. Preston is getting on in years, you know. Say, that gives me an idea. Carl, how'd you like to go on a fishing trip with Bradley and me? I've been promising to take him fishing for a couple years now. Weather's good. If it holds, we should go week after next."

Carl looked over at Elsa, who shrugged her shoulders and smiled.

"Sure. That'd be great," said Carl.

"Okay then, that's great. I'll be in touch when I firm up the plans for the trip. We'll leave early and go up to my father's old cabin on Lake of the Woods. You know, up by Kenora in Ontario. We can fish for three days and come home on the fourth day. Not sure yet what day we'll leave but we'll definitely be gone three to four days. Trip's hardly worth it if you don't stay for a few days."

"Sounds fine. I'll be ready anytime," said Carl. "Oh! Do I need my passport? I don't have it. It's back home in Illinois."

"No, you won't need it. We won't be seeing any border patrols. It's nothing but wilderness up where we're going. No one can tell where the border is, even if they cared, and why would anyone care anymore now that Prohibition is long over."

"All right, then. Just let me know. Elsa can bring me over in the boat," said Carl. "Say, you won't believe what Elsa brought up from the bottom of the lake the other day. We were trolling on the reef over by Black Duck Island when Elsa got stuck."

"I'm surprised, my dear," Irv said to Elsa with a smile, "I thought by now your husband would have taught you how to avoid that pitfall. What did you get stuck on?"

Elsa said nothing as Carl continued. "She brought up a human skull. Perhaps you'd heard the news that the county dive team was called in to recover the remains."

Irv took a breath before he answered in a dismissive tone. "Yes, I did hear some rumor or another when I was in Tower yesterday, but I didn't pay any attention to it. Was it some lost gold miner from the 1800's?"

"No, they think it is a man who was murdered mob style. Drowned with his hands and feet bound to a couple of anchors. They're pretty sure they'll be able to identify him because he had on a Northwestern University class ring."

Irv's face had turned white, and he had just grabbed the porch railing to steady himself when they heard a commotion and barking from around the side of the house. Carl and Elsa glanced at each other when they realized Bruno wasn't on the porch with them.

"Bruno! Where are you, big guy? Come on. Don't be getting into trouble," Carl shouted off the end of the porch.

A minute later, the dog trotted around the corner of the house, tongue hanging out. He casually walked up the stairs and went over to Katy, who had been playing with a couple of sticks, hitting them on the porch railing. He gave her a quick sniff over and a nose nudge to make sure she was fine, then he went to lie on the floor next to Carl's chair.

"You stay here, now," said Carl as he patted Bruno's head.

His timing couldn't have been better because just then a squirrel jumped up on the railing not far from Katy. As Bruno leaped forward to protect Katy or get the squirrel, which was probably one and the same to him, Carl's hand was right there on his neck to grab his collar. The squirrel kkkaa-kkaa-kkaatched at the dog and the dog barked back, teeth bared. Elsa jumped up to snatch Katy away from the fray, and the little girl started shrieking.

The hubbub went on for a minute, then subsided as Elsa calmed Katy, and Carl commanded Bruno to silence. The big dog was obviously frustrated, but lay still with his head on his paws, eyes focused on the squirrel, which kept chattering, still on the porch railing. Katy snuggled up to her mother as Elsa held her close and rocked back and forth.

Irv went up to the squirrel and started talking to it, and it stopped fussing, too. Then he turned to speak with his guests again, "Well, that was exhilarating."

The squirrel climbed down from the railing and crawled up the outside of Irv's pant leg. It circled around so it had access to Irv's pocket. Elsa looked concerned, Katy was staring, Carl was smiling, and Bruno was growling quietly. The squirrel had his head deep in Irv's pocket, and his bushy tail was flicking furiously. When he emerged, he had two peanuts sticking out of his mouth. He climbed down the pant leg and scampered off the porch and up a nearby tree.

"I always keep peanuts in my pocket for him. He's quite demanding, isn't he?" Irv said, staring after the critter. "He can get pretty damned annoying. One of these days, I'll just have to get rid of him. Twist his little head off. Won't be hard to do since he trusts me." He turned back to his guests with a smile. "Just kidding, of course."

Something in his look was unsettling, though, and Elsa and Carl quickly stood at the same time. "Well, we've got to be going," said Elsa as she picked up Katy.

"Nice seeing you, Elsa," said Irv. He shook hands with Carl, "I'll stop by your place to give you the dates when I firm up plans for the fishing trip with Preston."

As they pulled away from the dock, Elsa looked back through the archway to Shadowland. She could see nothing but darkness where she knew the shadows were.

Between 1850 and 1930, large numbers of Swedes immigrated to the United States because of the promise of religious freedom and economic opportunity. They were ambitious, industrious people and started many new companies and developed new, innovative products.

The first Swedes in Chicago settled just north of the Chicago River. After the Great Chicago Fire, the Swedish community moved further north, and by the 1890's they had consolidated in what came to be known as Andersonville around the intersection of Clark and Foster. At the turn of the century, Chicago, as a city, had the greatest population of Swedes, second only to Stockholm. In 1920, there were 110,000 Swedes in Chicago.

Swedish civil, mechanical, and structural engineers, as well as architects and developers, were instrumental in rebuilding the city after the fire and this established their place in Chicago's civil society. Their influence on the growth of Chicago as a hub of manufacturing and industry was celebrated by the Swedish Engineers Society, organized in 1908.

Swedish-Americans were very entrepreneurial and forward-thinking but also worked at keeping their culture alive through fraternal organizations, hospitals, and churches. The Chicago Swedish-American Tribune was the largest Swedish language newspaper outside of Sweden.

1927 CHICAGO

CHAPTER 15

One Sunday in early May, to celebrate getting his first automobile, Carl and his friends, Gunnar Erickson, Tord Nystrom, and Eric Lindberg, went for a ride in his new Star four-door sedan. They were looking for a place to have a bite to eat and a cup of coffee as they drove south on Clark Street.

"Take a right here. I've heard there are some good bakeries on Halstead. Maybe they'll be some good places to eat, too," said Tord.

After driving for a bit, Eric called out from the backseat, "Hey. There's a place."

A nice-looking establishment with samples of baked goods in the front window was on the left. The street was crowded with automobiles and people, so Carl turned into the next alley to find a place to park. Laughing and chatting, oblivious to their surroundings, they walked into the cafe and sat near the window - just a group of hungry, young friends.

The waitress came to take their order, and that is when Carl realized they were in an Italian establishment.

"What can I getta you, young gentamen?" said the buxom, dark-haired waitress in a puffy-sleeved white blouse, a tray cocked against her ample hip.

They ordered coffee and pointed at the cream puff pastries they'd seen in the front window on their way in. The waitress nodded, and they went back to chatting about the dive Irv had taken them to the night before. The Velvet Club was a speakeasy in No Man's Land, an unincorporated parcel of land between Evanston and Wilmette, suburbs along the Lake Michigan shore just north of Chicago. Several restaurants with less than hidden speakeasies in their basements had opened in No Man's Land, as there was no law enforcement in that short half mile of lakefront.

"Boy, Irv sure does know a lot of great places to have fun," Gunnar said. "Dat dame dat called herself Tina vas a real hottie!"

They had met several young women they hoped to see again and were talking animatedly about the ladies' respective physical attributes. It wasn't long before the waitress brought steaming cups of coffee and flaky pastries with a creamy filling.

Carl looked around while his friends ate and talked. The restaurant had a dozen or so tables. Along the back wall was a bar. It was obvious that just a few years earlier the bar had served liquor. But now the bartender was a barista, a cheery-looking bald man, wearing a white shirt with the sleeves rolled up, black pleated pants, and a long white apron, manning an espresso machine. The glass shelves on the wall held cups and soda glasses, not bottles of whisky. Leaning against the tall counter, a group of young Italian men had been drinking coffee and smoking when the Swedes came in. They all turned and stared at Carl and his friends silently for a while.

"Eh," the tallest of them called out. He was leaning back with his elbows on the bar, one foot in a smooth leather shoe crossed over the other ankle like a mannequin in a Marshall Field's window and dressed like one, too. He was addressing Carl, who happened to make eye contact as he looked around, "Whadda you talkin' over dere?"

"We're speaking Swedish," Carl replied.

After a pause while he chewed on his thumbnail with a sneer, the Italian said, "Swedish, eh? Well, here's what you gotta know. You wanna eat here, you speaka English, eh?"

"Dumb Swedes," said one of his buddies to no one in particular. The others in his group laughed and mumbled their agreement, jostling each other in anticipation of the upcoming confrontation. Carl said nothing and turned back to his friends. They had gone silent, watching the situation between Carl and the Italians unfold.

"I think it's time to leave," he said. There was no doubt the Swedes were bigger than the Italians, but they were outnumbered six to three. They all stood and fished in their pockets for money to pay the bill. The waitress hurried over.

"*Gracie, gracie*," she said as she picked up the money they were setting on the table.

"Let's go," said Gunnar, grabbing the last of the pastries from their plates, shoving the pieces in his mouth. As they left the restaurant, the Italian guys followed them. The Swedes quickened their pace, and when the Italians did too, Carl and his friends broke into a run. They ran down the alley, pulling garbage cans and stacks of empty crates over to fall behind them, hoping to slow down their pursuers. Carl had no idea how serious these thugs were, but he had heard that the mob were Italians and all kinds of terrible things happened to people who 'crossed' the mob. He wasn't sure what 'crossing' was, but he was sure he didn't like the way those guys had looked at them. Earlier, a couple of them had made a point of pulling jackknives from their pockets, pretending to clean their fingernails. Now they were being chased full speed, and Carl's heart was pounding in his chest.

As they ran, Carl shouted in Swedish, *"Gunnar, du måste kör. Ja ska' ta cranken."* Gunnar shouted back that he understood. They reached the Star a little ahead of the Italians, and Carl ran to the front, grabbed the crank from its clips, and inserted it into the front of the engine as the other three jumped in the automobile, Gunnar behind the wheel. Carl had begun to turn the crank as Gunnar opened the choke. The engine turned over. Carl felt a sigh of relief. But just then, the Italians caught up. The first one to reach the car slapped both hands on the trunk, just to be intimidating, shouting what the Swedes could tell was swearing.

Gunnar, who had only learned to drive a few months before and had been concentrating on starting the automobile, was startled by the slaps on the metal. His foot slipped from the clutch, and the car lurched forward into the brick wall of the building they had parked up against. He got his foot back on the clutch before the engine died, but the damage was already done.

Carl screamed in pain. His hands flew forward onto the hood of the car, trying to push it away. His legs were trapped between the car and the wall. The crank, bent with the weight of the car, was the only thing keeping the bumper from from crushing Carl's calves. He screamed to Gunnar to put the car in reverse just as the Italians surrounded the Star. The gears ground as Gunnar tried to shift into reverse, but he was too nervous. The engine died abruptly.

The young Italians swaggered around the car and jeered. They left Carl alone as he was already pinned down and couldn't run. They threw the car doors open and tried to yank Tord and Eric out of the car. Everyone was throwing punches, pushing, and shoving. Eric had swung around on the seat when someone pulled the door open. He started kicking at the guy, but they just grabbed his legs and dragged him out onto the ground. They had started beating and kicking him when a man's voice called out.

"*Ehi! Fermare che*!" The man had stepped into the alley from the back door of some business. He was well-dressed with a starched white collar and black tie showing under his open vest.

"You boys always make-a trouble. What you gonna do? Beata dese guys up? For what? Get yourselves back to where you suppose ta be. Go on! *Andare! Va via! Ora!*" He waved a hand high in the air, as if to brush away some flies.

The young Italian men backed off, heads down, grumbling and cursing under their breath as they retreated down the alley.

The man came over to the front of the car, where Carl was still pinned.

"Are you hurt bad?" he asked.

"No," replied Carl with a nervous laugh. "Not bad. But my pantalonis are no good no more."

With that, the older man laughed and laughed, repeating the Italian word "pantalonis" in Carl's Swedish accent. The young Swedes laughed too. When all the tension was spent and the laughter subsided, they gathered at the front where Carl was pinned. Together they pushed the automobile away from the wall and freed Carl as Gunnar hopped in to step on the brake.

"Are you sure you're not hurt?" the man asked Carl again. "You can come into my office. See how you are. Your legs, maybe. Rest a bit, maybe."

Carl replied as he leaned over to rub his calves, "No, no. Thank you. I'll be okay. Just bruised. Nothing broken."

The Italian stood for a moment, looking at the Swedes. "Eh, you guys know Irv Edgar? He's a Swede, too. He runs the funeral home just a few blocks from here. You tell him hello from Mr. Martinelli. I am sorry to say, it is better if you keep to your own neighborhood. I know these *giovani*, and too many of them have the hard head about newcomers, strangers, you know. Safer for you, you know, you stay on Clark Street. I wish it was not like this, but what can you do?"

"T'ank you, mister, for your help," said Gunnar. The others thanked him too. With a small salute of fingers to his forehead, the man turned and went back into the building.

CHAPTER 16

Gunnar and Carl decided they wanted some Swedish food this particular Saturday in summer. Gunnar pulled up in front of the small bungalow in Evanston where Carl was staying and honked the horn of his Renault KJ. When Carl hopped in, they headed south on Ridge Road into Chicago. Their destination was Andersonville, the fifty or so square block neighborhood just east of Rosehill Cemetery, where Swedish immigrants had settled after the Chicago fire fifty years prior. English was still a second language there.

Gunnar found a parking place on a nearby residential street. The two homesick young men spent the early part of the afternoon leisurely walking south on Clark Street, the de facto Main Street of the crowded Swedish neighborhood. They stopped in almost every store, browsing Scandinavian housewares, home decorations, clothes, and groceries, savoring the aroma of baked goods, and soaking in their native language being spoken in the stores and on the streets. They respectfully greeted the older people they passed, touching the brims of their hats as they politely said, "G'dag." But when young women were nearby, they jostled each other to be the first to introduce themselves and make small talk.

When they finally reached the south end of Andersonville at Foster Avenue, they agreed Villa Sweden looked like an opportune place to have an early dinner, so they went in and hung their hats on the rack near the door. The matronly hostess greeted them in Swedish, seated them at a table in the middle of the room, and handed them menus. As Eric concentrated on reading his menu, Carl looked around. He already knew what he wanted – *kåldolmar*, cabbage rolls stuffed with ground beef and pork spiced with nutmeg, pickled beets, and boiled potatoes.

The restaurant was small and pleasantly decorated in the bright blue and yellow of the Swedish flag with white woodwork and moldings. There were cheery blue and yellow checked curtains in the large bay window at the front of the room overlooking Clark Street. The wooden tables were covered with white linen tablecloths, and the small wooden chairs had curved backs and seats covered with fabric matching the curtains. A flight of stairs ran up from the foyer to a banquet room upstairs.

Carl noticed an elderly lady sitting by herself at a nearby table. There were only a few other people in the restaurant so early in the evening. He listened as she spoke to the waitress in Swedish. Her voice was so much like his mother's that he closed his eyes and listened to the lilting sound of it. He barely heard what she said, but understood that she was waiting for her son.

"*Väntar du för mej, mor?*" he thought. Are you waiting for me, mother? Oh, how he missed home. Just seventeen when he left Sweden, he had only been gone two years. The catch in his throat brought him back with a start. Gunnar was talking about what he was going to order. Carl cleared his throat and replied that he wanted cabbage rolls.

After the pretty waitress took their order, Carl looked back at the lady at the other table. Impulsively, he took a flower from the little vase on his table, stood up, and approached her table. He greeted her with a traditional Scandinavian bow. Leaning forward slightly at the waist, he nodded his head quickly down, then up to meet her eye. He gave her the flower and greeted her formally in Swedish. She smiled broadly and asked him to sit with her while she waited for her son.

"Idag är min födelsedag," she said. It was her birthday, she told Carl. Her son always takes her to dinner at a nice restaurant on her birthday, she said. She told Carl all about her husband, who had been an undertaker. When he passed away, their two sons took over the funeral business. They were chatting pleasantly about their hometowns in Sweden when her son arrived. Carl stood and pushed his chair under the table.

"Oh, Irv, dear. This nice young man has kept me company while I waited for you. Is everything all right?" she asked her son, concerned about his tardiness. He leaned over and gave her cheek a small kiss. Irv Edgar appeared to be in his mid-thirties and was well-dressed in beige linen slacks and a double-breasted navy blue jacket with a deep red and white polka dot silk tie and matching pocket square.

"Yes, mother. Of course. Some business came up, that's all. So sorry to keep you waiting."

"Irv, this is Carl Swanson. He's from Hälsingland not far from where your uncle Torben lives."

"Nice to meet you, Carl. I'm Irv Edgar. Her youngest and

sweetest son," he said to Carl, chuckling and extending his hand. Mother and son exchanged happy, familiar glances.

"Glad to meet you, Irv," said Carl. "I should be getting back to my friend." He wished Mrs. Edgar a very happy birthday and a pleasant meal. Then, with a nod to Irv, he joined Gunnar back at their table.

Carl and Gunnar finished their meal and indulged in their favorite dessert, *jordgubbstarta*, a whipped cream and strawberry cake, and a cup of coffee. The flavor of the fresh strawberries turned their conversation to home and the people they had left behind, who would be picking wild strawberries without them. As they stood and prepared to go, they were approached by the old lady's son.

"Say, gents. What have you got planned for later tonight? Anything exciting?" Irv asked the younger men.

Gunnar and Carl exchanged glances and shrugged. "No. No ting exciting," Gunnar said in his heavy accent. Carl's English was much better than Gunnar's, who after five years still dropped pronouns, couldn't pronounce a 'w' or 'th', and used Swedish sayings which he translated word for word, making them total nonsense in English.

"Why don't you guys meet me at the corner of Broadway and Lawrence later. Umm, say at nine o'clock," Irv said. "I'll show you a bit of Chicago fun. Whaddya think?"

"Yah, sure. We'll be there," said Carl. The three men exchanged handshakes and goodbyes. Carl went over to Mrs. Edgar and shook her hand as well.

"It was a pleasure to meet you, *Fru* Edgar," said Carl in Swedish. "You are a lucky woman to have such a fine son. I know you are very proud of him." He wished he had told his mother that he knew she was proud of him, too. He made a mental note to tell her that in his next letter home. He wrote her often, at least once a week, sometimes including newspaper clippings about interesting things in Chicago, especially if there was a photo in the article. He knew she would take the clippings to a neighbor's daughter who had spent some time as a nanny in England for her to translate them.

Carl and Gunnar left the restaurant full and intrigued.

"So, vat do you tink of our new friend," asked Gunnar.

"He seems like a cheery person. We should have some fun tonight. Perhaps there's a dance pavilion where he likes to go to."

"I don't tink so. Everyting here is inside de house. No out-of-de-door places to dance de schottische or hambo, like at home."

With a few hours to kill and it being such a pleasant summer evening, the two friends decided to walk over to the lake. They knew Lake Michigan was to the east, and the person they stopped on the street to ask how far it was pointed them in the right direction and told them it was about ten blocks away. It didn't take them long to get there because Chicago street blocks are not square but shorter east to west and twice as long north to south.

Brownstone two- and three-flats were interspersed with a few stores and courtyard two-story apartment buildings. Trees lined the streets, and a variety of flowers were coming up in small beds and window boxes. The sun was beginning to go down, and their shadows were long on the sidewalk in front of them. At the end of Foster Avenue, they turned south on Marine Drive. A block or so further, they saw a nice grassy area on the lakeside of the street. They sat down looking out over the water, and after a few minutes of talking, they slid down onto their backs, put their hats over their faces, and fell asleep.

* * *

"Hey! You can't sleep here!" hollered the policeman as he smacked the soles of their shoes with his billy stick. "C'mon, now. Get up. Move along or I'll have to take you in for vagrancy."

"Sorry, sorry, mister officer," Gunnar said, jumping to his feet, eyes wide with confusion.

The sun had gone down, and they could hear the waves of the lake in front of them. The lights of the buildings and street lamps barely reached where some bushes had sheltered them. There were a few cars on the small street. Carl stood and took his time brushing off his clothes.

"Thank you, sir, for waking us. We didn't mean to fall asleep. It was such a beautiful day, and we had such a good meal at Villa Sweden, I guess we just dozed off, "Carl said. "We've got an appointment to meet Mr. Irv Edgar at 9:00 so we had better get going. Do you know him? He owns a business over on Clark Street."

He wanted the policeman to know they had money and important things to do. He was hoping that dropping Irv Edgar's name would help. Carl had heard how vagrants were treated if they got arrested, and he had no desire to experience jail first-hand. He had come to the United States with a genuine appreciation for the opportunity to be a good citizen of a country where he could make something of himself. He was bound and determined to stay on the right side of the law. Most of the immigrant Swedes he knew were the same way, not so much on purpose but because they were ingrained with a work ethic that kept them out of trouble, even if they did let loose on their day off. There were a few, though, that Carl had met who were, in his opinion, dumb and lazy and tempted by the fast life. One or two of them had even been to jail.

"Mr. Edgar, you say," said Officer Doyle. "Well, if you have business with him, you'd best be on your way then. He'll break your legs if you keep him waiting." With that, he continued walking down the beach, looking for the desperate men and women hoping for a place to sleep for the night along the shore where the sound of the waves could wash away their cares. When the weather was fair, some of them would choose to be near the shore; otherwise, they found places in alleys where they could stay warmer. After the sun went down, he would stroll up and down the lake shore for the last few hours of his shift. It was easy and safe, as the vagrants were usually harmless drunks or just people who were poor, tired, and hungry with nowhere to go.

Officer Doyle often wondered about their past - how they had gotten to such a place in their lives, but he knew what their future would be. They would eventually get sick and die and be buried in a pauper's grave. Whenever there was a child with them, he would find a way to get the family off to the side and give them some money to at least feed themselves for a few days. He would admonish them to stay away from his beat and to find a job, or the next time he saw them, he would take their child away. He knew he should take the child to Social Welfare right then and there, but he couldn't bring himself to do it, so he acted gruff and hoped they would get a break somehow.

"Wait, sir," Carl called after him. "Can you tell us how to get to Lawrence and Broadway, please?"

"Lawrence is just a few blocks down," the cop said, pointing south, "and Broadway isn't far once you're on Lawrence. You gentlemen have a pleasant evening with Mr. Edgar and try to keep your noses clean," and he laughed.

* * *

As they walked, Carl and Gunnar talked about whether they really wanted to meet Mr. Edgar or not. They were a little confused by what the policeman said and why he had laughed that way. They had heard that mobsters broke people's legs for not paying them money, but Mr. Edgar didn't seem like a mobster, being a businessman and all. The prospect of getting in trouble somehow didn't seem very likely, they thought, so they decided they would go meet him. It would be fun.

Carl noticed the stately brownstones in that section of Lawrence Avenue with their tiny spot of grass and a small bush or two for a yard, and wide, steep steps leading up to beveled glass front doors. Crossing the street out of the residential neighborhood, a large stone building loomed on their left. As they passed, Carl glanced at the plaque near the impressive entry doors. "People's Church" it read.

The Aragon Ballroom, built by the Karas Brothers, opened in July of 1926 with a crowd of 8,000 people. Its design simulated a Mediterranean plaza, complete with a domed night sky 60 feet overhead, twinkling with stars. Built on springs, felt, and cork to accommodate the weight and movement of so many people, the vast all maple dance floor, almost an acre in size, was like none other. The brothers exerted control inside the venue to maintain a safe environment and attract younger people who wanted to dance. Proper attire was required, no alcohol was allowed, and chaperones were present to interrupt any untoward advances. Being adjacent to the L-station brought huge crowds from all over the Chicago area. Attendance ranged from 10,000 to 20,000 per week.

Big bands were the draw and once the events started being broadcast on the radio, the ballroom became famous all over the world. Freddy Martin, Wayne King, and Dick Jurgens were the resident band leaders with other big bands regularly playing as well. In the 1960s, the Aragon kept up with the times by hosting concerts and other events, which it still does today.

CHAPTER 17

Ahead of them, they saw the elevated train tracks cross over the street just past another large building at the corner of Winthrop. A huge vertical sign announcing "Aragon" in lights extended high over the roofline of the building on the Lawrence Avenue side. A brightly lit marquee above the street entrance announced the evening's performers – Charlie Spivak and His Orchestra. A crowd of people waited in a line that went all the way around the corner.

The spectacle of lights and people, the roar of the 'el' train, and the hubbub of the traffic was a stark contrast to the quiet lakeshore the young Swedes had just left.

They crossed the street and watched for a few minutes as droves of people came down the stairs from the elevated station and out onto the street to join the people in line at the Aragon. The young men in the crowd were wearing fine clothes, three-piece suits of shiny or pinstriped material and polished dark leather shoes. Some lingered in tight groups, jostling each other and laughing, while others came in couples, their dates for the evening on their arm. The women wore short, shapeless dresses, long beads and dangling earrings, and small, close-fitting hats with rhinestones or feathers adorning them.

Carl and Gunnar hung back by a lamp post to take in the scene. When their imaginations gave way to reality, they walked on. A block further, they saw Irv at the corner waiting for them. He made a show of looking at his wristwatch, tapping the dial with a finger, a stern look on his face. The two young Swedes stopped walking – and breathing.

"Oh, there you are," Irv said, smiling. "My watch stopped. I'm sorry, I just got here myself and thought maybe you weren't coming."

Carl and Gunnar exchanged a glance, then burst out laughing.

"What's so funny," asked Irv.

"Oh, nothing, really. We asked a policeman how to get here and mentioned we were meeting you. He seemed to know you and said we'd be in big trouble if we were late. I guess he was just having some fun with us," said Carl.

"Yeah, better be on time next time or I'll break your legs," Irv said with a serious face.

After a tense moment, he laughed and said, "Now, I'm having some fun with you. C'mon. Let's go have a drink."

"Are we going to have to wait in that long line," asked Gunnar.

"Nah. There's no liquor in there anyway. Just music and root beer. I'm takin' you to a spot you gotta know people to get in. You can go to the Aragon some other day, especially if you're looking to do the Shimmy with some spiffy flappers. Me, I'm no dancer. Come on," said Irv.

They had only walked a half block when Irv motioned them to follow him between the buildings. The small alleyway was littered and dark. A rat slipped behind a garbage can, startling the Swedes, which made Irv laugh.

He stopped abruptly at a wall of an old building pockmarked with cracks and broken bricks. He looked around for a moment, then knocked on the wall. It sounded hollow. One of the bricks disappeared inward, and a muted voice asked who was there.

Irv looked at the two Swedes and smiled. "Leif Erickson and a couple Vikings," he said.

They heard a laugh, "Oh, hi, Irv." Without warning, a large section of bricks moved into the building a foot, then slid to the side, exposing a doorway. Irv led the way. As they walked forward, the inner door opened and they stepped into the dark. Meanwhile, the sliding brick wall closed behind them. A light switched on, and they saw they were in a reception area decorated in dark green velvet. The burly doorman greeted Irv with a smile.

"How are you tonight, Mr. Edgar," he asked. "Who are your new friends? Not Federal agents, I hope." He laughed heartily. Irv introduced Carl and Gunnar to the doorman, who studied their faces and repeated their names. "I never forget a face. Just so you know, if I'm at the door, you'll be welcome as friends of Mr. Edgar," he said. "Have a nice evening." He gestured to the short flight of stairs leading down to the main club room.

Carl and Gunnar looked around and noticed that the employees were mainly Italians. They exchanged a glance as they followed Irv across the room. Gunnar tapped Carl on the arm as they walked and surreptitiously pointed to a guy leaning on the end of the bar. The man was not drinking, he was surveilling the crowd. It was the leader of the gang that had chased them in the alley off Halstead Street. On a whim, Carl had just begun telling Irv about that incident when the Italian spotted the Swedes. The tall, well-dressed Italian clicked his fingers in the air and immediately three other guys joined him as he walked toward Carl and Gunnar.

Irv, who hadn't really been focusing on Carl's story, stepped forward to greet the tall man. "Hey, there, Marcos, how are you tonight? These two young gents are friends of mine. Carl and Gunnar," he said. "This here's Marcos Vincenzo. Carl, Gunnar, you'd be smart to keep Mr. Vincenzo on your good side."

Marcos smiled but did not extend his hand. "You're pretty lucky for being dumb Swedes," he said with a smirk. Gunnar took a step forward, ready to fight anyone who called him a dumb Swede, but Carl grabbed his arm.

"If Mr. Martinelli had said to put an end to youse that day, you wouldn'ta made it out of dat alley. But for some crazy reason he liked you, so youse got a pass. And now I see youse here with Mr. Edgar. I gotta say, you got some kinda luck wid youse, knowing the right guys and all. What's with dumb Swedes and dumb luck, eh?"

Turning to Irv, Marcos continued, "Mr. Edgar, you let us know if dese guys give you a hard time," gesturing at Carl and Gunnar. "We'll take care of them, no problem. Like we done for you before, but then maybe you'll wanna take care of them yourself. I know youse got no problem wid dat. Have a pleasant evening, Mr. Edgar."

Irv laughed and put an arm around the two Swedes' shoulders while he answered the Italian. "We got no issues with these guys, Marcos. They might be dumb Swedes, but we like 'em anyway. And now, how about I buy everybody a drink? Eh, boys? Whaddya say?"

The bartender took their orders and returned in a few minutes with their highballs and beers. Marcos and his buddies thanked Irv and took their drinks on down the bar.

The three new friends were just getting comfortable on some bar stools when two young ladies mosied in between them. One perched herself on Gunnar's lap. He turned three shades red and stammered a few words to her, which made her laugh. The other doll put one arm around Irv and the other around Carl and whispered in Irv's ear. He laughed and bought the ladies drinks. They all toasted to the evening and were having a good laugh when the lights went out. Only a few lights under the bar remained on. The place burst out with shouting and screeches of tables and chairs moving and people trying to leave. The crowd started to run for the door as uniformed police were pushing their way in. The narrow passageway was jammed. The officers grabbed a few people, but weren't able to hold onto them in the melee. When the coppers made it through and into the bar room, they blew their whistles and shouted to stay in place, but no one paid any attention to them. People continued to pour out the door. The bartenders had disappeared.

Irv grabbed Carl and Gunnar by the sleeves and shouted, "Follow me. Hurry!" Carl focused on Irv and stayed close behind him as he ran behind the bar and through the curtained doorway to a storeroom.

Gunnar, never one to leave a glass with something in it and thinking this was all fun, had stayed to gulp down his drink. He was one of the few taken into custody during the raid.

"Where's Gunnar?" shouted Carl looking back.

"Don't know. Come on. Gotta go!" Irv pulled on a recessed handle near the baseboard which snapped back into place again. A trap door in the middle of the floor popped open a few inches at one end. He yanked it up, "Come on, Carl. He'll be okay." He shoved Carl down the narrow stairs to the darkness below and followed after him. When he was almost to the bottom, he reached up for the handle near the far edge of the opening and turned it. The trap door clicked tightly closed. Carl was waiting a few steps away as Irv flipped his Ronson De-Light to illuminate the tiny passageway.

"Come on. This way," said Irv as he headed down the dark corridor, lighter held out in front of him. Carl could see there was a number of tunnels and felt the air flow change when he passed by them. Irv turned without hesitation at several intersections. It was obvious to Carl that Irv knew exactly where they were going. Neither man spoke as they walked through the dark.

"Here we are," Irv whispered. "Now we gotta be quiet until I'm sure no one is above us." He closed the lighter and the two stood still for several minutes in an open area.

Irv re-lit the lighter and led Carl to the far side of the underground room to another narrow set of stairs. He climbed them, opened the trapdoor, and clicked it shut once Carl had made his way through it. They were standing in an office furnished with a desk and a couple of chairs and various cabinets and shelves. One window high in the wall above the desk shone with city night light.

Without speaking, Irv opened the door a crack and listened. When he was satisfied no one was around, he opened the door and beckoned Carl to come out. The two men walked through a hallway, turned down another one, then entered a large foyer with several ornate double-doors on the two long sides of the room. Carl could see a large auditorium with curved rows of seats and a stage beyond. Irv went to the last door on the other side, pushed it open and stepped out onto the sidewalk. "Come on," he said. "Let's go get a drink! I need one!"

As they walked away, Carl looked back at the building and the plaque that read "The People's Church."

1950 LAKE VERMILION

CHAPTER 18

Carl and Elsa tied up to the wide dock on Black Duck Island on the south side. A large house with dark cedar siding and many dormers sat at the top of the steep hill. Reverend Bradley came down the stone-stepped path, huffing; the air pushed out of him like a fireplace bellows with each heavy footfall.

"Hello. Hello. Well, well, you finally made it out to our humble abode up here in God's country," he said boisterously but breathlessly, as he shook Carl's hand. "I saw you approach from across the bay, so I came down to greet you. My wife says a little exercise is good for me, but this hill is a bit of a climb. But what a pleasure to see you!"

He turned to Elsa and took her extended hand into both of his. "Welcome," he said with a smile. "You must be Elsa. I've heard so much about you from your wonderful husband. Ahhh! And this must be the little girl. Let's see, what was her name?" He looked to Carl.

"Katy," said Carl.

"Yes, yes. Of course! Katy! What a lovely child!" Preston continued to fawn over the little girl, much to her distress, as she tried to hide behind her mother's legs. When there was no response from Katy, he abruptly turned back to the adults, "Well then, let's go up to the house, shall we? My wife will be anxious to meet our guests." With both arms extended, he gestured to the path dramatically.

Carl led the way, carrying Katy. Elsa followed with Preston bringing up the rear. The cabin could be seen through the trees directly up the hill above them, but a straight path would have been too steep. So, instead, the path led off to the right at a slight slope, then made a switchback winding its way up the hill.

Preston took it slow, but still labored up the incline. By the time they reached the expanse of yard in front of the cabin, he was out of breath and paused to rest at the front porch door, his hand over his heart.

"There is another lake access around the back of the island. I'm sure you've seen our boathouse back there. That path is a much easier climb and one which we use much more often, I assure you. Next time, please feel welcome to dock back there," said Preston, still breathing hard.

"Oh, you shouldn't have come down to meet us. I hope you're all right," said Elsa, concerned.

"Nonsense. I am fine. Nothing to worry about. Just a bit out of shape is all. I haven't even yet reached the venerable age of seventy. Although with my birthday coming up in August, that milestone will be accomplished with relish."

Carl set Katy on the ground and turned to Bruno. "You stay here, Bruno. Right here by the stairs," he said, pointing to a nice grassy spot. The big dog was casually looking around, so Carl tapped him on the muzzle. "Bruno. Pay attention. No chasing squirrels, you hear? You stay right here. Lay down and be a good boy." With a loud umph, Bruno flopped down in the shade of the steps, then relaxed even further onto his side, legs extended.

"Seems to be an obedient animal," said Preston with mild interest.

"Come, come, then," he said as he opened the door to the screened porch to let his guests enter first. "Let's go in and see what my wife has prepared. She does so love having company. It never ceases to amaze me how efficient the woman is."

Jane, wearing a flowered dress with a ruffled apron in a matching color, came out of the kitchen with short steps as if walking on it might break the floor. She ran her right hand down her apron, then extended it to greet Carl first, then Elsa, as Preston introduced them. Katy had run over to the large coffee table in front of the sofa where there were stacks of books, some with colorful covers.

"Book, mama. Book, mama. Book," she called to her mother and opened one, looking for pictures.

Elsa sat on the sofa and called Katy to come sit on her lap. "Okay, honey. But let's be gentle with the books."

"Do you mind if we look at one?" she asked Dr. Bradley.

"Of course not! Help yourself," he said as he seated himself in his overstuffed leather chair. "I see you are bringing up your child to love and respect books. That is a very good thing. It is only with knowledge gained from both experience and by reading about the experiences of others that we can truly understand how fragile and beautiful this life is and how we can help one another live life to its fullest."

Jane motioned to Carl to sit on the sofa too, and then she

went back into the kitchen without a word.

"Books are my favorite pastime and the source of much of my inspiration for all that I do. I read voraciously, although I must say I do not particularly care for the more, shall we say, base genres of fiction such as the frivolous romance and mystery novels that my dear wife seems enamored with." He gestured to a stack at the far end of the table.

Elsa reached over and turned the stack he pointed to, so she could read some of the spines. "The Innocent Heiress" by Barbara Cartland. "Dinner at Antoine's" by Francis Parkinson Keyes. "Remembered Death" and "Murder After Hours" by Agatha Christie. Further down, she noticed one on gardening and found it had colorful pictures of flowers and insects. She pulled it from the stack and held it so that Katy could see. The little girl was fascinated each time her mother turned a page.

"I just love the Tower Library, Dr. Bradley. It's so wonderful that you've given all those books to the public. I check out several every time we go to town," said Elsa.

"Why, thank you, my dear. It gives me great pleasure to enrich the lives of others. Besides, where on earth would I put them all?" He chuckled as he gestured to the overflowing shelves that lined the walls wherever there were no windows.

Jane returned with a tray of cookies, bars, some small plates, and a small jam jar with milk for Katy. She set it on the table as Carl moved a couple of books out of the way. Then she went back to the kitchen for the coffee pot and cups.

The four of them carried on a pleasant conversation while they ate bars, drank coffee, and watched the toddler explore the new space she found herself in.

As Jane stood and poured a little more coffee in each cup,

she said, "It was so nice of you to drop in. It has been a quiet summer for us so far. Although we are expecting some visitors in August."

"Say, that reminds me," said Carl. "We just came from Irv Edgar's and he said you and he are going to fly up to Lake of the Woods to go fishing."

"Yes, yes. That's true. We do have plans to do that, but he's been talking about it now for a couple of summers. Perhaps this year it will happen."

"Well, Irv asked if I would like to join you. How do you feel about that?" asked Carl.

"Wonderful!" Preston exclaimed. "That would be just wonderful. I thoroughly enjoy your company, Carl, and you would definitely be a grand addition to our fishing expedition. Have you ever been up to Lake of the Woods before?"

"No, never been there. I have been up in Irv's plane a couple of times. It's pretty interesting. Have you been up to Canada fishing before?"

"No, I haven't been up there either. I haven't even been up in his plane before, although I am well acquainted with air travel. I have to fly home to Chicago from Duluth frequently during the summer to conduct church services. We should definitely proceed with plans for this delightful sounding trip."

"Thanks for the coffee, Jane. The coconut chocolate bars are delicious," said Elsa.

Carl agreed, then continued, "Irv says he'll firm up the dates with you soon and let me know."

"It will be an interesting experience, to say the least. However, I am very glad that we will be staying in a cabin with real beds and not camping out on the cold ground. I am just a little too old for that. Irv assures me that the fishing lodge is quite comfortable. It was used by smugglers during Prohibition, you know."

"Oh, really? That's interesting. Who were the smugglers? I thought it was Irv's family's cabin," said Elsa.

"Irv's father was, shall we say, quite the entrepreneur during those years," said Preston. "And I must say Irv was an enterprising young man as well. Truth be told, we were all affected by Prohibition. To quote Dickens, 'It was the best of times. It was the worst of times.'" He laughed as he shook his head. "What we all went through back then to secure a mere dram or two of what we now so unthinkingly take for granted – our late afternoon scotch. Why even the churches had trouble securing wine for the sacrament. Fortunately, being Universalist Unitarians, we had no such worries. Speaking of which, perhaps you'd care for something a bit stronger than coffee."

"No, thanks," said Carl. "We really can't stay long. We've got to get back before nap time."

"Ah, yes. The noble sacrifice of parental responsibilities. My dear Jane and I have never shared in those responsibilities, but it is my observation that more often than not, the parents are significantly more relieved to remove themselves from the social fray than the erstwhile children are."

Carl and Elsa laughed. "Oh, now you've called our bluff," said Elsa. "But really we must be going soon."

"Did you hear about our recent misfortune, or should I say, our discovery of someone's misfortune? Right over there." said Carl as he gestured out the window toward the reef where they had found the skull.

"No! Pray tell. What tale have you got for us today?" said

Preston as he sat back even further in his chair. He turned to his wife for an aside, "Carl, here, is a wonderful storyteller. He often entertained me with tales of his homeland while he painted the interior of the church. You do remember I told you about him doing such a wonderful job."

"Yes, dear. I remember," Jane said.

"Please, Carl, continue. I'm afraid I have an intrepid habit of interrupting myself," Preston said with a laugh.

"Well, we were trolling the reef right over there off Fectos Point when Elsa got stuck. When we got her lure free, she pulled it up with a real human skull hooked on it. It was quite a surprise, believe me. Surely you saw the boat activity when the Sheriff's Department dive team was searching for the rest of the remains. They were out there for several days."

"Why, yes, we did note the many boats and people out there. We figured they were searching for something, but never dreamed it was a body," said Preston.

"Well, I guess you'd call it more of a skeleton than a body," said Carl. "They found a number of bones that seem to be all from one person at least."

"Who was it?" asked Jane, in a voice as pale as her face had become.

"The Deputy, Pittella, you know him, of course. Well, Pittella says they will figure out who the remains belong to before long," said Carl. "You see there were a couple of pieces of jewelry found with the bones. One was a class ring, so they know where the man went to college. And the second was a watch with some initials engraved on the back."

The conversation turned to other deaths on the lake. There was a lull of awkward silence, and as they all contemplated a watery death, Katy, who had been occupying herself quietly with a few small toys on the floor, climbed up on her mother's lap and started to fuss.

"Really, we must be going," said Elsa. "Thank you so much for the coffee and yummy cookies."

As they were saying their goodbyes at the porch door, Elsa insisted that Preston not accompany them back down the path to their boat. With much ado, Preston made it clear that it was a great disappointment to him not to see them off at the dock, but he would abide by her wishes.

Jane touched Elsa's arm and said, "Please come see me when our husbands go off on their fishing trip, will you?"

"Certainly. Katy and I would love to come visit. We'll drop by mid-morning one of the days they are gone. Thanks again for your hospitality."

* * *

After the Swansons had left, Jane and Preston went back into the house without speaking. After a bit, Preston said, "That was such a nice visit. I'm glad they stopped by."

He sat in his leather easy chair looking out the window where he could see Carl and Elsa's boat heading east across the water. He picked up a book and started to read.

"Ummhmm," said Jane in agreement as she stacked the dishes from the coffee table together to take them into the kitchen. She walked toward the door with them, then stopped. She turned back to face her husband. "You know, dear, I really regret not having adopted. We should have had a daughter. Or a son. Just think how wonderful that would have been and we could even have had grandchildren by now," she said.

Preston barely looked up from his book. "I thought you didn't want children, my dear. You...you know...had that...that procedure," he said with a slight hand gesture as if flicking a crumb from his memory.

"Procedure? You mean the abortion? All those years ago?"

"Well, yes. You told me you didn't want a baby."

"I meant I didn't want that man's baby. I mean he took advantage of me that one time. I didn't even really know him. I couldn't have had a baby then anyway. I was practically a baby myself."

She stopped for a moment, realizing they had never talked about this before. Pent up emotion was rising in her, and she could feel her cheeks redden. She gained control and continued in a calm voice.

"But, of course, I wanted a baby. I've always wanted children. I'm so sorry that I was never able to conceive again. That 'procedure', as you call it, must have damaged me somehow."

She sighed, "You were so kind to me and then after we were married you never pressured me about having children. It's one of the many reasons I fell in love with you. You were so kind and understanding. I'm sorry I was such a disappointment."

He closed the book and looked across the room at her. "Oh, my dear," he said. "You have it all wrong. It is I who am sorry. I thought you were happy not having children. That you didn't want any. You never said a word otherwise."

Lowering his eyes to his folded hands resting on the book, he continued, "And it is I who am damaged. Many years ago, when I was at one of my regular checkups with Dr. Farnsworth. He asked about you. When I responded that you were well, he asked if we had taken any steps to address our childlessness. And when I said no, he asked me a number of questions and ran a few tests." He paused for a moment.

"Evidently, my having had the mumps when I was in my early twenties rendered me unable to father any children. I am so sorry if you felt you were the cause of our childlessness. It was an unfortunate misunderstanding. But as you can see, we have had a perfectly reasonable relationship without the burden of children." He readjusted his glasses and turned back to his book.

Jane stood perfectly still as she listened to her husband. She stared at him as if he were a stranger. Finally, she said, "And you never thought to mention this to me, your wife?"

He looked up from his book with flat eyes. "It never crossed my mind that it mattered."

His words took the very bones out of her legs. She felt she couldn't stand. Her breath stopped in her chest. The cups in her hands were clattering as she turned and hurried into the kitchen. She set them on the table as she collapsed onto the kitchen chair. Bent over in despair, she pressed her forehead to the cool yellow and gray formica and sobbed silent tears.

Preston, comfortable in his chair by the window, turned a page.

CHAPTER 19

One day in mid-June, Elsa suggested to Carl that they take Victoria up on her invitation to visit Gold Island and meet her father. Coming across the east-to-west expanse of Frazer Bay, passing between Black Duck Island and Fectos Point, the Swansons stared at their destination: Gold Island, a thin piece of land almost a mile wide. The famous Muskrat Channel and The Narrows, which connected the eastern end of Lake Vermilion with the western end, were directly behind the island. Carl and Elsa had fished these waters many times but had never had reason to go ashore on the island, which everyone knew was private property. There was no mistaking the rustic opulence of the two-story house perched on the steep granite hill with a massive gable over the main center section. An impressive vignette of a wooden sun on the horizon was centered at the bottom with yellow wooden rays emanating from it out to the gable's edges like a geisha's fan. The rustic art was visible from far across the water.

Carl pulled up to the shortest of the three docks and tied up their boat. He got out and took Katy from Elsa, then gave her a hand up onto the pier. Elsa and Katy started up the path to the house. Carl couldn't help but be impressed with the beautifully crafted log boathouse with dovetailed corners. He ran his hand over the massive timbers as he walked toward shore. He came to the side door, which was slightly ajar, and with only a slight hesitation, he pushed it open and stepped in to satisfy his curiosity, hoping he wasn't visible from the house. The bays held a 16' aluminum fishing boat and a small rowboat crowded together in one, a 20' Chris Craft Sport runabout in the next, and an even larger cabin cruiser in the farthest. The walkways between them were lacquered parquet flooring. A dozen or so brass nautical-themed chandeliers hung in rows from the massive beams of the ceiling. Shelving and hooks lined the long back wall holding all manner of fishing equipment, paddles and oars, water skis and ropes, life preservers, and foul-weather gear. Carl gave a soft whistle as he stepped back out of the boathouse and closed the door.

Elsa and Katy were waiting for him at the door to the house.

"There you are, honey. What took you so long."

"I'll tell you later," he said under his breath just as Elsa's friend Victoria opened the door.

"I thought I heard a boat come up! Come on in. So nice to meet you, Carl." She hugged Elsa and extended her hand to Carl. Katy, like a hound on the hunt, ran off to find her playmate, Angelina.

Victoria led them from the foyer into the main salon where her father was looking out the expanse of window toward the lake. When he turned to greet his visitors, Carl immediately recognized him but wasn't sure how he knew him. He realized it must have been a long time ago when he had seen him, and maybe it was more than just once, but he was certain he had met him or seen him before. He searched his memory for the connection. Finally, it came to him. The man was much grayer now, and his age showed in the lines of his face, but somehow Carl thought he looked grander and happier. He glowed with paternal pride as he looked at his daughter and granddaughter briefly before he turned his attention to his guests. As the young mothers took their seats and the prolonged greeting unfolded, Carl was distracted remembering the chance encounter with Martinelli in that Chicago alley so many years ago.

Prohibition started abruptly on January 1, 1920. The law was written to appease those on a crusade to stem the evils of intoxicating liquors, but, in fact, it backfired. The national ban on the production, distribution, and sale of alcoholic beverages simply missed its mark, and instead of curbing immoral behavior, it drove it underground. Since it was not illegal to drink alcohol, individuals drank with abandon at home and flocked to speakeasies for good times. Two significant results came of this. Prior to prohibition, men did most of the drinking in establishments where women were not allowed. Men had to drink at home, so their wives started to drink with them without fear of social retribution. When speakeasies became popular, wives went along with their husbands and enjoyed newfound liberties. The second repercussion of prohibition was the transformation of gangs, which had always been prevalent in big cities, into more structured, interconnected business entities, controlled by the smartest of the lot.

In Chicago in 1928, over twelve hundred different gangs were roaming the streets, with specified territories and working agreements, although sometimes contentious. Bootlegging was big business, and those with the most business sense, connections, and ability to control the gangs profited.

While crime and gangs were prevalent, there were a lot of gray areas when it came to the law in Chicago. A balance between those who enforced the law and the criminals who broke it had long been the established norm. Under this status quo, Chicago remained a reasonable place to live, and most people went about their business and daily lives without fear.

CHAPTER 20

Carl's attention snapped back to the present as Katy squealed in delight at finding Angelina.

"Hello, Mr. Swanson. I have heard so much about your wife and baby, it's a pleasure to meet you," Martinelli said, shaking Carl's hand. He was dressed in a dark red velvet smoking jacket with black satin lapels over sharply pressed slacks.

"And nice to meet you, too," said Carl, regaining his composure.

"Who knew that pushing prams in Lincoln Park could lead to such a pleasant friendship? Young mothers!" the older man said. "And what a coincidence that we both have cabins here on Lake Vermilion. Life is full of coincidences, don't you think, Carl?"

"I'd hardly call this beautiful home of yours a cabin, Mr. Martinelli. We always admire it when we're fishing over here in Frazer Bay. Our cabin is in Daisy Bay. It's a, um, more traditional cabin," Carl said with a chuckle.

"Thank you, Carl. But please call me Antonio. And I can take no great credit for this magnificent house. You see, it was my wife's, although we never spent any time together here. And for years it sat idle, but once I visited here, I fell in love with it. It's been used for many things over the years, some pleasure and some business. Now, that I'm retired I intend to enjoy it with my family as much as possible," Martinelli said as he gestured around the salon with its wall-to-wall windows overlooking Frazer Bay. "Now, what can I get you to drink?"

"A rye and soda would be just fine, thanks," said Carl. Martinelli nodded.

"Ladies, may I make you a cocktail?" asked Martinelli, addressing the two women sitting near the toddlers who were playing on the floor.

"Do you have a Pimm's Cup?" asked Elsa.

"Of course," said Antonio.

"I'll have one, too, Papa," said Victoria.

Martinelli proceeded to the sideboard, where a silver ice bucket and a full array of crystal decanters were on display. He opened a lower door and took out the glasses he wanted, setting them on the silver tray next to the ice bucket. He proceeded to mix the drinks using the soda siphon while he talked to Carl.

"I find it exceptionally peaceful here. Yet, exhilarating at the same time. And it's amazing how many people we know here from Chicago. There are the Sandells over on Birch Point. The Edgar brothers, Irv and Gus. You know them don't you, Carl? They have the funeral homes in Chicago that cater to the Swedes. And, of course, the Bradleys, right over there on Black Duck Island."

"Of course," said Carl. "I've only met Gus once or twice when I've been at Irv's place over by Sylvan Dells. I met him and his mother years ago and I consider Irv a good friend. Up here at the lake, we get together a couple of times each summer. He's even taken me up in his plane. Boy, that's a real thrill, I'll tell you!"

"It's funny our paths have never crossed before. I've known the Edgars for years. I used to do a lot of business with the boys and their father during Prohibition," Martinelli said. He sipped his drink, then continued. "Those were some crazy times we lived through."

Carl took a swig from the glass Antonio had handed him. It was very fizzy from the soda siphon, and he had to stifle an embarrassing snort.

"We don't know the Sandells. But I've done some painting in Chicago for Reverend Bradley a couple times, and we dropped over to say hello to him and his wife for the first time a week or so ago. It's funny, this summer's the first time to visit them and the first time to visit you. We didn't come up last summer because the baby was so little. So, this is a summer for firsts, I guess," said Carl.

Antonia delivered the Pimm's Cup cocktails to Elsa and Victoria, who were engrossed in talk about the proper time to wean and potty train while the toddlers played on the floor between them.

"Thanks, Papa," said Victoria, smiling at her father.

"Thank you," said Elsa, taking the glass offered to her.

Antonio took a seat on the long leather settee. Carl sat in a matching leather club chair, and after a long draw, he said, "Speaking of coincidences, I think I have one for you," said Carl, looking out of the expanse of picture windows overlooking Frazer Bay. "Do you remember breaking up a fight in an alley off of Halstead Street, maybe 20 years ago? Young guys, some Italians, some Swedes, were having a tussle. I can't imagine you'd remember, but I have to tell you, you might have saved my life that day."

Martinelli looked at Carl for a moment, then said, "*Mio Dio, sei tu!*"

A big grin crossed his face, and he laughed, "Did you get new '*pantalonis*'?"

"Yah, I did, and I sure needed them," Carl laughed.

"Well, I guess I was wrong. Our paths have crossed before."

After sharing some Chicago stories, Antonio had made them another drink.

"So, tell me more about this beautiful place," said Carl, accepting the refill.

"It is beautiful, isn't it?" Martinelli said. "My wife's father built it in 1895. He was from Germany and had it fashioned to look like it belonged in the Alps or something. He spared no cost, and I am thankful it was kept in good repair all those years after his death."

"Oh? He passed away a while ago then?" asked Carl.

"Yes. Oh, sorry. I guess I neglected to say my father-in-law was Frank Hibbing, founder of the town just southwest of here. He was instrumental in starting the iron mines up here and amassed quite a fortune. He died just two years after he built this place which he left to his daughter, my wife. She was just twelve years old at the time, and I think she was badly affected by his death. She hated the place and refused to come here. But then, she hated everything about Minnesota after he died. It was only after her death, and I inherited Gold Island that I first visited Lake Vermilion. Basically, I came to inspect the property in order to sell it. But I fell in love with it and the lake. After all is said and done, I am very glad I kept it. It has served me very well as a business retreat for meetings and such over the years. Now it's just for family."

"So, how did you meet your wife if you hadn't been up here before?" asked Carl.

"She was very beautiful," he said, moving to the window to look at the distant shoreline. "And talented. She sang and danced beautifully and wanted to be on Broadway. She left home as soon as she could. I think she was seventeen at the time she went to New York."

Martinelli paused to take a drink of his highball. "She did well there. Made it into several musicals, but always as understudy or a secondary part. Then she was offered the lead in a traveling version of 'Leave It To Eve'. I happened to attend a production at the Shubert Theatre in Chicago and when I saw her on that stage, I fell in love. I wooed her and succeeded in getting her to give up life on the stage to marry me. Those few years we were together were the happiest of my life."

"I hope I'm not asking too many questions, but how did she die?"

"She died in childbirth. She was very fragile that way, I guess. The doctors told us they could save the baby or the mother but not both and we had to decide."

Looking out the window, he continued. "But if you were Catholic, you had no choice. She could have had a procedure to get rid of the baby and save her life, but she had become Catholic to marry me, you see, so it really is my fault. I knew that in such cases the Church decreed that the child is more important and the mother must give up her life to save the child. Now, I would give up anything – my unborn child's life, even my own life, if only she could have lived, but we had no choice then. She lived through her last few days knowing she would die never to know the joy of our sweet baby. She was the bravest person I know," he paused, then turned back to the room. "But look at what a wonderful young woman Victoria has grown to be. I see her mother's likeness in her in so many ways."

"That's such a sad story," said Carl, imagining Elsa in that horrible situation, his emotions clouding as he thought of how much he and Elsa had wanted a child. He tried to suppress what he wanted to say, but couldn't. "But, why?" he practically cried. "How could you let her die?"

The older man lifted his free hand and flicked away the question he had asked himself a thousand times. "They say 'God moves in strange ways' but the truth is that I don't believe in God anymore. I haven't been to church since she died. I didn't even bring our daughter up in the church like I should have or she might have wanted," he paused and looked at Carl.

"But you know, time passes, and life goes on. People die for a lot of different reasons. And even if we had a part to play in it, we have to move on and forgive ourselves. Now, look, we have the next generation, eh?" He waved toward the toddlers playing near the two young mothers.

Victoria caught his eye, "Papa, can you bring Elsa and I another drink?"

"Sure, my dear."

"We really should be going soon," said Elsa. "But okay, just this one, then we have to go."

When Katy started to rub her eyes, Carl and Elsa gathered her up, thanked their hosts, and made their way to their boat. The ride home was a smooth one, and Katy napped on her mother's lap. As they were going under the Isle of Pines bridge, a car happened to be passing overhead. The slapping noises of the loose boards as the wheels hit each one brought back another memory for Carl. He suddenly realized there was another time he had seen Antonio Martinelli.

Alphonse Capone's crime organization was based in Illinois in the Chicago area until his arrest and conviction on tax evasion in 1931. When local and federal law enforcement ramped up their efforts, Capone would often take refuge in Minnesota or Wisconsin. The most famous place he fled to was a 400-acre retreat in Sawyer County, Wisconsin nicknamed "The Hideout."

During the 1920's St. Paul, Minnesota was known as a safe haven for mobsters as long as they didn't conduct business there. While there is no evidence that Capone spent time in St. Paul, there were rumors that he and his entourage did stay at resorts in northern Minnesota.

1930 LAKE VERMILION

CHAPTER 21

The bridge creaked and groaned, loose cross boards clattering as the wheels of the new Nash Ambassador Carl was riding in passed over them.

"*Herre Gud!* It's going to collapse under us," said Gertrude in her stiff Swedish accent and lengthy rolled 'r's. Leaning forward from the back seat, "Careful, Verner, don't drive off the edge," she squeezed his shoulder, her black lacy sleeve tickling his neck.

"Jeez, Gertrude, let me drive already. We're almost over it, and I am being careful.," said Werner, her husband and the driver.

Carl laughed at his friends, who were taking him out to dinner to celebrate his newly acquired citizenship. The older couple was active in the Chicago Northside Swedish community, and they knew many of the new immigrants. They had taken a liking to Carl, the hard-working young man with a ready smile who showed up at almost every event or celebration, so obviously homesick. At one church potluck, Werner mentioned to Carl how much his place in northern Minnesota reminded him of back home. Whenever they met after that, Carl would ask Werner to tell him more about it. After a year or so, they invited him to come and stay with them for a week to help with painting and repairs around their cabin.

Half a mile farther on through the trees, the road ended where the resort was perched on the cliff, looking out over the western tip of Big Bay. It was a Tuesday at the end of July. The weather was beautiful, but there were no family groups on the paths or children's laughter coming from the swimming area when they pulled up to the supper club located in the main lodge building. Small cabins were scattered along the shore in both directions. As the two men got out of the Nash, a valet dressed in a crisp white shirt and black slacks opened the door for Gertrude, then drove the big sedan away to park it. Carl followed his friends into the grand lodge constructed of massive, hand-hewn timbers. A bear skin rug lay on the floor in front of the enormous stone fireplace, its glass-eyed face cemented in a ferocious grimace with bared teeth, silently warning not to tread on it. Chandeliers made of deer antlers lit the big room from high in the beamed ceiling.

At the podium, Werner asked for a table for three. They could see that, other than the large party at the far side of the dining room, all the tables were empty.

"I'm sorry, sir, but the dining room is closed," the maître d' replied. "A party from Chicago has the entire resort for the week. We'd be happy to welcome you back, perhaps next Monday?"

Gertrude stepped forward to explain that they were from Chicago too and that they were celebrating a very special event, begging the man to allow them to dine. While she was talking, Werner took a bill from his pocket money clip and gently laid it on the podium.

"I'm sure your chef could manage to make another three meals. We really would appreciate the exception you can make for us here," Werner said with a congenial smile. "We won't bother your other guests, I promise you."

"Wait here," the maître d' said. He crossed the dining room and spoke to the gentleman at the head of the table. When he returned to the podium, he nodded and picked up three menus from the sideboard. He led them to the table closest to the entry. It was covered with a crisp, white tablecloth, linen napkins folded like flowers, and a full complement of silverware. In the center was a vase of flowers and a silver candlestick topped with a small, pleated shade. The table offered a spectacular view of Big Bay in the early evening sunlight. Across the room by the back wall and the door to the kitchen, ten or twelve well-dressed men in pinstripe suits sat at the long table talking loudly over each other, toasting with highball glasses. As the maître d' leaned in to help Gertrude with her chair, he nodded his head toward the party of boisterous men and said close to her ear, "Perhaps you would like a table in our casual dining room? A little quieter perhaps? These men from Chicago can be a little crass."

"Oh, thank you, but the view here is too wonderful. It will be just fine," she replied.

After the maître d' lit their candle and left, Werner leaned forward and whispered with a grin, "They're probably mobsters."

The three laughed and picked up their menus. Their waiter appeared, and when Werner asked for highballs all around, he walked away. The maître d' came to the table, "May I help you? My waiter said you asked for something we don't have on the menu."

Werner discreetly slid another five-dollar bill under his fork and said, "We'd like to have the same ginger beer that those gentlemen are having."

"Of course, sir," the maître d' said as he palmed the money. "Ginger beer we do have on the menu."

They had a second cocktail and nibbled from the bowls of nuts and mixed olives before they ordered from the large hardboard menu. Gertrude had chilled tomato aspic, galantine of capon, au gratin potatoes, and a Waldorf salad; Werner had a shrimp cocktail, Beef Wellington, sliced potatoes and mushrooms with chateau sauce, seared brussel sprouts, and a salad etienne; Carl ordered herring bits, venison with cranberries, potato croquettes, buttered green beans, and a blue-cheese and bacon salad. Without asking, the maître d' served wine appropriate for each course.

Werner smiled after he set a glass down, "The maître d' is certainly accommodating. Either the tip did it or he doesn't want us paying much attention to the other guests who I'm pretty sure are mobsters."

"How's the venison, Carl?" asked Gertrude, ignoring her husband's idea with a dismissive snort.

"Very good. Almost as good as home," said Carl. "How is the little bird dish? Seems it wouldn't have much meat."

"Oh, it's absolutely delicious. Just perfect," replied Gertrude.

They chatted pleasantly the entire meal, ignoring the loud men who were also enjoying their meal. As Gertrude was speaking at length to Werner about their son's new job, Carl's attention turned to the other party. At the head of the long table was a short but imposing man with a very round face and a receding hairline. He was listening intently to a man whispering in his ear. When he straightened up to walk away, his message delivered, Carl saw it was Irv Edgar. Carl smiled when he recognized Irv and had begun to raise his hand in a friendly wave when he saw Irv look around the room, a dark expression on his face. Carl quickly lowered his hand when he realized Irv hadn't seen him and watched him hastily leave by the service door to the kitchen.

Carl knew the Edgars had a cabin on Lake Vermilion, so it was no real surprise to see Irv at the restaurant, but he wondered what the furtive encounter with the mobster was all about, and why he would leave through the kitchen. Gertrude's chatter had subsided, his attention returned to his companions, and he rejoined their conversation.

When the baked Alaska was rolled in from the kitchen near the long table and set aflame with a huge whoosh, everyone at the table shouted and hooted at the spectacle. The waiters served generous portions, then poured coffee and brandy. As all this was occurring, three black men came in through the service entrance and began to uncover musical instruments that were on a small dais set strategically so that the long table could see the musicians.

When the trio began to play, the men again shouted and hooted their approval. More brandy and more loud talk, but from where the Nelsons and Carl sat, the music was fabulous, and they ordered another brandy, too.

Carl noticed that man at the head of the table listened to the music more than anyone else, and every few songs or so he would tell the band what they should play next. Most of the group at the table were half-heartedly paying attention to the music. A few left and didn't return.

Werner recognized a few of the songs the trio played, and when the maître d' came by, he said to him, "That's some great jazz they are playing. Who are they? Where are they from? Not around here, I'll bet."

"No, you're right, sir. Our guests from Chicago bring their own musicians when they come up here once or twice a year."

"Too bad there's no ladies for them to dance with. No wives? Girlfriends?" asked Carl.

"No, no ladies allowed, although once they brought a lovely singer, Ma Rainey. She was fabulous."

"So, who are those guys?" asked Werner gesturing to the band.

"Well, that's Earl Hines on the piano. He's the main man. Zutty Singleton is on drums. Such a nice guy. And that's Eddie Lang playing guitar."

"This was really special. Thanks again for letting us have a table," said Werner after asking for the check.

"My pleasure, sir. I'll be right back with your check."

When the band took a break, Carl watched as three men got up, went to the man at the head of the table, and offered pleasantries before taking their leave. As they passed the Nelsons' table on their way to the main door, Carl recognized another face - the Italian who had interrupted the fight that day in the alley off Halstead Street. Carl couldn't remember his name, but he was sure it was him.

"Well, that was interesting," said Carl, nodding toward the door. "Do you really think they're mobsters?"

Werner laughed, "You must not read the papers much. That is definitely Al Capone sitting over there. For a lot of people, he's a kind of hero, you know?"

"Really? I didn't know that."

"There's a soup kitchen on South State Street that's his. I bet you don't get down to that neighborhood much, though."

"Nope. I got some advice to stick to my own neighborhood. Matter of fact, one of the guys that just left gave me that advice a couple years ago. Nice guy. He broke up a, um, uh, conversation we were having with some Italians guys down on Halstead. He told them to let us go and told us to stay in our own neighborhood," Carl said.

"*Herre Gud*, Carl. You need to be more careful where you go," said Gertrude, concerned.

"Yeah," Werner said to his wife with a shrug. "Well, you gotta go out and see things and do things when you're young. The Italians are nice people by and large, and not every Italian is in the mob. And even the mob doesn't bother regular people, so you must have poked a bear somehow."

"Yeah, well. I've learned my lesson. It's Clark Street for me from now on," Carl said to placate the worried Gertrude, and gave a wink to Werner.

The three finished the last of their brandy. Werner paid the check, and as they were leaving, he asked Carl to drive. "That bridge is awfully narrow and, to be honest, I'm seeing two of you right now, Carl," he said, laughing, and handed Carl the keys.

As they were going outside, Carl said, "Werner, why don't you two go get in the car. I've got to use the *toa*, I'll be right out."

A few minutes later, Carl followed the path to the parking

lot, which passed close to several of the resort cabins, each with a small deck facing the lake. The wind had died down with the sun's retreat, and voices from one of the decks carried in the stillness. Carl couldn't see them, but he could smell cigars. Not wanting to disturb them, he walked quietly but stopped for a moment out of sheer curiosity.

"Guess that's the last we'll see of Robert," said one voice.

"Why 'dya say that?" said a second, raspy and coughing.

"Martinelli told the boss he's some kind of spy or something. Now Irv's gonna make sure he takes a nap with the walleyes," said a third voice. They burst out laughing, and after a moment, they all puffed loudly on their cigars in silence, the smoke desicrating the sweet smell of pine.

"Too bad," said the second voice. "I kinda liked the guy."

1950 LAKE VERMILION

CHAPTER 22

On the Fourth of July, the Swansons went into Tower to enjoy the parade. It was a special celebration of sorts for them, because they had met on the Fourth twelve years ago. They loaded up the Frazer, left Bruno to snooze the afternoon away, and drove into town. They parked along the edge of the county road at the west end of town and walked to the main street. They preferred the long walk into town, which allowed them to head home whenever they wanted, rather than being stuck in the crowd trying to leave after the parade. Carl walked with the toddler on his shoulders, and Elsa carried a cloth satchel with a few toys and a small blanket.

They were chatting as they came up to Martilla's Drugstore, one of the first buildings on the west end of town, when Elsa happened to look in the window and saw Jane Bradley at the counter inside finishing her purchases. Carl continued walking as Elsa stopped to say greet her.

"Hello!" she said as the older lady came outside.

"Oh!" Jane screeched and jumped back, hitting her shoulder on the door as it was closing. She fumbled with her small purse and white paper bag containing her purchases. Her eyes wild with confusion.

"I'm so sorry I startled you. Are you all right?" Elsa apologized.

"Oh, uh, I'm sure I'm all right. I, uh, was, uh, just buying a few magazines about fishing for Preston. He's very excited about the trip you have got planned." And, with that, Jane lifted her shoulders and walked briskly away.

"That was odd," Elsa said to Carl after she caught up with him.

"Yeah, I guess we really surprised her."

"No, I mean that was really odd. I mean, she was carrying such a small purse."

"What's so odd about carrying a small purse?"

"She said she was buying her husband some magazines, but she didn't have any in her hand or under her arm. And they surely wouldn't have fit in her purse or that little white pharmacy paper sack."

"Hmm. I see what you mean," said Carl. "But I suppose she meant she was going to buy some but just didn't find any at Martillas."

"I guess. But it sure seemed like she said she had bought some. Oh, well. Never mind." And with that, they continued up Main Street to find a good spot to watch the parade.

* * *

Carl still had heard nothing from Irv by the following week. He had thought that the trip was going to be sometime around the middle of July, and surely they would need a few days to get ready. He was starting to think the fishing trip wouldn't happen. Perhaps, Reverend Bradley wasn't feeling well. He was just about to tell Elsa they should visit the Bradleys again to check on them when Bruno startled, jumped up, and went to the door. A loud fit of barking let them know a stranger was approaching.

Carl opened the door just as Irv was about to knock. They both laughed and talked at the same time.

"So nice to…Hello…see you…Sorry I…How've you…haven't stopped by…been…"

Irv joined them at the table where they had been eating and, after exchanging pleasantries, gave them the specifics about the trip. They would leave the following Monday and return on Thursday. He told them all the things they didn't need to bring - blankets, pillows, or towels, or even food basics, like Crisco for frying fish, flour, salt, sugar, or coffee. The cabin was well stocked, he said, and they would, for sure, be catching fish, but just in case, he assured them, there was plenty of Spam and baked beans if the big ones weren't biting.

"Have you talked with Preston? How's he feeling? He mentioned that he hasn't been feeling very well lately," asked Carl.

"Humbug! He complains, but I think he's just using his 'I'm getting old' card to get special attention. I'm sure he'll be able to go on the trip. He's a tough old geezer. He'll be fine."

"Well, good. It sounds like we'll get some real kicks fishing and all."

The Fishing Trip

For over one hundred years, Lake Vermilion has had one of the few mailboat routes in the United States. Steamers were the primary mode of transportation on the lake initially until combustion engines took over. The US Postal Service started the route around 1908 when people began building cabins on remote shores with no road access.

The Niemiste family, owners of Aronson's Boatworks, have run the mail route since its establishment. Russell 'Skibo' Thomas piloted the mail boat for 50 years and was a long-time friend of Dr. Preston Bradley, according to an article in the Mesabi Daily News in August of 1975. For many years, taking the 3-hour tour riding on the mail boat route has been a popular thing for summer visitors to do.

CHAPTER 23

On Sunday, Carl started his preparations for the trip. He packed his Army knapsack with underwear, khaki cotton T-shirts, woolen socks, two wool tan shirts from the Army that Elsa had taken the insignias off of, and a spare pair of wool combat pants. His army gear was well-made, comfortable, and practical. He was thankful he had been able to send home several trunks of clothes, army gear, and 'souvenirs' - which some people might have considered spoils of war. He had always appreciated interesting things, so, for instance, when an opportunity arose to remove a pair of large brass doorknockers from a looted, half-burned house near Lake Palermo, he took them, and many other odds and ends that fit in a pocket or knapsack. A foot soldier wouldn't have been able to take any 'souvenirs' or find a way to send them back to the States, but he had been the driver for a Colonel who appreciated Carl's level head and work ethic. The Colonel gave him lots of freedom to do as he liked, and he always had a jeep at his disposal.

Carl also put in the dark grey wool sweater Elsa had knit for him the winter before last. A toothbrush and a tin of Pepsodent Tooth Powder. A two-piece soap holder made out of Bakelite with a new bar of green Palmolive soap. A half roll of toilet paper. A small towel and a washrag.

Elsa was busy packing, too. She filled the red, two-handled aluminum cooler they had bought at Gambles recently with the food she knew Carl would like, assuming the others would like the same things. A large chunk of cheddar cheese. A dozen eggs. From Zup's, a pound of Canadian bacon and a good-sized summer sausage. She wrapped the dairy items and the meat together in several layers of newspaper, which acted as insulation to keep the items cold. She used cellophane tape to secure the tightly wrapped package. The eggs would be good for at least a week, but she separately wrapped a thick layer of newspaper around the cardboard egg carton anyway for extra security. A pint-size aluminum container with a screw-on lid carefully filled with soft butter, pressed to get as much in as possible. A round tin of oatmeal raisin cookies. A shoe box lined in waxed paper and filled with coconut chocolate bars. Another tin filled with hardtack. Two loaves of freshly baked bread. And a large box of raisins - great for a quick burst of energy, she thought, and a nice sweet treat, too. The items that didn't fit in the cooler went into a loose canvas sack.

After Katy was put to bed, Carl and Elsa sat together for a while watching the light of the day fade.

"This should really be a great trip. I wish you were coming along," Carl said.

"That would be fun, but really, I don't mind. Just be careful and come home safe and sound."

CHAPTER 24

It was early the next morning when Elsa woke up and realized that Carl wasn't in bed with her. She sat up with a jolt. Katy was making sweet baby snoring sounds in the other room. Elsa got up quietly and put on a pale cotton house robe, tying the fabric belt around her waist. In the kitchen, she saw the coffee pot on the stove. When she lifted it, she knew it was half full and still hot, so she poured herself a cup of coffee and went to the living room and sat on the sofa under the front window. It was still chilly in the house. She drew a knitted throw over her knees and pulled it up close to her chest. She looked out at the lake. A bit of fog hung over the water. Everything was the same color. Pale. Morning was not yet awake.

Outside the back of the house, the shed door slammed. "It must have slipped from his hand," Elsa thought and smiled. Carl was a quiet person. He would never allow a door to slam or a floor to creak if he could prevent it. His hypervigilance was a remnant of his experiences in the war, but she loved him for it anyway. It was what kept him alive when so many of his buddies died for being clumsy or inattentive. He had told her stories of clearing buildings in small Italian towns where Nazis or their sympathizers were holed up. Any creak of an ancient stair or a stubbed toe on an unseen threshold could mean your death. She shook her head.

Don't go there, she said to herself as she looked out on the beautiful lake. She sipped her cup of coffee and watched the light change as the sun rose above unseen treetops off to the east.

The door opened, and Carl came in with Bruno following close behind. The big dog's tail thwacked against everything he came near until he sat down next to Elsa and plopped his head on her lap. "Good morning, Bruno," she said, roughly scratching behind one ear with her free hand.

"Hi, honey. You're up early," she said to Carl.

"Yah. I checked over the gear we packed yesterday. I think it's good. Are you sure you and *lillan* are okay here while I'm gone?" Elsa could tell he was worried about leaving them alone because he only called Katy 'the little one' in Swedish when he was concerned.

"Of course, Honey. What's got you worried about this trip? It should be fun."

"Oh, I'm sure it will be. I just want to be sure you'll be okay without me for the week."

"You know we'll be fine. Besides, it's not a whole week. It's just for a few days. Bruno will be here with us, and we have the car if we want to go anywhere. I promise I won't do anything wild and crazy without you. Are you sure there isn't more to it?"

"No. Just my two sweethearts will be all alone without me."

Carl was on his way over to the sofa where Elsa was sitting when Katy called out from her crib in the corner. "Papa? Papa? Papa?"

Together, they went to the far side of the room where a folding screen hid the wooden painted crib from view. Katy was peering over the top rail, hair mussed, rubbing her eyes with the back of a chubby fist.

After breakfast, they loaded everything Carl had packed for the trip into the boat. Two rucksacks and a wooden crate held his fishing gear, some food, and other camping necessities. He packed as if they were going camping, even though he had heard that Irv's place was comfortable. *You never know what can happen in the woods*, he thought.

Still on the dock, Elsa put Katy's little red kapok lifejacket on, carefully fastening the straps. Bruno and Carl hopped into the boat.

"Well, I guess it's time we got going," said Carl as he fussed with the motor. When it started, he took Katy from Elsa so that she could get in, too. She untied the front rope, and Carl put the motor in gear and headed off toward Big Bay. He took the long way around Isle of Pines and then headed straight for Shadowland.

The morning was crisp and clear, the lake like glass, and they made good time over to Irv's. A sleek new Chris Craft was tied up at the dock.

Elsa slipped over to the back seat next to Carl so they could talk quietly as they motored slowly toward the dock.

"I guess Reverend Bradley is here already," said Carl, referring to the Chris Craft.

"That's a nice boat," said Elsa.

"I think it's Skibo's boat. Preston doesn't allow Jane to drive their boat, so I think he probably had Skibo bring him over."

"He's the mail boat pilot, isn't he? I've never met him," said Elsa. Then after a pause, "So, Jane doesn't drive their boat at all? So, she's stuck on that island by herself?"

"I guess so. But I'm sure Preston has arranged for Skibo to check on her and have him take her if she wanted to go to town. He does most everything for Preston. Anyway, somehow I don't believe she's just stuck there."

"You're probably right. It's not like this is their first summer here. How long have they had Black Duck Island, anyway?"

"Preston told me he first visited Lake Vermilion in 1916. But I'm not sure when he bought the island. It was many years ago, though. At least twenty-five, that's for sure."

They tied up, and as they began to unload Carl's stuff onto the dock, Irv came out of the shadows at the end of the pier. He had on a plaid shirt with a cable knit cardigan over it and dark brown gabardine hunting pants with several large pockets down each leg.

"Hey! Good morning! Why don't you pull into the cove and we can unload your things right onto the plane. Back that way," said Irv, pointing to the cove. "There isn't room for both your boats at the dock back there, so Skibo already unloaded and brought his boat back up here. They got here a while ago."

"Okay, will do," said Carl. He loaded his gear back on the boat, put the motor in reverse, and turned to head along the shore to the inlet.

With a wave, Irv turned and walked back into the dark woods to take the path to the plane's hidden harbor.

Carl motored slowly through the passage into the cove, then turned the corner toward the long dock where the plane was moored. Preston, Jane, and Skibo were standing near the luggage and boxes of supplies sitting on the planks.

Irv came to the dock and stuck his foot out to ease the heavy open boat's impact. Elsa tossed up the front rope with one hand as she held Katy close to her with the other. Carl turned off the motor and hopped onto the dock to tie up the back rope. He helped Katy and Elsa out of the boat, then he got back in and hoisted his gear up onto the dock.

After everyone greeted each other and Russell "Skibo" Thomas and Elsa were formally introduced, Carl began to explain what provisions he had brought. When he mentioned the bars and cookies, Preston laughed and patted his girth, saying, "I sure hope I can enjoy those, Elsa. Been a little off color lately."

Carl looked at the rotund little man and asked, "Preston, are you sure you're feeling up to this trip. Jane mentioned that you hadn't been feeling well. We could postpone it until later in the summer easily enough."

"I will be just fine. A little indigestion is all I've been having lately. We've been looking forward to this for some time. Wouldn't miss it for the world." Turning to Jane, he said, "You did pack my Milk of Magnesia, didn't you, dear?"

"Yes, of course. It's in your bathroom kit. But we put your medicine vials in your vest pockets. I just can't imagine why a fisherman needs so many pockets. I've dedicated one of them to your medications. Come here, Preston," Jane said, reaching around into various pockets. "See here. Here are your pills. Try to remember which pocket this is and don't put fishing hooks in this one," said Jane with a tight smile. "And it's time for you to take your Dramamine. Grab your thermos, there from the top of your bag."

Preston did as he was told with a show of husbandly patience and a roll of his eyes. "Yes, dear."

"Here, take these," and she handed him two capsules to swallow. "Now, Irv and Carl."

She waited until the two men were looking at her before she continued. "I want you to promise me you will be sure Preston takes these last two capsules just before he gets in the plane on the trip home. He gets nauseous when he flies." She clicked the little container shut and tapped it loudly with her fingernail to be sure they both looked at the pill box before she put it back into the vest pocket.

"Oh, nonsense, Jane," said Preston. "I'll be perfectly fine. It's not a very long flight. By the way, this Dramamine looks just like that one medicine I take in the morning. Isn't Dramamine usually a little white tablet, not a big capsule like these?"

"Well, this is a new kind, so swallow them like a good Preston, now," said Jane.

"He has other medicine to take every morning and just before bed. He's pretty good about remembering those, but you might remind him anyway. Being in a different environment, he might forget." Jane turned to Carl and tilted her head as if waiting for an answer.

"Okay," said Carl. "We'll make sure he takes them."

"You better believe it," said Irv. "Especially the Dramamine. I sure don't want any unpleasant mishaps in my plane."

"Yup," Carl said, "We got it covered."

"Thank you, boys," said Jane, and gave Preston's arm a wifely pat.

After all the gear was stowed and everyone said farewells and gave admonishments to be careful but have fun, Irv reviewed the plan for everyone standing on the dock. "We have about a three-hour flight up to Lake of the Woods, so we'll be there well before dark and get settled in. We'll fish for two days and leave for home on the third morning. That would be Thursday. If the fishing is wonderful or we're just having too much fun up there or the weather is bad, we might stay an extra day. That would mean we'd be back on Friday. So, don't worry if we don't show up on Thursday. But if we don't show up on Friday, call the Mounties. And if we don't show up by Saturday, call the undertaker." And with that, he laughed loudly and continued, "Oh, wait. I AM the undertaker!" and laughed some more.

Katy and Elsa gave Carl hugs and kisses. Jane and Preston exchanged pecks on the cheek. Preston shook hands with Skibo. The travelers began to get into the plane while the others moved back well out of the way of the propeller. Irv had already untied the ropes and stowed them in a compartment in the flip-up door.

Carl crawled in first behind the pilot's seat and sat on the small jump seat. The plane was built for two passengers with some cargo space behind the seats. Irv had a fold-up jump seat put in for occasions like this. He was careful not to take too much cargo when he had a third person on board. It was a tight fit, even for Carl, who was only 5 foot 8. The fishing poles went in next, laid on top of the gear next to Carl, with the reels to the front.

Irv went around to the other side of the U-shaped dock where Preston was attempting to get into the plane. Irv flipped down a small step, which made the entry easier for the older man. Once Preston was inside, Irv showed him how to fasten his lap belt. Then he released the latch that held the top-hinged door to the underside of the wing. Irv lowered it slowly and rotated the inset handle to secure it closed. He went around to the pilot's side, shut the door, and settled into his seat.

He flipped a few switches, adjusted a few knobs, pulled a few levers, and finally, the engine started. The wooden propeller rotated slowly at first, then whirred faster as Irv backed the plane out of the confines of the dock and reversed direction to head out of the inlet. The bushes were kept trimmed so the wings wouldn't touch them as the plane made its way through the short, narrow channel into open water.

Irv motored to the far side of the long bay, turned the plane to face west, and revved the engine. Then, with a whoosh of air and water stirred by the turbulence of the propeller, the Aeronca Champ accelerated until it slowly lifted off the surface of the lake. Below them, they saw Jane, Skibo, Elsa, and Katy waving from the dock. Irv tipped a wing and made a big sweep over them. Carl leaned forward and stuck his hand out of the small sliding window next to Irv to wave.

They were off on an adventure—fishing in the Canadian wilderness.

Prohibition was a socio-political movement that transformed the world. Religious and moral righteousness rose to such a fervor that prohibition became law in Russia in 1914, Iceland in 1915, Norway in 1916, Finland in 1919, and, most famously, the USA in 1920. Few had the insight to predict that the denial of alcohol to entire populations would lead to the rise of the Mafia in the US and to revolution in Russia.

In 1922, a prohibition referendum failed to pass in Sweden. Despite their freedom to make and drink alcohol freely, there was a strong temperance movement, and the societal compromise came in the form of a ration book. A person qualified to drink (by age, no previous misuse of alcohol, family status, etc.) could apply for a ration book with the government and be allowed to drink one liter of alcohol per month. Exceptions were made, of course, for things like celebrations, weddings, and other socially acceptable events where drinking was expected. The alcohol ration book was abolished in 1955, but to this day Sweden has strict rules when it comes to alcohol which can only be purchased in restaurants or government-owned stores.

While the Temperance Movement was very active in Canada, a national prohibition law was never passed. Instead, the provinces instituted

1950 LAKE OF THE WOODS

CHAPTER 25

The small jump seat faced inward, so Carl's back was against the curved wall of the airplane, and he had to lean forward a little or tilt his head. The plane flew canted slightly upward so Carl could see the sky out the front of the aircraft, but little else. *At least I can tell it's good weather and the propeller is still functioning,* he thought. The engine was loud, and conversation was limited to a few shouted words combined with hand gestures.

Preston, looking out the window, said, "What a great day! I'm just thrilled to be up here, high above God's Country. Glorious! Simply glorious!"

"What?" shouted Irv.

When Preston tried to repeat himself, he realized no one could hear him anyway, so he waved his hands in exasperation. Carl laughed out loud, as the elderly gentleman so used to pontificating became more and more frustrated, but, of course, the laughter couldn't be heard either.

Carl found that if he twisted forward, holding himself tight to the back of the seat in front of him, he could see out the pilot's side window. To the side, there were lakes and more lakes. The intermixing of rocks, trees, and water, the three elements of the Northwoods wilderness, was endless. In front, he could see strips of blue which seemed to grow wider as the plane approached; the strips turning into lakes sparkling and shimmering under the morning sun.

Although it was impossible to determine any contours of the land, Carl knew that the large patches of bare rock were higher. Occasionally, he would see a small open meadow, green and lush, but they were few and far between. He wondered why no trees grew there if grass could grow. Occasionally, he would see a small patch of old-growth timber, much darker green and sticking out above the heads of the younger, lighter varieties. The entire region had been clear-cut less than a hundred years before, leaving the faster-growing deciduous species to overrun what had been the home of one of nature's majestic wonders — the tall timber. On the flight north, Carl noticed very few boats on the lakes and even fewer cabins. Whitecaps on the water looked like lint on a blue serge suit.

They had taken off a mere twenty-five miles from the Canadian border, but it was a man-made distinction, and they weren't aware of crossing it after the first half hour of the flight. Lulled by the engine noise and gentle vibration of the plane, Preston nodded off, chin to chest. Carl felt his eyes grow heavy and wondered about Irv's capacity to stay awake. He pulled himself forward to talk.

"How are we doing, Captain?" he asked Irv.

"What?" shouted Irv.

"How we doing?" he shouted this time.

"Fine. Lots of fuel. Great conditions. Should be there in…" he consulted his watch and the instruments. "an hour or so."

"Okey, dokey," shouted Carl. He patted Irv on the shoulder and sat back in his seat.

A little later, Irv shouted over his shoulder to Carl, who moved close to hear, "This is Rainy Lake. Look to the left, there. That's Fort Francis. It means we're about half-way there."

They covered the 150 miles in a little over three hours. It was just after noon when Irv made a gentle sweep over his lodge, situated on the north shore of Yellow Girl Bay, pointing it out to his passengers as he went. Then he turned out over the bay where he would land. He made a pass close to the water to check the direction and intensity of the waves and scanned the surface for debris and deadheads. Hitting something in the water, even at a slow speed, could be fatal. He banked up steeply and came back around for the final descent. Flaps down, nose up, and splash, they were bouncing along on the lake at twenty miles an hour, the engine slowing to a purr.

"Welcome to Lake of the Woods," said Irv, as he slowed the engine and headed for the north shore of Yellow Girl Bay.

Fifteen minutes later, he guided the Aeronca Champ into the U-shape of the dock and turned off the engine. He popped open his door upward and latched it to the bottom of the wing.

A grand timber fishing lodge sat at the back of the huge mass of rock which sloped away from the shore. On three sides was the forest, thick and impenetrable. Two stories, made of whole logs bigger than any Carl had seen before, the entire width of the building was fronted by a screened porch. Wide wooden steps led up to the central screen door and main door to the house beyond.

"Just sit tight," Irv told the other two. "I'll come around and help you out, Preston. Carl, you can crawl out my side anytime if you don't clobber Preston with your clodhoppers."

"Yah, okay. I'll watch it." Carl said.

Preston was a bit wobbly on his feet as he stepped out onto the step, then onto the pontoon. Getting onto the dock required a little bit of a hop for him with Irv and Carl each holding a hand. The old man grunted loudly when he landed. Irv held his arm above and below the elbow and supported him as best he could, walking him off the dock and over to a wooden bench at the end of the path.

"How're you doing, Bud?" asked Irv. "Did you like the flight?"

"Yes, it was marvelous. Marvelous. I fly commercially on the occasions when I must and I will say it is quite exhilarating, but this was much more than that. Much more, I must say. I am veritably impressed with your aviational acumen, Irving."

"Hey, Irv," called Carl. "How do you want this tied down?"

"Pardon, Preston. I've gotta tend to my chariot," said Irv as he turned back to the Champ. "Carl, just loosen that rope, but hold it in place while I center the plane." After making sure Preston was comfortable on the bench, Irv hurried back to the plane.

The waves were coming straight at the dock, and Carl was doing his best to keep the plane centered in its berth. Irv lashed the front and back passenger side ropes, so the aircraft floated evenly from the dock on all sides. Then he rounded the nose of the plane and helped Carl tie off the other side the same way.

"Carl, could you get in and hand out the baggage and supplies?" Irv asked.

"Sure," said Carl, climbing back into the plane.

When everything had been carried up onto the front porch, Irv dug in his pocket and came out with a key to unlock the main door. Inside, it was welcoming despite a chill. The furniture was upholstered in a hunter green and brown plaid in the overstuffed it's-a-man's-world style. Several groupings of chairs and sofas were placed around the large room, interspersed with low tables and end tables with elegant brass oil lamps with glass shades. Bookshelves and gun cases stood along the walls. Heavy curtains made from a similar fabric to the furniture were swagged back to allow a magnificent view of the lake down the gentle slope of rock. The vaulted ceiling was crisscrossed with massive beams of pine, the knots untamed by the woodsman's plane.

Across the back portion, a second-level balcony spanned from left to right with several doors leading off to sleeping rooms. A long open staircase ran up the left side of the room, with several windows following the same angle as the steps. Along the right side of the room stood a long dining table of roughly hewn wood, as if part of the beamed ceiling had fallen into place there just to eat on. Twelve or fourteen chairs surrounded the table, too many for Carl to count quickly. A huge pine buffet and hutch filled the section of wall behind the table.

At the back under the second floor were two master bedrooms with the kitchen between them. An open door and a large pass-through from the main room afforded Carl and Preston a view into the large country-style kitchen.

"I'll take the supplies into the kitchen," said Carl.

"The icebox should have ice so go ahead and put whatever food Elsa sent along in it if you want," said Irv.

The icebox was literally just that. A large tin-lined wooden box, actually two such boxes, one on top of the other with ventilation holes between the two. The boxes had thick insulation between the tin and the outer wood layer and had chrome hinges and handles on doors that latched tightly with rubber gaskets. The top box held a large chunk of ice, which then kept anything in the lower box cold. A small drain fed the water from the melted ice down a tube to a container on the underside of the icebox. A block of ice could keep food refrigerated for a week.

Carl opened cupboards and drawers until he found what he wanted. He cut a plate full of salami and cheese and put it on a tray along with the knife and a loaf of homemade bread Elsa had sent. When he put the rest of the food in the icebox, he found it already contained cold beers, so he added three bottles to the tray.

With everything inside and put away, the three men sat on the front porch, beers in hand, looking out on the bay. They ate the simple fare as they talked.

"Well, the plane ride was really something," said Carl after a draw on the longneck Carling. "And this place is really something, too. How much land do you have up here?"

"My father said we own several hundred acres, but to tell you the truth, I don't think anyone has actually checked that out. I know for certain that no one in my family has walked the perimeter or even knows where the boundaries are. I don't think it much matters. It's not like Texas. We're not keeping herds of cattle here. Walleye maybe or lake trout would be good. But we sure don't need fences. So, who cares!"

"How do you keep up a place like this? You don't get up here that often and yet it looks great. I was prepared for spider webs and an inch of dust."

"Well, actually, we didn't do a great job keeping up the old boathouse. It stood right over there for years and we had a big old Chris Craft cruiser that we kept in Kenora. But one winter some years ago, the ice took the main supports and the boathouse collapsed. My dad was gone by then and my brother and I just didn't care enough to rebuild it as we should have.

"As for the lodge, the old ones like this come with a caretaker of sorts. Actually, that makes it sound much more romantic than it is. The truth is, years and years ago, my father contracted with a local family that lives on the lake up by Kenora, and they come down and keep the place free from vermin and so forth. They stock the icehouse in the winter, so we have ice all year and they clean it and keep the brush down now and again over the summer so whenever we come up it's ready for us. They've been on the family payroll for thirty years or so."

"So that's why there's cold beer in the icebox!"

"Yep, there's no way I could bring up enough stuff in the Champ. So, I have a standing order for certain things, like Carling. Have you had it before? It's a great Canadian beer. Anyway, how about a little fishing before nightfall. Maybe we can catch dinner and then we won't have to eat Spam."

"Boy, much as I appreciated Spam when we had to eat it, you know, over there in Italy during the war, I sure would rather have some fresh fish."

"Let's go then!"

Irv and Carl got up, but Preston remained in his chair. "Hope you don't mind, gentlemen, but I'd prefer to take my afternoon respite right here on this lovely porch. The view is spectacular, the air divine, and this chair well suited to my current needs."

"Suit yourself. Make yourself at home. The bedroom on the main floor to the left of the kitchen is yours. The loo is down the hall there. We'll be back in a couple of hours with the freshest fish you've ever tasted. Help yourself to whatever you can find, too, if you get hungry before we get back," said Irv.

* * *

The main rock on which the lodge was built ended near the shoreline, and the dock was built just to the east. A short way farther down the shoreline, a 16-foot aluminum Crestliner Runabout, covered with a canvas tarp tied with ropes, was pulled up on a small boat ramp equipped with rollers. Carl went to work folding up the tarp while Irv retrieved the fishing gear from a shed tucked back in the trees, not far from the icehouse. Before long, they were casting in a patch of weeds, hoping for a nice big northern pike to have for dinner.

The two men were comfortable with silence and enjoyed long periods of it between chats about times long past. They reminisced about their early days in Chicago and how they had met at Ann Sather's Restaurant. Carl recalled what a sweet woman Irv's mother was and how proud she was of him. They laughed about how, later that night, they escaped the police through the underground tunnels under Lawrence Avenue and ended up in Reverend Bradley's office. And those stories led to many more, parsed with the sound of fishing line flying off the reel.

When they got back to the cabin, Preston was still in the chair on the porch, snoozing.

"Hey! How's the fresh air treating ya?" Irv said.

Preston stirred and snorted as he awoke, "Fine. Fine. Just

fine! How're the fishermen? Were you gentlemen successful?"

"Wait until you taste this honey of a bass!" said Carl with a big smile, holding up a one-pound smallmouth bass as he headed for the kitchen with the catch. Carl and Irv cooked up the fish, boiled potatoes, heated two cans of green beans, and set the table. Preston kept them company from the dining room by leaning on the wide ledge of the pass-through opening in the wall. With the addition of a large wedge of butter and the loaf of Elsa's home-baked bread, dinner was served.

* * *

"So, the people that take care of the place don't come and do the dishes?" asked Preston, who was standing in the kitchen looking lost. Carl had cleared the table, and Preston thought he should help with dishes, but didn't have a clue how, and so there he stood mid-kitchen, hands on hips, contemplating how to proceed.

Irv laughed. "Nope. They live about an hour away by boat in Kenora and there are no roads here. So, we've got to do our own dishes. Sorry about that."

Carl laughed, too, and said, "Reverend, you and Irv, please retire to the front room. I'll have the dishes done in a jif."

After Carl finished drying the last dish and putting it in the cupboard, he stuck his head through the pass-through. "Anyone want coffee?"

They all opted for a whisky instead. Irv took a bottle of Famous Grouse and three lowballs from the huge built-in pine hutch, set them on the barrel coffee table, and poured a generous two fingers for each of them. They chatted for a while about this and that until Preston started to nod off.

"Well, guys. I think I'm going to hit the hay. No wives here to make us get up and do chores, so sleep in as long as you like. We'll get some fishing in tomorrow whenever we feel like it. We just have to catch something, or it will be fried spam and eggs for dinner," Irv said with a chuckle, "See you in the morning."

"I will also take leave of your wonderful company, my friends. May a restful peace fill your sleep." Preston followed Irv to the back of the house and into his bedroom.

Carl took a stroll out the front porch and down onto the dock. He stood there for a while, hands in his pockets, looking into the moonless dark. A falling star and then another caught his eye. The sky was filled to the brim with specks of light like tiny bubbles of champagne in a fine crystal glass held against a black velvet gown. The fabric of the Milky Way seemed to fray at its edges and blend into the velvet. Carl thought of his wife and baby and smiled. As he turned to head back to the lodge, without thinking, he said, "Come on, Bruno. Let's go to bed."

CHAPTER 26

Carl and Irv had finished their second cup of coffee when Preston emerged. The big room was filled with light even without direct sunshine, and the older man shielded his eyes as he joined them.

"Well, well. I must say that bed was most enjoyable. I slept like the proverbial baby."

"Good morning. We had some of the potatoes that were left over from last night's supper. There are still a few in the icebox. And we fried a slab of bologna and a few eggs with them in butter. Would you like some?" Carl asked.

"Not just yet, thanks," said Preston. He went into the kitchen, poured himself a cup of coffee, and joined the other two at the table. "What's on the agenda today, gentlemen?"

"Well, we were just planning our busy day," laughed Irv, "We decided we should relax until after lunch, then go for a boat ride and throw out a line or two and see what we catch."

They sipped their coffee and chatted about fishing and eating for an hour, when Carl said, "Say, Preston, aren't you hungry? You didn't have any breakfast. And did you remember to take your medicine that Jane sent."

"Why yes, I did take my medicine when I was in the kitchen, but, as for breakfast, sure could use some. My stomach is very picky and I'm not sure how to deal with it."

Carl got up and stood in front of Preston, "Come on. We'll bring a chair and you can keep me company while I fix you some breakfast, and I'll fix Irv and me some lunch."

And so, the next hour was spent in pleasant conversation and wonderful cooking smells. They ate together and sat back with a triple sigh.

"Oh, my. We'll have to take a nap before we go fishing," said Preston, leaning back in his chair. Carl was concerned about the old man's color but didn't say anything.

Irv must have noticed his pallor, too, but scratched his head and said, "Okay. Well, the air out there will refresh you. Let's clear the table and get ready to go out in the boat. C'mon, the great outdoors awaits us!"

An hour later, the three were trolling the lakeshore hoping for a walleye or two. While the big body of Lake of the Woods, some ten miles to the southwest, had the deep water needed for lake trout, the eastern section of the lake where Yellow Girl Bay was located was much more like Lake Vermilion — lots of islands, reefs and a convoluted shoreline, perfect for northern and walleye, bass, and crappie.

Preston got stuck several times. Carl could tell that the old man wasn't paying attention to his lure, letting way too much line out and letting it sink, but felt the old man's pride was worth more than exposing a fishing flaw or two, so he didn't say anything. The afternoon passed amicably, and when the catch included several nice walleye, Irv asked, "Well, boys, are you ready to head into the barn?"

The consensus was yes. Dinner and drinks were calling, and who could resist the pleasant lodge with comfy chairs on a big screened-in porch.

After dinner, Irv announced that he would break out the 'good stuff'. They had just brought out cushions from a storage closet for the oversized wooden chairs on the screened porch and were settling in for some camaraderie and cigars. Preston was ensconced in the center with the two younger men on either side. The magnificent view of the wilderness spread wide in front of them.

"I liked the Famous Grouse from last night. But are you saying there's something even better?" asked Carl.

"Come with me," Irv said and gestured for them to accompany him into the house.

"If you don't mind, Irv. I'll wait for you here. It's just ever so pleasant here. And to tell the truth, my gut isn't feeling quite right, despite your wonderful cooking and that magnificent specimen of cold-water aquatic gill-bearing vertebrate you served," Preston said.

"Well, okay. Carl, you want to come along?"

"Sure." He followed Irv across the main room and into the bedroom off to the right side of the kitchen.

Irv led the way. A long, low dresser made of knotty pine resided under the wide windows looking out into the backwoods. The large bed's headboard was against the interior wall, affording a lovely view of the trees. Two side tables matched the dresser, and a Native American rug of brown and rust colors, patterned with diamond shapes, covered most of the floor.

First, Irv pushed the dresser off to the side, then he went to the foot end of the bed and pulled it away from the wall. Carl watched with interest as Irv got between the headboard and the wall and rolled the rug back in a tight roll. He stood up to face Carl with a grin.

"Come on. Give me a hand."

Irv showed Carl where to pry away the baseboard, exposing the end of the flooring, some of which wasn't nailed down. The heads of the nails were there, but they had been cut off on the back side and didn't bite into the joists below. Together they lifted the section of the floor and put it off to the side. A set of steps led down into a dark space. Irv reached down and flipped a switch, then led the way into a crawlspace which stretched twelve feet in three directions, ahead and to the left and right, but was just barely six feet tall. It was paneled in rough plywood, as were the floor and ceiling. Across the subterranean room, the wall directly in front of them had a ladder attached to it. A few thin strips of pale light on the floor were filtered from a hatch directly above the ladder.

The front of the house was built on a giant rock bed, which sloped toward the lake. The back of the house was built over dirt. There was a small stoop by the back door, and next to the stoop was a good-sized enclosed firewood bin about three feet tall, with a sloped lid hinged at the top, and it was here the interior hatch opened.

Irv explained that the space had been used during prohibition to store cases of high-end liquor waiting to be transported to the US. The hatch opened into the bottom of the woodbin outside the back door. This made it possible to load the space without carrying crates through the house, as well as allowing for a stealthy escape should it have been necessary through a hinged half door. Stacked against the left wall were several dozen cases of liquor and wine. The paper labels on some had curled and faded. Others were stamped directly on the wooden crates. Cases of scotches, whiskeys, cordials, wines, cognacs, and some liquors Carl had never heard of were lined up, some three high.

"So, this is what's left after all these years. But, there's still some really nice liquor down here. Just imagine this completely filled," Irv waved his arm across the room. "Sometimes, we'd have just a path to walk from here to there. Stacks piled up to the ceiling. Boy, those were some wild times."

Carl whistled in amazement.

"Well, let's start by taking up this crate. These are open bottles left from previous trips. I always leave some cheap stuff upstairs in the dining room cabinet so if anyone breaks in, they don't keep searching for the liquor. Sorry about the Famous Grouse last night but I was just too bushed to deal with coming down here."

"I liked the Famous Grouse just fine," said Carl. "Here, let me help with that."

Irv handed over the half-filled case of opened bottles, and Carl went up the steps with it. Irv poked around in the crates for a few minutes until he found what he was looking for. He was rolling back the rug when Carl returned from the main room to help put the furniture back in place.

* * *

Irv let the smoke ring dissipate before he spoke. "Ahhh. That's more like it." He lit his Cuban cigar and poured the 100-year-old cognac into crystal glasses. The three had finally settled in again on the front porch. The air smelled less of the '612' mosquito lotion that Preston had used now that the cigars had been lit.

"All right. It's a fine night in this beautiful place. I'm so glad you two decided to finally take this trip with me. I do so love it up here. I dug this particular bottle of cognac out from the storage room because it has such wonderful flavor and carries with it so many wonderful memories – exciting memories of a younger time, a younger me. I remember we received over fifty cases of it with our first order and when we cracked open the first bottle, I was wowed. I had never tasted anything so good. Our customers agreed and we must have ordered it twenty times over the ten, eleven years we worked the border. It was a huge money maker."

"Worked the border?" asked Carl.

"Irv's father was quite the, shall we say, entrepreneur - despite being Swedish." Preston laughed heartily at his own joke. "Swedes had a reputation in the old days as dumb prudes."

Irv's face soured but quickly returned to his normal bonhomie.

"Well, since both my father and brother have passed, I guess I could let you in on a secret or two," Irv said, addressing Carl. "Preston knows all our family secrets already. You know my father started the mortuary business in 1913 in Chicago, and that we mainly served the Swedish community.

"But what you didn't know is that one day in early 1918, my

~206~

father was approached by a guy from Torrio's mob who wanted a small, secure, and discreet funeral for an 'associate.' It seemed at the time they were afraid that an Italian funeral parlor would be the perfect set up for an ambush. Since it was a very lucrative proposition, my father agreed to take the body, hold a private wake just for the family, and take a back route to the Catholic cemetery. The family agreed not to go to the burial and the plan went off without a hitch."

He paused for a few long puffs and sips before he continued, "What ensued was a business relationship with the mob that lasted for years. And while quite a few guys did sleep with the fishes for sure, there were also quite a few whose bodies spent their last seconds in the heat of our crematory.

"Another part of my father's working relationship with Torrio and later Capone was as a protected middleman for high-end liquor, which we brought in from Canada. What made it work was that they knew my father was very good at keeping secrets, and he never asked for much in terms of getting paid. I think they saw him as, you know, kind of like an appliance or an automobile — unthreatening, didn't cost much, you only need one of them, and just keeps doing a very specialized job without any trouble.

"My father had this place built in the early 1920s as a fishing lodge, but he was a far-sighted man and, I think, he knew exactly what he was doing in choosing this place and especially in how he had it built. He was born in Iowa, and for reasons I'll never understand, he traveled up here to Ontario as a young man. And it was here in Winnipeg that he learned undertaking. He was wild and crazy and dabbled in all kinds of things. So, he knew that Ontario, Kenora, and this big lake were wild, open places.

"During prohibition, he saw an opportunity to get liquor in Ontario and fly it down to our place on Lake Vermilion. He had learned to fly up here as a bush pilot for Laurentide Aviation and so he had the connections to buy a Curtiss H2-2L seaplane from them at just the right time. They had had a whole fleet of seaplanes bringing men and provisions to the gold mines in Kenora. How they came to sell my dad a plane I have no idea, but he made the most of it, that's for sure. He'd buy top quality liquor imported from Britain, Ireland, and France and fly it down himself. Then my brother and I would drive a hearse filled with cases of the best European liquor from Minnesota to Chicago. We'd do the trip without stopping – except for gas. Boy, my brother could hold it longer than any person I know."

After a few more puffs, he chuckled, "I remember when Einar Sponberg… Do you know Sponberg? Had the Standard Station on Ridge Avenue in Evanston?"

"Yah. He's a great guy. He helped me get my first car back when I first came here. Bought the thing outright, handed me the keys, and said to pay him whenever I could. And I hadn't even asked him! He just thought a good-looking guy like me should have a car. That's what he said," Carl said, laughing. "Anyway, back to your story."

"Well, we got Sponberg to beef up the suspension on that hearse so we could carry much more than that hearse was meant for. We told him it was a rush job, that we had a 400-pound dead man and that his family wanted a heavy mahogany casket. That it was being specially made for him. Einar just couldn't get over it – somebody being that big and all – but he did a great job on the hearse. Only thing is, we'd blow out a motor running that weight and have to get it replaced somewhere else because we never wanted Einar to know what we were up to. He was such a nice guy. And, if I told him what we were doing, I mighta hadta kill him," Irv laughed. "Some things are a need-to-know, you know? Anyway, that was a long time ago now. He must be really up in age if he hasn't died already."

All of a sudden, Preston snorted. His head had fallen forward shortly after they started talking, but Irv and Carl had assumed he'd been listening. "Ah, me. I guess I must have dozed for a moment," said the Reverend, running his hand over his face. "Perhaps I'd best put myself to bed."

He stood but faltered. Carl quickly rose to grab his arm and steady him. "How about I give you a hand there?"

When Carl returned, Irv asked, "Hmm. So how's the pastor doing? Does he seem okay to you?"

"Yeah, I guess. He seemed like he was just really tired. I asked him if he'd been taking his medicine and he said he had, but I don't know, he looked kind of pale."

"Well, we should give him the option of staying here when we go fishing tomorrow. Better yet, let's head out early, and he'll be spared the decision to go along or not," Irv said.

"Sure. That'd work. I think he'd enjoy himself just as much from this porch as from the boat."

"And we should catch enough to take some fish back with us, so we might be on the lake too long for him."

"Okay, then. See you in the morning," said Carl, and they called it a night.

CHAPTER 27

Up early and out on the lake by sunrise, Carl and Irv had great luck fishing and returned just before noon with a full stringer. Preston, who had slept in, greeted them from his favorite chair on the porch, still in his pajamas.

"Hail, oh, fearless fishermen!" he called from the porch. "Home are the hunters, home from the hills and the sailors, home from the sea." He tried for a hearty laugh, but that caused a fit of coughing.

Carl and Irv exchanged a concerned look and waved hello as they made their way up the massive rock to the lodge.

As they ate a simple lunch of leftovers, Irv told Preston that he had decided they needed to head back to Vermilion.

"Today?" asked Preston.

"Yeah, Carl and I talked about it, and we think the weather might change and it would be good to leave before that."

They had discussed how peaked the old man looked, and even though Carl had been making sure he took his medications,

Preston was looking worse each day.

"What do we need to do in the house?" asked Carl.

"Nothing really. The Klemsons will come next weekend and clean out the icebox and take the laundry back with them to do at their house and tidy up."

"Well, then," said Preston, "despite the lack of the proper saying of grace, I declare this to be an absolutely wonderful final meal. I'll gather my things and be ready whenever you say. And by the by, boys, I want you to know how much I appreciate being included on your manly adventure to this glorious piece of God's earthly paradise. Your hospitality and inimitable…"

Irv stood, cutting short the upcoming speech, saying with a grin, "You're more than welcome, Preston. But now we've got to get moving so we'll make it home by dinner time."

For the next hour, Carl and Irv tended to the boat and the fishing equipment, packed the morning's catch in the red cooler, stowed away the liquor in its hidey-hole under the floor, packed up what they had brought with them, and hauled their belongings down to the plane.

Standing together at the water's edge, they both noticed the gathering clouds to the northwest. "Does that look like anything much to you?" asked Carl.

"Well," said Irv, "I've learned never to take nice weather for granted or to think you can outrun the bad. Then again, if you wait for bad weather to pass, you're kind of a pussy, if you know what I mean." He laughed as he got in the plane to prepare for the flight.

Carl laughed too, but his laughter soon faded with concern. They were leaving early because of the old man, but now there was a potential for bad weather. Not good, not good at all, Carl thought. He headed to the lodge to bring Preston and his belongings down to the plane.

Preston wasn't on the porch and was nowhere to be seen in the main room, so Carl waited a bit, thinking he would appear any minute from the bedroom. Carl looked around the place to take in its character, thinking about the bootlegging days and the crazy illegal things that had gone down there.

"Preston, are you ready to go?" Carl called out.

No answer. "Preston?"

Carl went down the hall. All the doors were closed. He tapped on the bedroom door. "Preston, are you okay?"

No answer. He opened the door, and Preston was lying on his back, coat and shoes on, hands folded across his chest. Carl rushed over and shook his shoulder, "Preston. Preston."

The old man opened his eyes and slowly sat up. "Yes, that's me. What's all the fuss about? I just closed my eyes for a moment to contemplate a particularly bothersome question while I waited for you. The Lord Almighty hasn't called me to his side just yet. He, he, he. Are we ready to go then? Be a good man and carry my luggage for me, would you?"

"Sure. Here, I've got it," said Carl as he reached for the suitcase. "Let's stop in the kitchen for a minute."

He set the brown leather portmanteau on the floor by the sink and ran a glass of water.

"Let's dig out your medicines I'm sure you forgot this morning, and Jane said to be sure you took the capsule with the Dramamine so you won't be sick in the plane."

"Ah, yes, my lovely spouse, ever patient and caring of my welfare, has yet again succeeded in protecting me from my own failings. You know, of course, by that I mean she has enlisted your assistance in ensuring I take such medications as the dear woman and the doctors, of which there seem to be endless numbers, believe will best serve to keep me upright. My feet planted firmly on terra firma," Preston said as he worked at finding two vials in the large pockets of his fishing vest, which he was wearing under his flannel-lined oil cloth coat. He tapped capsules into his palm, popped them into his mouth, and drank from the glass Carl handed him. Carl washed and rinsed the glass in the sink, then dried it with a dish towel. "Okay, now we're ready to go," he said, putting it in the cupboard.

But Preston had already started out the front door. Carl noticed the medicine containers on the counter, shoved them into his jacket pocket, picked up the suitcase, and rushed to catch up with the elderly man.

Together, arms linked, Carl and Preston made their way carefully down the path to the dock where Irv waited by the plane. Carl took Preston's luggage with him as he climbed into the jump seat. Irv helped the old man into the passenger seat and buckled him in. He stood for a minute, checking the clouds and wind in the trees. He stared at the darkening horizon to the northwest before he climbed in.

As they taxied away from the dock, Irv said, "Damn, I left a couple of Cubans in the sideboard. I meant to bring them with me. I mean we gotta smoke 'em before we die. Can't do it after!" Carl didn't hear the words, but he laughed too when he picked up on Irv chuckling to himself.

Carl leaned around the pilot's seat and said, "Sorry, Irv. Can't hear you back here."

"Oh, yeah. Well, nothing important," Irv replied. "Let's get this baby in the air before that front gets any closer."

Irv guided the nose of the plane into the wind and revved the engine. The propeller engaged, and they started gaining speed. Just another long minute and they would be in the air.

Carl leaned forward to speak to Preston. "Isn't this exciting? Boy, I wish I knew how to fly a plane." Preston's head was forward. His chin was pressed to his chest like it was when he was taking a nap in the porch chair.

"Preston, are you sleeping?" Carl leaned close to Preston's face to see his eyes and was greeted with a distinct smell, sort of like the smell of almonds. He'd smelled it before. In that instant, he was with his platoon in Northern Italy. They were on patrol near Lago de Garda when they came across two German SS officers whose vehicle had broken down and were making their way on foot north to Austria. Carl's platoon shouted for them to stop when they started to run. But they hadn't run far when the two men stopped and looked at each other and nodded. They were just far enough away that they had time to sit down, so with steady hands, they could get the cyanide capsule from its secret pocket in their uniform and place it in their mouth. Carl ran to the closest one and kneeled down to try to save him, to fish the deadly pill out of the man's mouth if he could. The German's last breath smelled like Preston's now.

Carl jerked away in surprise and back to reality, practically falling into Irv's lap and shoving Irv's hand on the control stick sharply to the left. Both men shouted as the plane barrel-rolled upside down, slamming into the water.

CHAPTER 28

For a moment, everything was still. There was no noise except for the lapping of small waves on the windshield. Disoriented, Carl lay on his back on the ceiling of the plane above the front seats. His hands at his sides felt the water first. He slapped them up and down like a child patting a puddle, trying to come to terms with where he was. Irv and Preston hung just inches above him, suspended by their seatbelts.

Irv shook his head to clear it and said to Carl, "Are you alright?"

"Yeah, I'm okay. But Preston isn't doing well. He was asleep when we flipped. I'll get his seatbelt. Do you need help with yours?"

"No. You focus on him. I'll be all right. The wings will slow down our sinking, but we don't have much time to get out of here."

Carl kneeled and reached up to unbuckle Preston's seatbelt, but his full weight hanging on it was making that impossible. Irv was having the same problem and struggled to shift his weight around to get to the buckle. The water was coming in faster now. When it reached the top of Preston's head, and neither seat belt had released, Carl remembered his knife in his backpack. He reached into the back and felt around in the water for it. He found the knife inside the pocket where he always stowed it - a five-inch blade with a reindeer antler handle sheathed in leather. He clipped the sheath to his belt loop and removed the knife.

"Move your hands out of the way," he shouted at Irv, who was struggling to keep his head out of the water. In just a few seconds, Irv was freed. As he untangled himself from the instruments and worked his way out of the plane, Carl turned his knife to Preston's seat belt.

He stopped when he realized that Preston's body would trap him if he stayed where he was. He reached the passenger door, turned the recessed handle, and the door flopped downward onto the wing, which was now submerged in a few feet of water. Carl stepped out onto it, then turned to cut Preston's belt. He had been trying to keep the man's face out of the water, but it was impossible to cut the belt and do that too. Finally, it gave way, and Carl quickly ducked under the water to release Preston and pull him out of the doorway onto the wing.

The waves and the buoyant body he desperately hung on to pushed Carl around, and he had a difficult time getting his footing. There was no way Carl could get his arms around Preston to try to resuscitate him. The man is just too rotund.

"Come on, Preston. Just help me a little here, and keep your head up. You're gonna be okay," Carl said. Holding on to the long metal strut with one arm behind him and his other arm hanging on to the old man, Carl managed to get Preston's back pressed against the side of the plane. Face to face and only their heads above water, Carl used the strut as leverage, pushing his body against Preston's chest in small thrusts, trying to get him to start breathing. With each compression of air coming, Carl smelled the ominous odor coming from the dead man's mouth.

The plane tilted as the air pocket inside disappeared and filled with water. Carl could no longer stand on the wing, but with one arm, he continued to hold onto the wing strut. He had given up trying to keep Preston's body upright, but he would not let it go. The body would never be found if it sank in the deep waters of Yellow Girl Bay.

"Irv! Irv! Where are you? Are you alright?"

"I'm coming around to you," shouted Irv.

The wind had picked up, and Irv fought with the waves as he maneuvered around the propeller. He froze when he saw Preston's body floating face down next to Carl.

"Come on, Irv. Irv! Come on!" shouted Carl.

"Oh, my god. Is he dead?"

"Come on, Irv. Irv! Look at me. We have to get moving. Can you hold on to Preston for me? I have to get in the plane and get some stuff. Irv! Can you do that? Irv! Come on!"

Dazed, Irv followed Carl's orders and managed to hang on to the body while Carl dove into the cab and retrieved a long rope from the crate where Irv kept the mooring ropes. He was pulling himself through the doorway when suddenly the cab was totally underwater. The door jam slammed into his shoulder as the plane sank, and he was dragged downward several feet further. The rope tangled on something he couldn't see behind him, and he had to let it slip off his injured shoulder. He pushed to the surface; his air almost gone.

Irv hadn't fared any better when the plane sank a few feet; he was floundering in the water, trying to hold onto a pontoon. He had let go of the body, which was no longer in sight.

"Irv! Where's Preston?"

"I don't know. I just couldn't hold on anymore," he cried.

Kicking hard, Carl managed to pull himself up onto the pontoon. Sitting astride it, he shimmied to where Irv was desperately trying to hold on to the edge.

"Come on, Irv. Kick really hard. You've got to get up here and rest," said Carl, yanking on Irv's arms. The man was twenty years older and had never chopped wood, but he did have Carl's enthusiasm for living, so he put every effort into getting out of the water. Carl helped him get to the center of the pontoon, so that if he did fall off, he would be in the middle of the cross braces, which held the pontoons apart front to back. Irv began to shiver and was very pale. Carl knew he was probably going into shock, and he had to hurry.

"Are you okay here? Irv, are you okay to stay here? I've got to find Preston and get supplies from the plane. Just hang on, Irv," Carl shouted.

He looked out over the surface of the lake. There were white caps now, and the sun had disappeared behind the approaching storm clouds but no Preston.

"I'm going back in the plane. It can't sink anymore. Just hang on, Irv. Keep your eyes open. Hang on," he said as he slid back off the pontoon. He found the wing strut and pulled himself underwater to look around. To his amazement, Carl could see the body floating under the surface, not far away, and made his way toward it. Preston seemed to be flying, outstretched arms waving gently, reaching upward to the light and sky above. Carl found it was Preston's foot, wedged between the strut and the end of the wing, that tethered the body to the plane. He tested how secure it was and decided to leave it for the moment. Other things needed his attention more.

At the surface, Carl wasted no time, one deep breath in and went back underwater. He knew the rope could be a literal lifeline, but the rope, now caught in several places, was writhing like a trapped snake inside the cab. Carl had to fight with it as the currents made by his movements wrapped it around his limbs. To his surprise he spotted his knife, which had dropped onto the windshield after he cut the seatbelts. He grabbed it and cut his way out, holding onto the pieces of the rope that came free.

On the surface again, the waves slapped his face as he gasped for air. He struggled to put the knife into its sheath and snapped the leather tab to hold it there. He tread water for a minute to gather his strength and his thoughts, not realizing he was drifting away. Once he realized how far from the plane he was, panic propelled him through the water back to the plane where Irv sat, pale and shivering on a pontoon. He grabbed onto a cross brace to rest.

"Irv! I'm back! How are you doing?" shouted Carl.

With one arm slung over a strut, he tied the pieces of rope to the it, except for one, which he tied to his belt loop.

"I'm so cold," said Irv in a flat, quiet voice.

"Hang on, Irv. Just bit longer. Have to go back inside. Be right back."

With the rope gone, Carl was able to get in the cab easily. He found his backpack and put it on. He grabbed the cooler, which was floating at the floor, and tied the rope to the handle at one end. He pushed it out the door in front of him, holding on to the rope, then let it float upward.

On the surface again, he made his way to where Irv sat, feet dangling in the water. He pulled himself up onto the pontoon, drew the cooler close to him in the water, and holding the lid open, tipped it to bring it empty up onto the pontoon. It was hard work and took several tries to get rid of its contents.

"Okay," said Carl. "Phase One complete." Words he had used when he and his platoon had been on maneuvers in Italy. "Now for Phase Two." He slapped Irv on the arm as encouragement.

He slid back into the water on the cross brace side and untied the rope pieces. He secured his backpack to the brace with one, then he tied several of them together with a knot he learned as a child – one that wouldn't come undone. With a big breath, he dove to where Preston's body was still reaching for the light. Using the same knot, he tied Preston to the wing strut in several places. He knew the fish would peck at the body, but the birds would do the same thing if it were tied to the pontoon on the surface - if he could even manage to get it up there. Carl had to shake away the memory of when he had kept scavenger birds away from a friend's body. Tying the older man under the cold water was the best he could do for his friend, so with a touch, he bid farewell to the preacher and pushed for the surface.

He made one last trip into the cab of the plane to retrieve a wooden paddle and the two kapok seat cushions. Back on the surface he gave them to Irv.

"Hang on to these. Irv, hold these tight. Don't let go," Carl said.

Irv sat with glazed eyes, clutching the cushions to his chest with one hand and held the paddle with the other as Carl pulled himself up on the pontoon.

"OK, now give that to me, Irv," Carl said, reaching for the paddle.

Irv seemed frozen in place, not responding. "Irv!" Carl shouted. "Hand me the paddle."

After Carl grabbed it from him, Irv finally said, "Okay. Okay."

"Okay, now the cushions."

Carl arranged the cushions across the middle of the paddle and tied them together with several crossed pieces of rope so that Irv could place his chest on the cushions with the paddle under his armpits. He knew the flotation contraption wouldn't last, but it was the best he could do.

Carl took off his coat and shoes and put them in the cooler, latched the lid, and set it in the water. It floated.

"Now, Irv. It's your turn. Hand me the cushions," Carl said. "Irv. Look at me. I know you're cold, but you have to take off your heavy coat." Irv groaned and protested. "Come one, Irv! Take your coat off. I know. I know. But you have to! Hurry up!"

Carl put Irv's coat in the cooler, shut the lid quickly, and pushed it into the water. A small miracle. It still remained afloat.

"Now your boots, Irv. Hold up your leg and I'll unlace it for you." Carl added the boot to the cooler. "Now the other foot, Irv."

Carl knew from experience that swimming with boots and gear was exhausting. Even the young, strong soldiers he had crossed the Po River with in Italy had struggled. It was much better to swim unencumbered by heavy coats and boots. And he knew from experience that you could work up a good sweat swimming in cold water. As a youngster, he and his friends had liked to swim in Stor Sjon near his home in northern Sweden until late in the fall. The thin new ice formed on the edges of the lake had been no deterrent for the young and hardy. Hollering and whooping, the boys would emerge from the water, red-skinned from both cold and exertion, exhilarated and feeling alive.

Carl slid into the water and motioned for Irv to follow. He gave the shivering man the tiny raft and suggested he hold it under one arm and use the other to paddle.

"Now we have to really work hard at this, Irv. Kick with all your might. We have to make it to shore. Kicking will warm you up, but we have to hurry!"

Getting into the water, Irv found it warmer than the air, and his survival instinct kicked in. He began to swim, frantically flailing his arms.

"Whoa, Irv. Slow it down. Hurry, yes, but don't waste your energy. Take long, hard strokes and keep your arm in the water as much as possible," said Carl, who was doing the side stroke, keeping his head above water; the cooler on its long rope bobbed along behind.

Irv started to talk, but Carl encouraged him to be silent and concentrate on the shore. "Look at one tree or one rock and aim for it. Get a pace and keep it up. I'm right here beside you."

The older man calmed down and did as he was told, looking at the shore, which seemed so far away. His legs were tingling but in a good way, he thought, and the only part of him that was really cold was the shoulder that was out of the water. Carl had to swim slowly to stay near Irv, but truth be told, the cooler tied to his waist slowed him down even more. He was glad he hadn't been able to bring his large backpack on the plane; its large metal frame and heavy canvas would have been an albatross. The small backpack he was wearing was lightweight and easy to swim with. It was the waves that were concerning him, continually slapping the two men in the head. Irv coughed and sputtered, visibly becoming disoriented. He often stopped to rest, no longer concentrating on the shore.

"Irv! Come on. Look at me! Irv! You've got to keep going. Come on. Look at the shore. It's just a little farther," Carl cried out to him.

"I can't. I just can't do this," Irv managed to say. His head rested on the cushion, and the water splashed his face continuously. He continued to cough and made no effort to move.

Carl treaded water for a minute, thinking. He pulled the cooler to him and untied the rope from it. He watched as it quickly floated away on the fast-moving white caps - in the wrong direction. He made note of the shoreline and trees where he guessed it would eventually wash up as he wound the rope around his arm and pulled it up on his shoulder.

"Come on, Irv. We can do this!" Carl adjusted the paddle in front of Irv so that he had both arms over the cushions. He tied a smaller piece of rope he had in his pocket to the paddle on either side of the cushions, then tied the long rope from his shoulder to the loop the first one made. He had seen this technique used for pulling water skiers behind boats. Maybe, he hoped, it would make a small difference here.

"Okay. Irv. Let's see how this goes." Carl said, giving Irv a pat on the shoulder.

Within minutes, Carl's legs were screaming with the strain,

but he kept on swimming. It was slow going, but when he looked back to see Irv alert and holding on, he was heartened and swam all the harder. Twenty minutes later, Carl thought they might be close enough to shore to try for the bottom, but the drop off was steep, and the rocky bottom remained elusive. He tried again after a few minutes, and when his feet touched bottom, relief ran through him like a shot of good whisky. He pulled Irv to him, then pivoted to push the tiny raft and its passenger onto shore. Irv rolled off and sat in the shallow water, not even noticing the sharp rocks. Carl tossed the paddle contraption onto dry land and yanked at Irv's arm.

"Come on, Irv. Get up! Out of the water, man. Come on! We made it!"

The two men lay back on the rocky grass and panted. Then Carl began to laugh. He poked at Irv, who started to laugh, too. Together they laughed until they couldn't anymore.

"Now what?" said Irv, looking toward the oncoming storm. Small drops of rain were starting. Their mood changed quickly.

"I noticed a place over that way that we could use for some shelter. Can you walk in your stocking feet okay, Irv?" Carl asked as he gathered up the makeshift raft. He patted his knife, silently thanking it for staying in its sheath.

"I sure can try. I think I've got my second wind. We'd better hurry. The rain might start any time. Lead the way," said Irv, shivering but smiling.

They followed the shore, breaking through brush and cursing the rocks and stubbed toes. In less than ten minutes, they came to the place Carl had spotted from the water. It was a small clearing with an outcropping of solid rock to one side. Fortunately, its face was in the lee of the wind. It would be the place to try to build a fire. It had started to drizzle harder.

"Gather whatever wood you can for a fire, will you, Irv? Let's set up camp over there against the rock wall." Irv headed for the trees, and Carl cleared an area for the fire close to the massive rock, moving stones into a circle. He filled the little fire pit with lichen and pine needles and piled a few pieces of the wood that Irv had gathered on top.

Carl retrieved the small metal screw-top film container where he kept matches from his backpack and lit a fire. Irv brought another armload of firewood and tucked it close to the giant boulder wall. The wind had picked up and the rain was coming down

"How can we keep this dry," shouted Irv over the wind.

"You keep piling it up there. I'll see what I can do about a cover," answered Carl.

A short while later, the wood pile was substantial and covered by large pieces of birch bark Carl had stripped from downed trees and held in place with rocks. "That should keep us through the night at least," he said. "That's if this doesn't turn into a big storm."

Irv gestured across the bay to the grey wall of storm and rain that was coming their way. "No such luck," he said.

For the next thirty minutes, they sat on the kapok cushions, backs to the big rock, and watched the fire sputter and go out in the downpour. Both men shivered uncontrollably.

"The lake water was so much warmer than this damn Canadian ice water rain!" said Irv.

"It's the wind, too, that makes it so cold," replied Carl. "We might have to get up and dance like Indians doing a rain dance to get warm again!."

At last the rain stopped, and the wind died down. Carl lit another fire, and they finally started to warm up. They took their clothes off and, piece by piece, dried them suspended on branches held over the fire. They ate the few pieces of hardtack from the backpack, still dry in the little flat tin Elsa had packed for Carl.

"I usually snack on Elsa's hardtack when I'm fishing," Carl said.

"Boy, I sure wish we had some of our catch to fry up right now."

"So, Irv, I've been thinking, I need to go get the cooler before it's dark. August is practically fall this far north and the nights can get really cold. And here we are in our going-home-to-eat-dinner clothes and stocking feet."

"How on earth are you going to do that?" asked Irv, rubbing his hands together by the fire.

"Well, I guess I'll go for another swim," Carl said with a grim smile.

Leaving his pants, socks, and shirt draped over the little woodpile, Carl set off swimming along the shore in the direction the wind would have carried the cooler. This time he swam as fast as he could, watching the shoreline for any hint of red. After almost a mile, there was still no sign of it. Ahead and to the right, he could see open water and the far shore in the hazy distance. If the cooler had been carried past the end point of land he was nearing, it could be anywhere, miles away by now.

He was just about to give up hope and turn back when he spotted it stuck between two large rocks on the shore. It was banged up pretty good, but the latch had held fast, so it still floated. Carl tied it to his waist again, this time he tied the rope around his body, and started back. It seemed twice as long on the way back with the waves and wind against him, and he had to rest on shore several times.

It was almost dark as Carl dragged the cooler up from the water to the campsite. His face pale and drawn, he lay down next to the fire, exhausted.

"Hey, look what the lake spit up! Man, you look like hell!" said Irv in a weak voice.

After recuperating by the fire and getting dressed, Carl opened the cooler and dragged out the boots and coats. It was hard work holding the wet coats near the fire, so they jerry-rigged a makeshift clothesline using the rope and some sturdy branches.

As Carl was about to close the cooler, something caught his eye. There on the bottom was a small walleye. It somehow managed to stay inside the cooler as the plane flipped over and even when Carl had tried to empty it.

"Hey, Irv! You got your wish! Look what we've got for dinner!"

The small tin mess kit Carl always carried in his backpack worked just fine to fry the fish. Carl made short order of the scales with the serrated back of his knife. There was no butter or lard, but it didn't matter that the skin stuck to the thin pan.

"I believe this is the best fish I've ever tasted," said Irv, licking his fingers.

As soon as the coats were dry enough to put on, they each took a cushion and lay down by the fire. The slight breeze helped keep the mosquitoes to a minimum as the sun went down.

"I can't believe that Preston is dead. I feel terrible we had to leave him there." As Carl spoke, his hand touched the medicine vials deep in his jacket pocket, and he remembered Irv's last breaths.

"Like in the old days, I guess. He gets to sleep with the fishes," said Irv sadly.

After a while, Irv was snoring and breathing fitfully, uncomfortable on the cold, rocky ground. Carl dozed, leaning up against the rock wall, thinking of his wife and child. He fed the fire several times during the night and worried that they might not be found.

The Search

Lake Vermilion is a large lake, spanning over 61 square miles and featuring 365 islands. The Ojibwe originally called the lake Nee-Man-Nee, which means "the evening sun tinting the water a reddish color." French fur traders translated this to the Latin word Vermilion, which is a red pigment. In comparison to Lake of the Woods, it is a puddle.

Lake of the Woods covers 1,679 square miles, has over 14,552 islands, and stretches 70 miles north to south. It transects the borders of Manitoba, Ontario, and Minnesota. French explorers named it Lac du Bois in the 1730s. At the northernmost point of Lake of the Woods sits Kenora, Ontario, originally named Rat Portage, referring to the numerous muskrats in the area. Despite its remote and almost inaccessible location, the town has a strong history of trade and commercial enterprise. The Hudson Bay Company set up a trading post there in 1861. In 1863, the Canadian Pacific Railway was completed across Ontario with a station in Kenora. Although gold was discovered in 1850, it wasn't until 1932 that a highway was built that passed through Kenora.

THURSDAY

CHAPTER 29

Irv's groans woke Carl from his last attempt at sleep. Daylight was breaking, and it was cold. Carl prodded the embers and got the fire going. His optimism revived with the flames. He had always been practical and a problem solver, and along with those traits comes some small amount of positive thinking, else why bother?

"Morning, Irv," he said.

More groans and grumbling from the older man confirmed he was coming around, and he joined Carl sitting by the fire, boiling water in his tin pan. He poured some in the cup portion of the kit and offered it to Irv.

"It will warm you up at least, even if it doesn't taste like coffee," Carl said.

After Irv finished and Carl had drunk a cup too, he said, "I've been thinking. The plane probably isn't visible from a boat unless you're getting close to it and then you'd give it a wide berth thinking it to be a reef. Only another airplane would see it with just the bottoms of the pontoons above the surface. We've got to figure out how to attract some attention to where we are. A fire is fine, but people camp and have fires all the time, but it's still our best bet."

"What are we going to eat in the meantime?"

"I'll be back in a bit, hopefully with some berries at least."

Carl took the pan and walked into the woods. He stumbled on a few juneberry bushes and filled the pan in short order.

As he and Irv ate them, Carl said, "I'm going to explore where we are. Perhaps there's a cabin nearby. I'll be gone for a while, so you've got to keep the fire going. Use any pine or damp wood that will give off lots of smoke."

"Okay, I can do that, but I'm so hungry," said Irv.

"Take some of the pine sap, roll it into a ball and chew on that for a while. It will trick your stomach into thinking you're eating. Just don't swallow it. And you can boil some more water."

The sun was low in the sky when Carl came back with the bad news. They would have to hunker down and wait to be rescued. They were indeed on an island. He hadn't made it all the way around the shore but at one place there was a steep rock outcropping. He climbed it and shimmied up a big pine at the top. From that vantage point, he could see water almost everywhere.

"Eventually, someone will come looking for us," Carl said. "They expected us home earlier this afternoon, so they'll send a search party soon, I'm sure." He did his best to keep his voice light and hopeful. He knew there would be no search for at least a couple more days. After all, they had said if the fishing was good they might stay an extra day.

They spent the rest of the day gathering wood and pine boughs. "Boy, what I wouldn't give to have a hatchet."

"Okay, but what are we really going to eat?" Irv's mantra now.

"Crayfish!" exclaimed Carl suddenly. "It's a Swedish favorite – boiled crayfish. Have you ever had them?"

"I've had crawfish at a restaurant in Chicago that served Louisiana food," said Irv. "It wasn't bad. I presume they're the same thing – crayfish, crawfish."

Carl stripped down to his skivvies in case he fell on the slippery rocks. The mosquitoes and the deer flies took advantage of the newly exposed skin, and he had to put up with their bites as he crouched in the shallow water. He could see hundreds of the gray-brown shellfish skittering over the rocks just inches below the surface. At first, he set his sights on catching the biggest ones, but soon gave up and tried for any size. The small lobster-like creatures move backwards very fast, and Carl figured out a technique to catch them by placing his tin cup behind them and scaring them with his other hand. It took a while, but finally, he had the pan filled with wriggling crayfish, frantically crawling over each other as they tried to climb out. He added water and set it on a rock in the fire pit to boil. When they were a rich reddish color, Carl declared that dinner was ready and set the pan in front of Irv.

"There isn't much meat in a crayfish so you each this batch, Irv. I'll catch more for me when you're done." Carl showed him how to break off the head and suck the juices from it. Then, using his thumbs on the belly, cracked open the two-inch-long shell and extricated the tiny morsel of meat tucked inside. It took a while, but when Irv was finished, he exclaimed, "Well, that was really good. I think I'll have a cigar and some cognac now."

His attempt at humor fell short, and neither man laughed.

The daylight was fading by the time Carl finished his pan of crayfish. The two men fell into silence as they waited near the fire. The night sky darkened, and thunder rumbled in the distance.

"I sure hope they come for us tomorrow," said Irv, as the rain began. The two hustled for shelter against the rock.

"Good night, Irv. I'm sure they will come soon. But tomorrow first thing, I'll head back up the hill and find some berries for breakfast. And maybe I'll find some mushrooms. Back home when I was a boy, I'd go with my mother into the woods and help her pick *svamp*. That's Swedish for mushrooms. My dad sure loved when she cooked with them. Anyway, don't worry, now. Get some sleep," Carl said.

The rain only lasted a short while. The main part of the storm moved past them to the west. Irv fell asleep quickly. Carl quietly sang some folk songs his mother used to sing, and eventually, he dozed off with the familiar smell of a wood fire for company.

* * *

On Thursday afternoon, the day the men were expected home, Elsa, Katy, and Bruno took the boat to Black Duck Island as planned, where they would wait for the fishermen to return. Jane had planned a light supper for all of them – a simple hotdish that just needed to stay in the warm oven and a tossed salad already made and waiting in the icebox.

Elsa and Jane sat outside on the broad porch chatting about nothing of import as they watched Katy occupy herself with some clothespins and a few wooden toys. After the conversation on the porch with lemonade and cookies became tiresome and filled with awkward silences, Jane suggested they move to the garden where Katy could run around on the grass. Bruno ambled down the steps and along the path to join them.

The two women sat on the bench overlooking the bay. Bruno canvassed the area, then settled nearby. Katy, happily and noisily, ran around and back and forth between her mother and the dog for a bit. When she tired of that, she played with some rocks and sticks that suited her imagination, making funny noises as she bounced them along Bruno's back and head.

"You are so fortunate, Elsa, to have such a lovely little girl."

Jane's tone was warm and sympathetic. Elsa felt a connection with the older woman, but was aware that something felt off, something she couldn't put her finger on. She decided to share more than usual, hoping it would encourage Jane to reveal what was making Elsa uneasy.

"Yes. I think we are so very lucky. We thought we wouldn't be having any children. We were married seven years before Katy came along," Elsa paused to gather herself. "It was hard. First, we blamed ourselves, then we blamed each other. It was really, really hard for us during those years, but we managed to stay together. Finally, after we'd been to all the doctors and had all the tests, we found there didn't seem to be a reason we didn't conceive. It just didn't happen. Then one day, it did."

"I love babies and children. I would have done anything to have had some of my own," Jane said with a change in her voice, her lips tight.

"Do you have any brothers and sisters? I mean for you to enjoy nieces and nephews?"

Elsa could see Jane considering her options: keep her own

counsel, or reveal a little of herself. Their eyes met for a moment before Jane looked out over the lake and began.

"I grew up on a dirt farm in central Illinois. My mother had ten children by the time I left home for Chicago. I was the oldest. I was dead set against having children. I saw what it did to my mother. She was too tired to care for us properly, I know that now. My father was strict and whenever he was in the field or not around, the kids would be mean to each other, especially the boys. They fought each other and bullied the girls. I suppose that comes from not having enough to eat. And to answer your question, I never kept track of my siblings. Being the oldest and often put in charge, they hated me when I had to make them do things. There was never time for play, except of course for the babies. And once a child was old enough to carry a bucket, they were sent to work on other farms, even if only for a few hours a day after school. I honestly don't know what happened to any of them. I suppose that's a horrible thing to say."

She was pensive for a while, her shoulders mimicking the sadness in her face. "One of the youngest was my favorite. She was frail and often clung to my side. She died of fever just before I left. Helen was her name. A sweet child, like your Katy."

"That's such a sad story," said Elsa. "I'm so sorry it was like that for you, and for all of them, too."

"Later, when I worked with children at Hull House, I began to hope someday I might be a mother. When a particular child or another would respond to a kindness or a little attention, it was all worthwhile. And when a crying infant would quiet in my arms, my heart ached for such a thing to be mine."

They sat in silence for some time, and when the daylight started to fade, Elsa considered leaving for home. She was about to say they would be leaving when, from the high vantage point of the garden bench, she saw the boat approaching.

"Look! Here they come!" She gathered Katy in her arms and hurried down to the dock, Jane following behind. Bruno immediately took the lead.

"Greetings, ladies!" Skibo shouted as he pulled up to the dock. "I waited at Shadowland all afternoon and I don't think they'll be coming yet today. Even if they slept in and hadn't left until noon, they would have been here by now. It's only a three-hour flight. So, I guess we'll do this again tomorrow."

The three chatted about the weather and fishing and what they guys were probably doing.

"Skibo, after you drop Preston off tomorrow, would you mind bringing Carl home?" asked Jane, a stiffness returning to her face. "There's no need for Elsa and Katy to spend another whole afternoon here. The little one would be better off napping in her own bed."

"Oh, he doesn't have to do that. We don't mind boating over to wait with you," said Elsa, confused by Jane's withdrawal.

But Jane insisted and, despite Elsa's protests, pressed Skibo to comply.

"Well, of course, then, I'll be happy to," he finally said. So, it was settled. They would wait separately.

FRIDAY

CHAPTER 30

Today they will begin to worry when we don't show up, and tomorrow, for sure, they'll send a search party, thought Carl, even before he opened his eyes. He had a pain in his neck from the crooked way his head had been resting on the rock wall, and his back felt like it would never be straight again. He stood and groaned like a troll in a children's tale, loud and scary.

Irv had slept lying on his side on a bed of pine boughs. The plane's seat cushion under his head. He stirred but didn't rise, when Carl groaned. "You okay?" he asked.

"Yeah. I'm fine. Just a little stiff."

The morning was rising over the water in a pointillist's palette of peach and pink and light blue. The steam that rose along the shoreline, a portent of a warmer day to come, added to the pastel scene awaiting some painter's brush. Not a ripple blemished the mirror surface of the lake, nor was there a single bird call interrupting the absolute stillness of the chilly morning.

Carl walked to the water's edge and squatted to splash some

on his face. As he raised his head, his face dripping, he was overwhelmed with the beauty around him. He leaned back on his haunches and took in the amazing sunrise. The sliver of yellow gold sun gently slid away the delicate curtain of dawn exposing the true colors of the day, bright and real and confident.

When he turned back to the makeshift campsite, he saw Irv had fallen back asleep. He picked up the pan without a sound and went into the woods to find berries for breakfast.

The day passed slowly. Irv was quiet and withdrawn, although Carl could see nothing physically wrong with him, he seemed unwell. Several times, Carl pressed Irv to move around or talk to him, but he barely responded except to express how hungry he was. Carl provided berries and more crawfish, but neither was very filling. He racked his brain for ways to catch something else to eat but had no success. He knew about spring traps set using bent saplings, but that just seemed like a hopeless endeavor. He also knew that people could survive a very long time as long as they drank water, so he coaxed Irv to drink as often as possible. He added a few juniper berries to the boiling water to give it a little taste, and Irv found it easier to drink.

When the sun was high, he set off to see if there was anything else he could learn or find on the island. He had explored the high parts of the center of the island already, so he headed along the shore to the south. The brush was thick, but soon he saw a deer path that ran parallel to the shore for a good distance before it led down to the water's edge. As he looked out over the expanse of Lake of the Woods he thought he could see a boat in the distance. He waved his arms and shouted. Then he realized how ridiculous that effort was. He couldn't be seen from that far away if he couldn't even be sure that dot was a boat. Despair, like a determined deer fly, buzzed around his thoughts, and every time it landed, the idea of never seeing Elsa and Katy again was as painful as the fly's sting. He swatted those painful thoughts away and kept going on the path.

A little further on, the path split in two; one path continued along the shore, and the other led into a clearing to his right. The little meadow, filled with milkweed, dandelion, coneflower, goldenrod, and silky asters, was a sea of timid colors, topped with butterflies and birds flitting here and there, unable to land on the waves of wildflowers and grass. Carl smiled at his good fortune and stuffed all his pockets full of dandelion greens.

Along one section, straight-line winds of a long-past storm had devastated a section of trees that now lay in a tumble, dry and ready to burn. Carl took off his jacket and laid it open on the ground. He broke branches to a manageable length and piled as much wood on the jacket as it would hold. Using the arms, he hoisted the bundle over his shoulder and returned to the camp.

"Hey, Irv. Look what I found. A whole bunch of dry firewood. And there's lots more where this came from. At least we don't have to search for one piece at a time now."

"That's good," Irv responded in a weak voice. "I kept the fire going, see. Did you find anything to eat?" He attempted a smile.

"No, not yet. But how would you like some delicious crayfish with dandelion greens? The chef recommends it!"

After catching and cooking what passed for their dinner, Carl went back for another load of firewood. And the evening passed without rain or incident – just worry.

* * *

Elsa was awake before dawn and, sure that Carl would be home for dinner, she began planning a happy homecoming meal as she lay waiting for the sun to flood the tiny cabin. The day passed slowly, and in the early afternoon, she began the meal preparations. When there was nothing else left to be done, she took Katy down to the dock to watch for Daddy to come home. Bruno joined them, paws hanging over the edge of the dock, to keep watch, too. It was almost dark when Skibo's boat arrived. His news was neutral again, but not what Elsa wanted to hear. The fishermen had not come home, and there was no news from Lake of the Woods.

"I'll bring him tomorrow, for sure," said Skibo.

"No, that's very nice of you, but I'll take our boat over to Black Duck. I'll go wait with Jane. She must be worried sick."

After a few tries to convince her to stay home, he finally gave up. "Okay, then. I'll see you tomorrow afternoon. Don't worry, now. They're having a good time and just wanted to fish some more, I'm sure," he said as he backed away from the dock.

"Okay. Thanks for all you're doing. See you tomorrow," Elsa said with a wave of one hand, the other holding tight to Katy's. Worry seeped from her into her daughter like an icicle chills the hand that holds it. When Katy looked up and asked with a tiny, furrowed brow for her daddy, Elsa said, "He's catching a big fish, I'm sure. We'll see him tomorrow, sweetie." And the three of them went up to dinner and to bed.

SATURDAY

CHAPTER 31

By Saturday, Carl had more than being rescued to worry about. Irv was starting to act listless and disoriented. He had lost weight and, without his daily medications, he was visibly going through some difficulties. He had given up fending off the flies and mosquitoes, even with the switch that Carl had made for him from some ferns. Carl kept pressing him to drink water and eat. He tried to get him up to walk around, but Irv just wanted to lean back against the granite. *It's like he has battle fatigue*, Carl thought.

Carl had to be careful not to let the fire go out. There were only a precious few matches left in the little film container. Since he could no longer trust Irv to keep watch over it, he realized he had to improve the fire pit or he would never be able to leave for more than a few minutes. After thinking about it for a while, he came up with a plan of action and got to work. He removed the ring of odd-shaped stones he had hastily assembled the first day. Using flat rocks retrieved from an outcropping of slate on the shoreline, he built walls around the fire pit by stacking them on top of each other. When he had a u-shaped structure about two feet tall, he placed a wide flat stone across the back section of the top opening. It would serve as a stove top and keep at least part of the fire dry if it rained. He sat cross-legged on the ground in front of it and thought of the stone fireplace he was building in Half Bay. He missed Elsa to his core. He knew she was worried and wanted to comfort her. With his head in his hands, he spoke out loud to her words he didn't know were coming until they were spoken. He wiped his eyes and stood.

He was exhausted, but the threatening sky and rumbling in the distance spurred him to push on. The firewood from the windfall was vulnerable lying in the open where he had dropped it. As valuable as gold at this point, he had to keep it dry. He considered the options and chose to stack it against the rock wall near their sheltered spot. Covered with birch bark held down by stones, it would stay dry, would break the wind from that direction, and was even more convenient to the pit opening. At that point, he had done everything he could think of, and there was nothing else to be done but hunker down and keep the fire going. The storm lasted all day and seemed as if it would never pass. They ate the few berries and mushrooms that Carl had stockpiled in the cooler and sat hunched against the storm. When the dark became even darker as night fell, Carl made Irv change position to lie facing the wall and covered him with some pine boughs he had set aside for kindling. Irv gave no resistance and stayed where Carl put him, never speaking and barely opening his eyes.

Carl didn't dare lie down. He was so tired, he was afraid he'd fall into a deep sleep and let the fire go out. Sitting up, he might doze, but he knew he'd jerk awake just like when he was on watch in Italy during the war. He had to keep the fire going - that was the only thing that mattered.

* * *

Elsa waited until the afternoon to head to Black Duck Island. By that time, she was angry at Carl. He should have insisted that they come home yesterday. He could have, she reasoned, said that he was anxious to get back to his family. When she pulled the boat up to the dock at Black Duck Island, she was fuming. Jane was there waiting, hands clasped, knuckles white.

"Hello, Elsa. Thanks for coming and waiting with me. I'm sure they'll be here any time now."

At dusk, they were again waiting on the dock when Skibo arrived with the news that the fishermen still hadn't shown up. Jane, in a quivering but no-nonsense voice, asked them to accompany her up to the house to talk.

"What are we going to do? Where are they?" she demanded when they had settled around the kitchen table.

Elsa reached for the distraught woman, who waved her away. "They should be here by now. Preston isn't healthy. He needs to be home."

Elsa realized how close to hysteria Jane was and took charge in a calm voice, "You are right, Jane. They should have been here by now. Skibo, I think we need to alert the authorities. Can you please go to Shamrock Landing and contact Deputy Pittella and tell him what is going on?"

"Sure. That makes sense. I'll call him and come back here to tell you what he thinks we should do."

Jane put together a small meal of leftovers for Elsa and Katy as they waited for Skibo to return. The small talk they shared was strained and filled with platitudes. Katy fell asleep on Elsa's lap as darkness fell.

Skibo knocked as he opened the front porch door and rushed through to the kitchen area in the back where the two women were sitting. The tension in the room was heavy like the mud on gardening boots after a rain. The women focused strained eyes on the bearer of no news.

"The Deputy says to go to bed. He'll contact the Canadian authorities, and in the morning it will all be figured out. He'll be out to talk to each of you first thing. There's nothing to worry about. Just go home and go to bed. Oh, you are home, Jane. Elsa, can I take you and Katy home?" He spoke to the two women in a flurry of concerned words, his hands flapping like birds trying to perch on a branch blowing around in the wind.

Elsa stood with Katy in her arms, determination visible. "Thank you, Skibo. I think we should take our boat now and head for home. I'm sure we'll be fine. It's a clear calm evening, and I know the way."

Jane and Skibo started to protest, but Elsa insisted. "We'll be fine. Come down and see us off if you like." She made her way through the house and down the path to the dock, carrying the toddler in her arms with Jane and Skibo in tow. Bruno jumped into the boat first. Jane set Katy on the dock and got in. She made a smiling face at the sleepy toddler as she reached her arms out for her baby and put the tiny red kapok life jacket on her. "Come on, honey. Let's go home before it gets dark."

She sat Katy on the floor between her feet, held her tight with her legs, and rotated to start the motor. Skibo untied the ropes and waited to toss them into the boat.

"Thanks. See you tomorrow," she said stiffly, too many worries to even express her concern to Jane, as she pushed away from the dock.

Once out on the water, Elsa realized how quickly the dark of evening was turning into the black of night with only a sliver of a moon. She was a few minutes away from the dock when she realized Katy should be in a better place, that if she had to move quickly, she might actually harm the child. She put the motor in neutral and picked up the toddler with cooing words of comfort. She stepped forward, grabbed the pile of life jackets, and moved them to the floor in front of the back seat, positioning them close but not under her feet. She arranged them with a kick or two and set her sleepy child down on the lumpy bed with kisses and sweet night-night words. She took off her coat and covered the baby.

As she got her bearings after drifting those few minutes, she put the motor in gear and started out. At least it was calm, almost no wind.

I've got to turn right at Vermilion Dells, but will I recognize the channel? What if I miss the turn? If I don't make the turn, oh no, that would not be good. There are reefs there on the way to St. Mary's Island. But if I make the turn, will I even know the way after that? I thought I knew all the channels, but it's so different when it's my hand on the throttle control. Doubt flooded her mind like too many people on a crowded bus, pushing and shoving her to the point of panic.

The sliver of moon in the east stood out against the clear, dark, and star-filled sky. She looked down at her sleeping child, her sweet face barely visible in the dim light of the moon and gathered her thoughts. *I need to follow the shoreline until the channel appears*, she thought. *I can do this. Carl can do this, well, so can I.* She was angry with him, and it bolstered her confidence. *Why had he put their child in this situation? He should be here. But who needs him! I can do this! First, he almost lets Katy drown, and now he abandons us for a frivolous fishing trip. Men! So reckless and thoughtless and stupid! Just wait, Carl Olaf! You're going to get a piece of my mind when you get home.*

She could still see the shoreline and the occasional white of a cabin or boathouse, but when clouds started covering the moon, she was unsure. She closed her eyes and recalled the memories of what she saw as she sat facing forward on the front seat, the many times Carl drove the boat. She concentrated on the shoreline, the subtleties of the dark and the even darker trees, the tall and the even taller trees, the light spaces where granite rock masses pressed through the darkness around them, and most importantly, the space where the water opens through the dark. She opened her eyes and took a deep breath.

"The turn is coming up soon. It's here," she said out loud. She slowed the boat and turned into the gap of the channel, a narrow glisten of pale moonlit water that beckoned toward home.

She knew there was a reef on the east side of the channel, and then remembered Carl mentioning that there was light on it now. Once she spotted that, she veered to the right toward the open body of water. But her focus was to the south, where Isle of Pines was a harbinger of potential disaster. A reef, marked by several buoys, guarded the passage under the bridge.

It was so dark now with cloud cover that she had to reach down and pat Katy to be sure she was still there. "We're almost home, Katy. We'll find the way, sweetie."

As she crossed the expanse of water between the narrows and Isle of Pines, she shouted at Carl, "Where are you? Why

aren't you here with us? You'd better come home tomorrow!"
When the shoreline to the right showed itself in the blackness,
she gasped and turned sharply left, slowing even more. The
bridge appeared as if it was a dream trying to wake the sleeper,
insistent and unrelenting, it loomed in front of her. Elsa was
going at a snail's pace, but she was still startled at how close the
marker buoys were when she finally saw the center arch of the
bridge and steered through the narrow span into Daisy Bay.
Almost home.

From there, she chose to skirt the School Teacher's Island to
stay far from the reefs that surrounded it. It was so dark now
that she began to doubt where she was. When she recognized
the unique shape of the rocks at the tip of Horseshoe Island, she
realized she had gone too far and had to double back across the
bay. Home should be directly north of where she was. She swore
a few choice words and made a wide turn to head in what she
hoped was the right direction. The far shore seemed a long way
away until the white of their boathouse appeared like an
apparition. *Home! Thank goodness! Carl, you'd better come home
tomorrow.*

When the boat was secure in the boathouse and the baby in
her crib, Elsa turned off the lights, poured herself a shot of
aquavit, and sat on the sofa looking out at the bay. Bruno looked
pensively at her, and, breaking her own rule, she patted the
cushion to tell the big dog he could join her on the sofa. He
circled and settled with his chin on her lap. She rubbed his ear
absently.

"You miss him, too, eh, big guy?"

Clouds caused the moonlight to flicker ambivalently on the
calm water, not caring if Carl was safe or not. She took small

sips of the sharp caraway liquor and squared her shoulders, defying the elusive moon to dispute her logic. He's fine. He's made it through so many hardships. *Whatever is happening now isn't a problem for him. It's just an inconvenience, a matter of time. He'll be here soon because this is where he belongs.*

* * *

Pittella was about to go home when Skibo called the Sheriff's office from Shamrock Landing. "Whoa, whoa. Slow down, Skippy." The two had been friends for many years, and Pittella was the only one Skibo allowed to use the diminutive nickname. "Ya gotta talk slower for me to understand what's going on. Okay, now start over again."

After a few minutes of questions and many convoluted answers, Pittella fully grasped the situation. "Okay. Go back to Black Duck and tell Jane and Elsa that everything's under control, and I will come talk to each of them in the morning." After Skibo left, he reached out to his supervisor in Duluth and started the process of connecting with the Canadian authorities in Kenora. An hour or so later, his boss called back.

"This'll be a joint effort, seeing as the missing men were Americans presumably lost on Canadian soil or, er umm, water. I'll send someone from here up to Kenora in the morning. I think we'll charter a plane so the department's unit can stay here in case something comes up. Is there anything else you and Korchenko are working on right now?"

"No, sir. Nothing at the moment," Pittella answered.

"Okay, then. Have Korchenko take over the daily work and you concentrate on this case. You'll be the liaison with the families. Stay in close contact with the Canadians and keep the families informed. We'll handle the transport arrangements for the men, or the bodies, when they're found."

Pittella's choke was muffled, but his boss heard it well enough. "Deputy, we have to be prepared for all contingencies. Stay focused. Let me know any developments there."

"Yes, sir."

When he put down the receiver, he left his hand on it for a long moment. He knew his boss was relieved not to be the one to deal with the families. It was the most difficult part of any missing person's case. But his irritation at the assignment was minor. His thoughts were on the youngest Swanson. *Don't let anything happen to those men. That little Katy needs to grow up with her papa.*

* * *

"Boozoo, Minnie," he called out as he came into the house and hung his weapon belt on the hook behind the door and his jacket in the hall closet.

"I'm in here," he heard her call, and went into their bedroom. She was sitting in the armless rocker near the small window which looked out on the side yard. Wearing a simple blue nightgown, she held a darning egg with a grey sock stretched over it in one hand while the other hand swooped the darning needle, up and down, back and forth, through the stitches like a butterfly touching flower petals. Seeing his face, she put her work down and went to him.

"Carl Swenson, Irv Edgar, and Preston Bradley are missing. They were supposed to fly home from Lake of the Woods in Irv's float plane on Thursday." He sat on the edge of the bed and unlaced his work shoes, took them off, and slid them under the bed. He slipped on his moccasins, then sat up straight, hands on his thighs. "The Canadians will start a search tomorrow."

Minnie sat next to him and put her hand over his. "The weight of worry shows on your face. Do you fear they have passed? Or is it something else?"

"The little girl. Katy. Carl and Elsa's baby. I keep thinking what her life would be like without her father."

"So, you do fear something has happened." She turned to look him in the eye. "What will be your role in this?"

"Duluth has Korchenko taking the office, and I'll be coordinating with the families. I have to go talk to both Jane Bradley and Elsa Swanson in the morning. How will I tell them?"

"Harvey. What do you have to tell them? Nothing. You do not know that anything has happened. This worry has you turned over like a turtle on its back. Sleep with a clear heart, concerned, yes, but only that. Tomorrow, you will be righted, your feet back under you so you can show the concern you feel, not the despair. Concern walks holding the hand of hope. Despair walks alone."

As Minnie slept with peaceful puffs of breath that imitated the small movements of the sheer curtains in the breeze, Harvey spoke out loud to himself, "I think I am getting too old for this job."

CHAPTER 32

Carl knew before he even opened his eyes that there would be no rescue today. The wind had picked up, and the sky was dark and ominous; another round of storms was imminent. Whitecaps already dotted the lake, but fortunately, the wind was from the north, so their shelter was in the lee. He stood and stretched, then went to relieve himself in the woods. It started to rain before he got back to the smoldering fire. He quickly stirred it, added some wood, and got it stoked into a roar.

He turned his focus to Irv, who hadn't sat up yet, although he had pushed off the pine boughs.

"Hey, Irv. How are you doing? Stiff, I bet! I tell you, our beds are going to feel so wonderful when we get home."

When Irv didn't respond, Carl continued, "Well, today we'll be hunkering down because of this storm. I sure hope you're not sick of my company yet because I'm sure that we're not getting rescued today."

Carl helped Irv sit up against the ledge wall. "You want to go take a leak?" After Irv nodded, Carl helped him stand and guided him to the nearest bush.

As the rain beat down, the options became evident: get drenched and have berries to eat, or stay dry and be hungry. Carl looked at Irv and made the decision. He put more wood on the fire, took off his coat, shirt, and undershirt, and went into the woods to forage. Putting on the fire-warmed clothes when he got back made it worthwhile. They nibbled on what Carl had managed to gather.

Just to have something to do, Carl brought his backpack to his lap and began opening its many pockets. He found nothing of help or interest. But when he peered into the bottom of the main compartment, he saw a corner of a piece of paper peeking out from one of the gussets where the canvas folded in on itself to make the pack's shape. Curious, he pulled it out.

"Irv! Look! Look at what I found!" he cried. Without waiting for a response, he stood up and practically danced, "We're not going to be hungry anymore! I found fishhooks stuck in the bottom of the rucksack! I'm going to go catch us dinner."

The small envelope contained five hooks with a leader line and swivel attached to each one. Carl took a length of rope and carefully unwound it to extract one of the thick threads it was made of. He tested it and decided it would hold the weight of a small fish. He dashed into the rain, cut a thin straight poplar sapling with his knife, and brought it back to the shelter. He tied the rope strand to the flexible stick where small branches stuck out at the end, so it would be secure, and tied the other end to the swivel of the leader. He looked on the ground nearby to find a likely place for earthworms and used his knife to dig up the dirt a bit. The slippery flesh-colored bait was plentiful, and in short order, he had one on the hook. Carl added wood to the fire, checked on Irv, and took off his clothes down to his skivvies.

On the shore, a short distance away, was a fallen tree that extended into the water. Carl made his way out to the end, sat down straddling the trunk, and dangled the baited hook in the water. The rain beat down on him patiently, chilling him to the bone. His feet and calves, submerged in the water, felt warm in comparison.

Some fishermen believe that sunny weather is not the best time to fish; that rain and overcast weather are more favorable. Others argue the opposite, justifying their stance by saying no one should be on the water when lightning is possible. Carl had no opinion either way. The persistent hard rain pelting his skin made him all the more determined to land a big one. Like a hound at the base of an oak tree staring up at a raccoon, he would stay as long as necessary. When his shivering made it hard for him to hold the makeshift rod, he realized he might be getting hypothermia. He was considering giving up when the pole was almost torn from his fingers. He jerked hard to set the hook and reached for the string to pull it up out of the water. At the end was a chubby smallmouth bass, big enough to share.

When he got back to the camp, the fire was almost out. Only the part tucked under the stone cover was still smoldering. He cursed himself for being so careless. He should have gone back once or twice to put on more wood. He did that, then warmed himself before putting on his clothes. This time, he cleaned all the scales off the fish, gutted it, and put the whole thing, head and all, to boil with some juniper berries. He would eat the fish skin and everything he could off the head, if Irv would eat more of the meat.

The rain continued the rest of the day, and when night fell, the sky cleared, and the moon came out, just a thumbnail of light, bravely fighting the dark. Irv fell asleep sitting up, and Carl gently repositioned him onto his bed of pine needles and life jacket pillow. He added more wood to the fire and walked down to the shore to share the sliver of moon with his love.

Good night, Elsa. I miss you. Kiss Katy for me. I'll be home soon.

* * *

It was raining when Pittella stopped in at the Sheriff's office to check in with Korchenko and let him know the plan for the day.

"Morning, Harvey," Korchenko said. Pittella took no umbrage at being called by his first name – at least in private. In front of others, the patrolman always maintained the appropriate demeanor and correctly addressed his superior officer. In the five years Korchenko had been in the Tower office, Pittella has found him to be very professional, easy to work with, and reliable beyond expectations.

"This is really something. Three of our citizens missing," the younger man continued.

"Any word from HQ?" Pittella asked as he sat at his desk.

"Yeah, the Sheriff called just a bit ago. Kendall Johnson made the last flight to Kenora yesterday and is at the RCMP office there. The Sheriff was happy to have saved the cost of a charter. Unfortunately, the weather is even worse to our north so there will be no search flights today. They are sending a boat to Edgar's cabin on Yellow Girl Bay. Kendall will go with them. Evidently there is a man that lives in Kenora that takes care of

Edgar's cabin, or fishing lodge as they're calling it up there, and he will go with them, too. Sorry, I didn't catch the local man's name."

"Did you or the Sheriff get Edgar's wife's information? I need to call her before I head out to break the news to the wives."

"Yes, I got that from their Chicago home address in our property records, then called the operator there. Here's the number to call." Korchenko handed him a slip of paper with the seven-digit phone number.

"Thanks," said Pittella.

Dialing 'O' on the rotary phone, he gave the operator the information needed to connect him to the Edgar residence in Chicago. After a prolonged period of ringing, the operator came on to ask if he would like to continue. "No, I'll try again later," he said to the distant but cheery voice.

"Well, you've got things under control here, then, eh?" Pittella asked.

"Yeah. No problem. I'll stay close to the office in case there are developments. What's your plan?"

"Given the weather, I think I'll take the patrol car and drive to the Swanson's first. Then I'll try to find Skibo over at Shamrock Landing to take me out to Black Duck Island. He usually hangs out there for a bit in the middle of his mail run. Say, will you give them a call and tell them to keep Skippy there. I'll stop back here when I'm done."

Korchenko nodded his acknowledgment as Pittella got up and headed out the door. "You've got this," they said simultaneously, which made them both laugh.

"Yes, we do," said Pittella.

* * *

Bruno was already at the end of the drive when Pittella pulled up and got out.

"How did you know I was coming, Big Guy?" he asked, scratching where it was important. "Let's go see the ladies." Bruno led the way. The gravel crunched under his feet as he approached the cabin. He pulled his collar up as branches and trees whipped around in the strong wind, hurrying him on like a school crossing guard, knowing the light was about to change.

Elsa opened the door before he had a chance to knock. Katy stayed behind her mother, her face peeking out enough to see her smile. He smiled back at the toddler and wiggled his fingers at her.

"Are you both psychic?" he said, gesturing to Bruno, trying to lighten the situation.

"No, of course not. I just knew you would be coming soon with news," said Elsa seriously. "And I heard your tires on the driveway. Oh, I'm so sorry. Please come in. I'm just on edge, I guess. Come in. Come in."

"I won't stay long. I don't really have any good news, except the good news is that I don't have any bad news," Pittella said, shutting the door behind him.

"Well, come in anyway. Sit, please. Just talk to me. I've been sick with worry."

Elsa felt like she was going to burst, she was wound up so tightly. Pittella held information she wanted desperately to hear, but she took a breath and asked if he'd like something to drink. Tea, coffee, perhaps?

"No, thanks. I know you want some good news, but unfortunately this is all I can tell you for certain." He continued

~259~

to stand.

She clutched Katy to her and listened while Pittella told her the little he knew. He promised to come by as soon as he heard anything more concrete. He was sure they would start air searches as soon as possible when the weather broke.

After he left and Bruno returned to the cabin, Elsa set some blocks on the floor in front of Katy and sank onto the sofa. *He's made it through so much before, I know he'll do whatever it takes to get home. Tomorrow. He'll be home tomorrow.* Elsa's mind wandered to Jane and how she must be worried, too.

The day dragged on. On the third round of negative thoughts, she took charge. No more of that. She pulled the little box off the shelf that held her recipes and began to bake. First, some limpa bread, then while that was rising, she made Carl's favorite cookies. Then Katy's favorite. Then hers. A pan of bars. Cardamom braids. She stopped now and then to play with Katy and took her for a short walk with their raincoats on. But she forced baking to take center stage. When the last batch of cookies and the last loaf of bread were done and Katy put to bed for the night, she made herself a Manhattan with extra cherry juice, just like Carl would make for her. She cried a little but took another sip and set that mindset aside. *You'd better be home tomorrow. Damn it! We can't eat all this by ourselves!*

* * *

Pittella left the Swansons and drove to Shamrock Landing, which wasn't far by road. He almost missed the turn off, he was so distracted by his thoughts. He pulled up to the big boathouse and got out to see if the message had gotten through. Sure enough, Skibo was sitting in the open-air cabin with his feet up on the gunwale, waiting for him to show up so he could resume his mail route.

"Hey there, Skippy. Thanks for waiting for me."

Skibo waited for Pittella to climb on board.

"I need to get to Black Duck," he said.

"You have news about Preston?"

"No, not really, but I need to let Jane know that we're doing our best."

"Sure. I get that. Hang on. We'll be there in no time," he said as he started the engine.

The passage across the small stretch of water was rough, and he was glad he had worn his slicker. Green-grey clouds hung low, and whitecaps dotted the bays of Lake Vermilion like cake sprinkles on swirls of blue icing.

The rain began to let up a little as they pulled up to the dock on the island. Pittella said, "Do you mind waiting for me and take me back to my vehicle. I won't be long."

"Sure. Should I come up with you? Maybe Jane needs something."

"No. Stay here. I'll ask her."

"Okay."

Pittella hustled up the steep path to the cabin quickly and was panting when he knocked on the door. "Shall we sit here on the porch for a minute?" Pittella said when Jane opened the door, mainly because he needed to sit down.

"Of course." Jane sat on the wicker settee and gestured to the opposite chair. The wind was blowing hard but from the back side of the house, so it was calm where they sat.

"I have no news for you. But really, that means there's no bad news." He proceeded to bring her up to date on the little that he knew and talked positively about the air search they would conduct the following morning when the weather broke. He promised to come by as soon as he had any further news.

Jane had been sitting calmly, back straight, waiting for Pittella to finish. "They're dead, aren't they?" she blurted out quietly.

Taken aback by the question, Pittella sat for a moment, took a breath, then responded, "There's absolutely no reason to think that at this point, Mrs. Bradley. We haven't begun to search, there hadn't been any bad weather prior to this storm, and the three men are healthy and resourceful. I'm sure they'll find shelter. We have to be patient. They'll be found tomorrow, I promise."

As he got back into the boat with Skibo, he felt unnerved. He had botched that interaction. He should never have promised they would be found tomorrow. But what really bothered him was the older woman's question. *Why would she jump to that conclusion?*

CHAPTER 33

The next morning, Pittella was sure he would arrive at the office before Korchenko. He hadn't slept well and was up before dawn. He moved about quietly so as not to wake Minnie, but as he bent to kiss her goodbye, she reached for his arm.

"Promises you can't keep are heard by those who can. Walk not with despair."

She met his lips and touched his cheek. He left, pondering her words.

"Morning, Harvey," said Korchenko, not looking up from his writing. "I'm catching up on reports."

"Morning. You're here early. I thought I'd be here before you. Any news?"

"No and yes. The Kenora RCMP has secured a search plane from River Air, a local company that flies tourists and fishermen to and from fish camps and other remote destinations. They have been hired and will be searching for the lost Americans."

"When will they start? What's the weather up there? It's fine here. What are they waiting for?" Pittella showed his frustration, then breathed in and said, "Sorry. It's just that this has been so hard, knowing the missing men and all."

"Yes, sir. Understood, sir. Well, the only holdup, as far as I can determine, is that Kendall Johnson hasn't arrived yet. He got to Kenora yesterday evening but hasn't shown up yet at the docks where River Air float planes depart from."

"What? Why? Have you heard anything from HQ in Duluth?"

"Not so far. Other than what I just said."

"Okay. Well, we'll see what we can do from this end. Let's put up maps of the area over here. We'll call the radio stations and find out what's expected in the whole region including Lake of the Woods. Let me know if they give you any flack and I'll talk to them."

"Yes, sir," Korchenko went to a file cabinet and pulled out large, folded maps and began tacking them to the back wall of their office.

"Here, I'll do that. You call the radio stations and see what you can get regarding the weather," Pittella said, his impatience overwhelming him.

After reviewing the information from the weather experts, Pittella felt confident that the search would begin today and could continue unimpeded by weather for as long as it took. He had one positive thing at least to tell the wives. Still, he waited.

At last, the word came from Kenora that Johnson had arrived, and the first search flight was in the air. The pilot was a young man, born and raised on Lake of the Woods, and with ten years of experience, he had already assisted in two other rescues.

* * *

"I guess we're ready to go," Josh said to the dock boy. The tall Canadian pilot had finished his equipment check and was waiting for Officer Kendall Johnson from Duluth to gather his gear and get on board. "Let's get this show on the road. We've got people to find," he said in a cheery voice as if this was an everyday occurrence.

"Yeah, yeah. I'm hurrying," the older American said, huffing up the ramp.

Seated in the front seats of the float plane, they discussed their flight path, looking at the map of a small section of Lake of the Woods spread out across the instrument panel.

"The guy's cabin is on Yellow Girl Point. Before the storm, the wind was mostly out of this direction, so I'll bet anything they took off in this direction," Josh said sluffing his fingers across the map like he was getting rid of a piece of dust. "I think we should check this area first," tapping on a particular spot on the map.

"Okay. I see where you're coming from, but I used to fly back a while ago, and I think he would have angled the takeoff this way. Let's start at the outer limit of where that would be and work our way back to the area you're suggesting. That way we won't miss anything," said Johnson.

"But, I'm not sure that makes sense. I mean…"

"Yep, let's start here and work our way this way," Johnson interrupted, pointing at a different part of the map.

Josh shrugged, "You're the boss." He folded the map and started the takeoff procedure.

Hours later, Josh announced that fuel was running low, and they had to return to Kenora. Johnson lowered his binoculars and gave the okay. Half an hour later, they pulled into the dock at River Air.

Johnson went inside to use the phone and report to Duluth that they hadn't found the men. A short while later, Korchenko passed the news on to Pittella. With this meager, but hopeful, information, Pittella went to visit Elsa, then Jane, promising to return with more information the next day. The reactions were the same as before. Elsa was worried but confident that Carl would return. Jane was morose and without hope.

* * *

Carl heard the plane, jumped up, and shouted, "Irv! They're here. Get up! Wave your arms!"

The older man stayed where he was, staring at nothing.

Carl searched the sky but couldn't see a plane to even wave at. He could tell the aircraft was off to the west, not visible from their camp, and by the sound of it, it was making wide turns, moving farther away with each one. His spirits sank like a skipping stone after its final tiny bounce on the water's surface.

During Riva Ridge, when hopelessness lurked behind every word and every action, he never felt the despair others in his platoon had felt. But now he was beginning to understand why some of his fellow soldiers faltered, what they had felt. He had no wife or child at the time. Now, his life was more than his own. He leaned forward, elbows on his knees, and gasped, "Elsa!"

TUESDAY

CHAPTER 34

On Tuesday morning, as Carl was filling the tin cup in the lake, he saw a plane far to the east, too far to hear it. He waved and jumped around to no avail. It circled but moved farther east and eventually went out of sight to the north.

I've got to find something they'll see, he thought. I don't have a mirror or even anything shiny. I wish I had my red kerchief or Katy's orange blanket. Our clothes are all dull colors, even my undershirt is Army-issue green. Nothing to make a flag with. Maybe Irv's undershirt is white. But I can't do that to him, make him undress. Wait. The cooler. It's red!

Carl took some rope and the cooler to the top of the granite ledge they were camping beneath. He set the open cooler upside down over the top of a short, sturdy fir tree that stood near the edge of the cliff overlooking the water. He tied the rope through the handles and around the base of the small tree to keep it in place. The cooler tilted awkwardly but showed bright red skyward like a giant's ornament on an elf's Christmas tree.

* * *

When Pittella arrived at the Swansons' Tuesday evening, Elsa was visibly nervous, less confident, but she still didn't press Pittella for more information. She trusted him and knew that he would give her any information he had. If there was none, it wasn't his fault. But that didn't make it any easier. This time, when he left, he stepped forward and gave her a comforting fatherly hug.

"Don't worry. My gut tells me they're okay."

"I know. I appreciate your being honest with me," she responded. "Thanks for coming."

Pittella hurried to Shamrock Landing, where Skibo had been waiting. The reception at Black Duck Island was much more intense. Jane peppered him with questions, wringing her hands and holding back tears.

"Mrs. Bradley. They've only been missing for a short while. People get lost in the Northwoods all the time for much longer periods and are just fine when they're found."

No amount of consolation would calm her down. Skibo suggested that he could take the Deputy to the mainland and then come back to make her something to eat and sit with her for a while, to which she finally agreed.

When Pittella got home, Minnie was waiting for him.

"Come, sit," she said, leading him to the kitchen table. "Tell me."

"Again, there's nothing to tell. The plane went out for as long as it could without finding a trace of them. No plane. No people. No signal. Nothing."

"It's a huge area, I understand," said Minnie. "People can survive for a long time in the wilderness if they just listen to it.

It is the way of the eldest, in the face of death, to sit and wait, to ease the journey into the final night. But the young want to face it, stare it down, fight it. The young man, Carl. I think he will take care of the others. Unless he is mortally injured, he will not give in easily. What will happen tomorrow?”

“The weather seems to be holding, so that is good. No rain or storm is expected for the next few days. The search plane will go out again tomorrow. Let’s hope for the best.”

Pittella reached for her hand across the table and soaked in her warmth and her smile.

“You are like a cedar, my husband. You do not shed needles or leaves, but stay green through all seasons, giving shelter and hope to all who come beneath your boughs.”

WEDNESDAY

CHAPTER 35

The River Air pilot had put up with the American for two days. Just because he was young didn't mean he shouldn't be listened to. He went into the office at the end of the long, plank dock and knocked on his boss's door.

"Yeah, Josh. What's up?"

"That guy from Duluth is a real fat head. He's in charge, I know, but he don't know diddlysquat about our lake. I've got a strong hunch where to look and for two days, he's made us look elsewhere."

"Okay. I get it. I'm sorry it's not me flying these days, but I just can't with a bum ankle, you know. Listen, I will talk to the guy. I'll tell him you call the shots from here on out."

"Thanks, Bruce. I appreciate that. I'd best be getting in the air, then."

Josh joined the dock boy and made last-minute checks while Bruce had a talk with Johnson, who was sitting on a bench outside the office. When he completed the pre-flight check, Josh waved for Johnson to get in, and they taxied away from the dock.

"Hope you get why I have to be in charge," said Johnson after they were airborne. "It's a chain of command thing. But your boss explained that your hunches are usually right, so today it's my choice to go where you think best."

"Got it," said Josh with a side glance at the older man. "Let's go find these people."

An hour later, Josh caught a glimpse of something in the water. Maybe it was just the bright morning sun flitting across the water. Better to loop around and take a second look than miss something, he thought.

"Hey, why the tight circle back? Did you see something?" Johnson asked.

"I'm not sure. Maybe it was nothing, but..."

"Look!" Johnson exclaimed, pointing to the submerged plane's pontoons. "Man, that would be hard to see from anywhere except up here.

Josh did a second loop around closer to the water. It was apparent there were no people alive.

"Do you think anyone survived?" asked Josh.

"I don't know," Johnson responded. "But let's radio this in. This has got to be Edgar's plane."

Josh let Johnson take the mike and make the report as he continued to make larger and larger circles from the wreck.

"They're sending boats with divers now," Johnson said as he repositioned the binoculars he had been using and started searching the shoreline again.

"I'm going to head over that way," said Josh as he headed for the nearest islands to the west. "If there were survivors, I think they would have headed there. It looks like it's the closest land to where the wreck is. Of course, the plane could have drifted a long way. But still, it's worth a shot."

After a few minutes, Johnson, with binoculars pressed to his forehead, suddenly exclaimed, "Hey! I think it's Christmas!" He gestured at the upside-down ice chest hanging perched on a tall bush.

When Josh circled near the blob of red, he laughed out loud. "That's one way to get our attention!"

Johnson radioed Kenora that they had found the men as Josh buzzed closer to the campsite, where a man with a big grin on his face was waving both his arms.

Josh maneuvered the plane to an appropriate landing angle and set it down without incident. He taxied close to the shore, checking for a place to pull up on land. Carl waded into the water and grabbed the rope that Johnson threw out to him. After he moored the plane temporarily by tying it tightly against the fallen tree, Josh jumped down onto the rocks. Johnson decided to stay in the plane.

"Well, how are you doing?" Josh asked Carl when they were both on dry land. "You look like you could use a bath and a good meal."

"I just want to go home," Carl answered. "Thanks for searching for us." He gestured to follow him. "Please come with me. My friend needs help. I think you need to get him to a hospital as soon as possible."

The two men walked quickly to the campsite where Irv was still sitting, with his back against the rock wall. He barely acknowledged Josh when Carl introduced them. His face was pale and drawn, his eyes drooped, and his hands lay at his sides.

"Yeah, he looks in bad shape," Josh said. "Let's get both of you back to Kenora."

Together, they helped Irv stand, and with his arms over their shoulders, they walked him to the plane.

"I don't think we can get him in without hoisting him up on the pontoon. There's no way he can navigate walking on the downed tree. We'll all just have to get wet."

Although he protested, Irv was too weak to put up much of a fight, and it wasn't long before they had him in the passenger seat next to Josh.

"Okay, Carl you climb in on this side and take the back left."

Johnson had already climbed into the back right seat."

"I'm not going," Carl said.

"What? Why?" exclaimed Johnson.

"There are boats on the way, aren't there?"

"Yes. Oh, I get it. You don't want to go in an airplane again."

"Well, I would do that, and I really want to go home, but I need to stay until Preston's body is found. I owe that to the old man, and I might be able to help find him."

Josh spoke with the RCMP on the radio and found that the Kenora RCMP's 24-foot cruiser was on the way. It would arrive in under an hour and had a team of divers on board.

"Really. You should get going. Irv needs to be in a hospital. I'll be fine here until the boats arrive."

After a few more attempts to convince Carl to come along, Josh started the engine and backed away from shore.

After watching the float plane taxi and take off, Carl returned to the fire to dry off and warm up. He looked around at the few belongings they had subsisted with and began to pack them into his rucksack. He climbed up the ledge, retrieved the red cooler and ropes, and returned to the campsite. Exhausted, he sat down and waited, his eyes focused on the north where the rescue boats would be coming from.

When the RCMP boat came into sight, he gathered the cooler, the life jackets, and his rucksack and carried them to the shore, where he waited to be rescued.

The *Kenora*, a large wooden cruiser, set anchor offshore. Carl waved as crew members lowered a small inflatable over the side. A single RCMP officer steered toward where Carl was waiting. He waved back.

"Is that all you have that needs to come with you?" the officer asked as he approached the shore.

"Yes. I'll hand them to you so you can stay back from the rocks," Carl said as he waded to the dinghy.

"Got 'em. Here, give me your hand," the officer said, and helped Carl slip over the side of the tiny boat.

Once on board the Kenora and wrapped in an RCMP-issued blanket, Carl relayed all he knew about the position of the plane and how he had secured the body of his friend to the wing struts.

The captain and the dive crew discussed a strategy to retrieve the body, and the crew members set to work. They searched the area where the upside-down plane was thought to have been and, after an hour or so, discovered it a short distance to the east.

Once the Kenora anchored near the wreck, the divers suited up and entered the water. Carl had told them the location of the body, and it wasn't long before they surfaced and signaled they had success. Carl watched from the deck as they brought the remains of Dr. Bradley onboard and gently placed the body in a zippered body bag.

The trip to the docks in Kenora was uneventful. An ambulance and the coroner met the boat and took responsibility for the body.

Carl agreed to ride in the ambulance to the hospital and be checked out, even though he thought he was fine.

"Have a seat," said the ER doctor, pointing at the exam table. "I'll try to make this brief."

Carl sat on the padded table patiently while the doctor poked, prodded, listened, and then sat in the chair across from the table, going over all the symptoms to watch for after such trauma.

After the doctor had determined he was suffering no long-term effects from the ordeal, the RCMP officer, who had been stationed outside the hospital exam room, stopped him when he was leaving.

"The RCMP would very much appreciate it if you would accompany me to headquarters to give a statement about what has transpired since you came to Canada. I'm Peace Officer Melvin Schmidt by the way." He extended his hand in greeting. "I hear you've been through quite the ordeal."

Carl shook the young man's hand and replied, "You could say that. Do you think I could get something to eat before the statement requirement?" Carl asked.

"Yah. We can arrange for some grub for you. Do you have a preference?"

"Sure. I'd love to have a steak or pot roast or beef stew, some red meat, with vegetables and potatoes. Fish and berries were all we had there for a few days."

"Yah, sure. I'll order you something from my favorite place. Come on," said the young officer with a smile.

They walked to the Ford 4-door sedan, and Schmidt drove

to the station house. An older peace officer, wearing a name tag that said "Olaf," manned the reception desk with a cheery smile.

"Well, we are sure glad to see you in person, all hale and hearty. We've been rooting for ya, here at the station. You musta had quite a time of it over here on the Canadian side of the lake, eh?"

"I guess so," said Carl. "By the way, my middle name is Olaf. Nice to meet you." The two shook hands over the high desk.

"Same here. Alphonse is waiting for you in the back."

Schmidt led Carl through several corridors to a large room where a man in full RCMP uniform was waiting. He stood when Carl entered and extended his hand.

"Carl Swanson. Nice to meet you. I'm Detective Constable Alphonse Meyer. I know you must be tired and hungry, but we really need to deal with these formalities. Please, take a seat."

The interview had been going on for about an hour when there was a knock on the door.

"Food's here," declared Schmidt as he brought in food. The mood changed from somber to jovial in an instant. Meyer was the first to fill his plate and grab a Carling. Several other officers joined them, introducing themselves and engaging Carl with questions about his time in the woods and the rescue. The red cooler had become a major point of interest with speculation about the contents that had to have been sacrificed so it could become the 'red ornament of hope'. Carl laughed and relaxed. He relished the camaraderie and the good food, but his mind kept drifting to Elsa and Katy.

When they finished eating, the Detective Constable turned to Carl and said, "I'm sorry to ask this of you, but we need to finish your statement." He glanced around the room, and everyone quickly gathered the remnants of the meal and left.

By the time the interview was over and the statement typed up and signed, it was too late to fly to Minnesota. He would have to go home the next day. Meyer informed him that he had instructed Officer Olaf to arrange for River Air to fly him directly to Lake Vermilion. Someone would pick him up in the morning at the motel where Olaf had booked a room.

Schmidt offered to drive him, and, as they passed the reception desk on their way out, Officer Olaf stopped them to wish Carl a safe trip home.

As Schmidt and Carl left the station, Carl asked, "Do you think we could stop at the hospital to see how Irv is doing."

"Sure. That's no problem. It's on the way."

The receptionist at the hospital asked them to wait while she contacted the head of the ward where Irv was. Her head bobbed several times as she spoke with the doctor.

"No, I'm sorry. Mr. Edgar isn't able to have visitors now. He is very ill. The doctor says they will be transporting him to a hospital in the US as soon as possible."

"Thank you, miss. I appreciate your checking for us," said Schmidt.

As they walked back to the vehicle, Schmidt turned to Carl and said, "It sounded to me like they didn't want another American to die here in Canada."

"Yeah, it sounded like that to me, too," said Carl.

"Well, nothing we can do about that. Come on. Let's get you to your room. You look like you're about to fall over. The Tower Motel isn't far from here, and it's not from where I live."

"Now there's a small coincidence," said Carl.

"What's that?"

"The closest town to our cabin on Vermilion is Tower, Minnesota and there's a Tower Hotel there."

"Ya, that's a funny one, that is," replied the peace officer with a head shake.

When Carl got out at the motel, Schmidt reached across the seats and shook hands. "Take care, now. Safe travels home."

"Thanks for everything," Carl said. "If you ever find yourself on Lake Vermilion, come look us up."

When his head finally hit the pillow, for the first time in what seemed like forever, he fully closed his eyes and slept.

* * *

Korchenko was in the office early as usual, wondering when his boss would arrive, when the call came from Duluth that the missing men had been found. Korchenko immediately drove to Pittella's house and knocked loudly on the front door.

"They've been found, sir!" he declared from the stoop. Minnie opened the door as Harvey was putting on his gear. He grabbed his gun belt from the hook and, with it dangling at his side, leaned down to kiss his wife goodbye. Their eyes met in a shared expression of mutual concern, relief, and comfort. No words were needed.

Korchenko, always the silent stoic, couldn't keep from repeating the news, "They were found not more than two miles from the Edgar lodge. They were on an island. But there are only two men, sir. The report is confusing, sir."

"It's okay, Korchenko. It will all get sorted out. Maybe the third man is injured or lost in the woods. They'll find him. Let's just get back to the station and we'll hear all about it," said Pittella.

In a short time later, Pittella got the complete story. Irv Edgar's small plane had crashed in Yellow Girl Bay. Two men survived the crash. One did not. An RCMP boat was heading to the crash site. Updates would follow.

Deputy Pittella finally had the news he wanted to deliver. He had already given thought to the different ways things could have played out - everyone safe, someone hurt, or someone dead or, heaven forbid, never found - and what he would say to the bereaved family. On the spot, he decided to take Korchenko along to make the announcement of the death of one of the parties. Pittella hoped the younger officer would never have to draw upon the experience he was about to have, but he knew that wasn't realistic. People die for many reasons, mostly health-related; crime and passion create regrettable circumstances sometimes; and, once in a long while, nature takes a life. Lakes, beautiful but full of hidden peril, and the elements surrounding them posed the most dangerous threats. People go about their vacation or workdays in the northwoods and ignore how close and pervasive those threats are. Hypothermia in the winter and drowning in the summer being the most common, but those can happen at any time. Add to those direct 'natural' causes are actual natural causes exacerbated by the lack of communication systems or quick access to health providers or hospital.

"Let's lock up the office and take the boat. It'll get us out to Black Duck quicker, but we'll stop at the Swansons' first."

* * *

Elsa was finishing the breakfast dishes while Katy jumped up and down on a recumbent Bruno's back, squealing at the top of her lungs. She was unceremoniously dumped onto the braided rug when the big dog headed for the door at a sound only he could hear. Elsa opened the door for him, gathered Katy in her arms, and followed the dog down the path to the dock as the Sheriff's Chris Craft rounded the point.

"Hello, again, Big Guy," said Pittella, with an ear rub. He had tied up the bow and was waiting for Elsa to join them on the dock. It was a beautiful day with perfect puff clouds lounging on a sky of adonis butterfly blue.

"You have news?" Elsa, no words wasted, out of breath.

"Yes. Good news. Carl's okay. Let's go inside and I'll give you the details."

"No need. Is he hurt? What about the others? Where are they?"

Korchenko watched as Pittella calmed his demeanor and spoke softly to Elsa. "Are you sure you don't want to go into the house?" When she shook her head, he gestured to the bench on the dock, and she sat down, settling Katy on her lap.

"Just tell me."

"There was a plane crash. Carl and Irv swam ashore to an island and managed to tough it out until they were rescued. Preston Bradley died in the plane."

After a moment, with tears running down her face, Elsa asked, "May I come with you to tell Jane?"

"Yes, I suppose that'd be all right."

Elsa went to the boathouse door and reached inside for Katy's little red life jacket hanging on a hook.

"Can you be a big girl, Katy, and stay on the dock for a minute with Deputy Pittella while I run up to the house?"

Pittella nodded that she would be fine and proceeded to put the life jacket on the little girl, standing with her arms out, ready to put it on.

"C'mon, Bruno," she called to the dog to follow her to the cabin, where she grabbed her and Katy's jackets and locked Bruno inside.

* * *

Jane was sitting on the front porch as the four of them came up the path. She didn't greet them or even look at them. She was staring straight ahead at the trees. Pittella exchanged glances with Korchenko and Elsa. He spoke from the bottom of the steps. "Hello, Jane. Do you mind if we come up and join you? I have some news."

Jane didn't respond. Pittella climbed the stairs and moved a chair to be in front of her. Elsa sat on the bottom step where she could see both Jane and the Deputy, pulled Katy close to her on her lap, and peeled the wax paper from a Zweiback she had in her pocket to give to her daughter.

"Jane," continued Pittella. "I have to tell you that there was a plane crash when they were taking off to come home." He tried to get her to look at him, but she avoided his eyes.

"Jane, I'm so sorry to tell you, Preston didn't make it. He died in the plane crash."

"Good," Jane said and walked into the house.

Elsa hustled up the stairs and followed as Pittella went in after her. Without thinking, she handed Katy to Pittella and rushed to Jane who was walking toward the kitchen. She wrapped her arms around the older woman and mumbled her sorrowful empathy. Jane stood stoic for a minute, but Elsa's embrace finally broke through, and she began to cry.

"Let's sit for a moment, shall we?" asked Pittella, handing

~281~

Katy back to her mother.

Seated on the sofa and the side chair, Preston's empty chair became the focus of their gaze. Korchenko closed the door and stood to the side. Jane composed herself, smoothing out the imaginary wrinkles in her skirt. At last, she looked up and from one to the other.

"I'm so sorry. The waiting was just too much to bear. I hope you understand I didn't mean 'good that he's dead.' I just needed that part of my life to be over."

"Oh, dear, Jane. What will you do now?" asked Elsa, her brow showing her empathy.

"First, we have a few things to tend to," interrupted Pittella. "Are you up for this right now, Jane? Or should we come back tomorrow?"

"No. No. I'm fine and really would like to have all of this behind me. Please proceed."

"Well, I really am sorry to have to ask these things."

Jane waved a hand, staring at the wall.

"The first thing we need to do is to confirm that the deceased was, in fact, your husband. Since two friends of his were with him at the time of death, would you accept their identification of the body or would you prefer to do that yourself?"

"Of course. Who is the one to do that? Carl?" She looked at Elsa when she asked.

"Yes. Irv is hospitalized with double pneumonia and is very ill. Carl assisted in the water rescue of the body. He made an official identification at that point, but it is your right to make your own."

"I trust that young man. Look at the beautiful wife and child he has. He would never lie to them."

Pittella and Elsa exchanged glances again.

"So, of course, I'll accept his identification. I have no need to see that face again."

Elsa reached forward to console Jane, who drew back and asked, "What else?"

"The Canadian Medical Examiner would like to do an autopsy but because Preston was a US citizen, he will need your permission," said Pittella.

"No," she practically shouted. "No autopsy. Preston wouldn't have wanted that. No."

"All right. Take a breath, Jane. I know this is hard." He leaned forward and patted her hand. "The final decision we need for right now is - where do you want the body sent?"

Jane drew herself up tall in the chair and said, "Please have my husband's remains delivered to the Edgar Funeral Home on Clark Street in Chicago."

Their departure was awkward. Elsa wanted to console a person who didn't want to be consoled. The Deputy Sheriff expressed his condolences and asked if there was anything his office could do for her.

"Would you like me to call someone to stay with you?" he asked.

"No. I'll be fine. Skibo will check on me tomorrow and I'll leave then for Chicago to start arrangements for the funeral. After that I'll be back here until Labor Day. Will you need anything else of me?"

"No, m'am. I don't think so," said Pittella, standing and beckoning Elsa to leave. "Please let my office know when you return. Again, my condolences."

Elsa attempted a condolence hug but was met with a stiff,

"Thank you, Elsa. I'll be fine. Thank you for coming."

On the way back to Half Bay, Pittella reviewed what he knew with Elsa and speculated that the RCMP would facilitate Carl getting home. This is what he would do, and he assumed his Canadian counterparts would do the same.

* * *

Elsa could hear Bruno barking inside the cabin as Korchenko pulled up to the dock in Half Bay.

Hold on, Bruno. We'll be there in a minute, and your dad will be home soon.

Pittella hopped up on the dock first to help Elsa and Katy disembark the cruiser. Without thinking about it, Elsa gave him a big hug.

"Thank you!" she said.

"Get some rest, now. I'll be in touch as soon as I hear any news. Bye, sweetie!" he said, smiling at the toddler.

After Katy was fed her dinner and put to bed, Elsa could barely contain her thoughts. How was he? Was he injured? How would he get home? Train to Duluth, then to Tower? No, there's no train to Duluth from the north. And they can't possibly drive from Kenora. That would take forever. Ah. He must be flying home. So, there's an airport in Duluth. Oh, and one just opened in Hibbing. Maybe he'll fly into Hibbing! I can make his favorite...

Her brain rambled on. She finally started to relax on the sofa after a few sips of manhattan. When the sun woke her, she found she had pulled a throw over herself, and her glass was on the floor. Bruno looked up at her, chin on paws.

"He'll be home today, Bruno!" she said, then looked over at

Katy, who was still sleeping. "Wow, it must be early. The princess is still asleep."

She let Bruno out and freshened up for the day. Katy was standing at the crib rail, smiling and singing her own song, when she came out of the bathroom.

"Good morning, honey! Your daddy's coming home today," she told the little girl as she took her out of the crib.

The next few hours were agony. Waiting for Pittella to come. Waiting for some kind of instructions on where to pick Carl up. Waiting. Damn. The last week had been nothing but waiting. She was happy but angry at the same time. Where is he? The myriad of questions returned.

* * *

"I don't know how I can thank you, Josh," said Carl as the float plane took off from the narrow bay where Kenora had been built along the rocky shore of Lake of the Woods.

"No problem. First, I'm getting paid," the young River Air pilot laughed. "But more important, I told them I had to be the one to bring you home. How are you holding up?"

Carl smiled, "Couldn't be better! I actually got some sleep last night. But, hey, can't you fly any faster?" He added with a laugh. "I want to get home!"

Carl held the folded map up so Josh could see it whenever he was asked. Josh adjusted course several times. Finally, he said, "I think we're coming up on Lake Vermilion from the northwest. I hope you'll be able to recognize where you want to go."

"Can you go a little lower?" Carl asked.

"Sure. See if you can spot some landmarks."

"Yes! That's the Vermilion Dam. Keep going. I think Muskrat Narrows is right over there."

After a few minutes, Carl said, "Look. I think that's Black Duck Island. The guy who died lived there. If you head east a little, then follow the shoreline, we'll pass over the Isle of Pines bridge. Then Daisy Bay will be right there. Our cabin is on the north shore of Daisy."

Once they rounded Gruben's and the bridge, Carl pointed, "There! That white boathouse in the little bay there! That's Half Bay!"

"Ok. I got it," said Josh. "I'll take it from here."

Carl did as he was told and battled to keep his emotions in check. The last time he was in a small plane approaching a water landing, it didn't end well, and this time his family was waiting and probably watching, too.

* * *

Elsa and Katy finished lunch and had just put their bathing suits on to go for a swim. As they walked down the path to the swimming spot on the lakeshore, Elsa heard a plane. Bruno barked and ran ahead. The float plane made an east-to-west landing in Daisy Bay, then turned and made a beeline toward Half Bay.

"Come on! Let's go see who's coming," she said as she scooped Katy up in her arms and began running to the dock.

The lake was calm, and the propeller forced tiny wavelets toward the shore with wispy trails of mist blowing off each one, like angels' kisses.

Josh coached Carl on how to disembark and backed the plane as close to the dock as he could. Carl tossed the cooler with all the gear inside onto the dock as Elsa and Katy came running.

"Stay back," Carl called and leaped off the pontoon to land on the dock, too. He turned back to the plane, which had begun pulling away.

Josh taxied out of the small bay, then angled the plane so he could see the people on the dock. He waved, and they waved back. A few minutes later, they watched him take off and head back to Canada.

Carl embraced Katy and Elsa as one, never wanting to let them go. Bruno barked and ran circles around his people. Elsa pulled away and hit his chest with her fist as hard as she could.

"I am so angry with you. Don't you ever go risking your life like that again," she said, tears rolling down her cheeks.

Carl didn't respond with words, just a bigger embrace. Katy wiggled and squealed. He let them loose and held his arms out to Katy. Elsa relinquished the toddler to her daddy, and Carl took the little girl in his arms for a much gentler hug.

"Come on. Let's go inside," said Elsa, wiping her eyes with the back of her hand. "I baked you a little something while you were gone."

The Telling

1950 LAKE VERMILION

CHAPTER 36

The Tower News covered the front page with the news of Preston Bradley's death, praising the long-time summer resident's devotion to the area, and included a lengthy biographical section in a sidebar. There were several photos of Reverend Bradley: at the dedication of the library, on his boat with his friend Skibo at the helm, a close-up with his wife, and a wide view from the air of Black Duck Island. Details of the funeral, which had been held in Chicago, implied it had been attended by thousands of devoted parishioners of The People's Church, where he had been the pastor for many years.

When Elsa finished reading the article, she passed the paper to Carl. "I had no idea he was such a big deal!" she said. "I mean, I knew he was a minister, but not how big his congregation was. I just thought he was a simple, elderly man with a knack for talking in a pompous way, oh, and had a sweet lady for a wife."

Carl nodded as he glanced at the article. "He was a genuinely nice guy. He'll be missed big time in Chicago, I'll bet."

"We should try to visit Jane when she gets back. She seemed so lonely before, I can't imagine what her life will be like now that she won't have a husband or her position in the church anymore. She'll have to move out of the manse, right?"

"For sure she will. If I know anything about churches, there's a committee that's already chosen his successor, and they've already had all of her and Preston's things packed up. Churches are big business, you know. They have to keep the donation plate full, so they'll get someone else who can preach the coins right out of your pants pockets."

Elsa reached for Carl's hand, her eyes searching his face for the concern she knew he was hiding, and said, "Do you want to go into Virginia and see Irv?"

"Yeah, I guess I should do that. The one time I went right after we got back, he sure didn't look good. He could barely speak and I'm not sure he even recognized me."

"Okay, then. We'll go first thing in the morning. Katy and I can explore the park across the street."

Katy had woken from her nap and was singing to her dolly.

"Come on. Let's take Katy outside and get some fresh air."

CHAPTER 37

The next day was rainy, so they drove the car to Gruben's. Elsa picked out a few things from the grocery shelves while Carl used the phone to call the hospital to see if Irv was able to receive visitors. He was told that Irv was still quite ill and would be kept in the hospital for at least another few weeks, but that visitors were welcome on a limited basis during certain hours.

A few days later, the Swansons left Bruno to guard the cabin and drove into Virginia to the Municipal Hospital. After parking the car, Carl went up the short flight of steps into the three-story stone building. Elsa and Katy waved to him and walked across the street to Olcott Park. They wandered along the path until they found the playground, where they would wait for Carl to come and find them.

* * *

The young woman behind the large semi-circle reception desk greeted him with a pleasant smile, "May I help you, sir?"

"I'm here to visit a friend. Irv Edgar is his name," said Carl.

"Of course. I'll have someone take you to his room," she replied with an even bigger smile. She pressed a key on the intercom and requested an orderly to come to the front desk. A teenage girl in a red and white striped uniform and a crisp white cap showed Carl to Irv's room, opened the door, then quietly backed away.

Carl stood in the open doorway for a minute, looking at his friend of so many years, now lying pale and drawn, the covers up to his chin. Carl thought about leaving and was about to turn around when Irv's eyes opened.

Carl went to the bedside, pulled a chair up close, and sat down. Irv turned his head, and Carl could see recognition in his eyes. "How're you doing, Irv?"

Irv struggled to free his arms from the covers. Carl stood and helped him get them on top of the blanket. Irv grabbed his hand with both of his and gave a feeble smile, but didn't speak.

"Are you in pain?" Carl asked. "Are they treating you okay?"

A raspy breath escaped the thin lips. "Yeah. Fine and dandy." Irv's attempt at hardiness caused a prolonged coughing spell. When his breathing was under control again, he said, "How are you, Carl? How's Elsa and the little one?" Irv's eyes wandered to the ceiling and lost focus.

Carl pulled his hand from Irv's grip and pulled the chair closer. "Take it easy, Irv. I'm here. Close. I can hear you just fine. Just rest for a minute. I'm not going anywhere."

Irv's eyes closed, and his breathing slowed to almost nothing. After a few minutes, his left hand patted around the bedding looking for something. When he found Carl's hand, he squeezed with all his might.

"I'm on my way out, Carl." He turned his head to look at his old friend. "I'm tired beyond tired."

Carl returned Irv's grip and said, "I'll be here. We can talk if you want, or I can just keep you company. We can pretend we're fishing. You know, just going along the shore, watching the lake and trees and stuff. I'm too tired myself to cast, so let's just keep trolling."

Irv was silent for a while, but a thin smile crawled across his lips. "Remember the lake trout we caught up by the dam. Everyone said there weren't any lake trout in Vermilion. But we got one. It was a beaut, wasn't it?"

"I remember. You brought it home to Ruth and invited some friends over for dinner. She said she wouldn't even touch it because it was too big to fit in the oven." Carl chuckled. "But you always knew how to make things work, so you just sliced it into huge steaks, and she finally agreed to cook those. That was quite a party!"

Irv seemed to doze, then opened his eyes to a slit and coughed.

"I'm sorry Ruth can't be here with you," Carl continued. "How's she doing?"

"Talked with her doctor on the phone. She's not doing too good. Doesn't know where she is or even who she is." Irv shook his head, which caused another fit of coughing. "We had a good run. So many years." His voice faded away.

"You want to get some rest, Irv?"

"Nah. Stay for a bit. I might not be here next time you come to visit."

"Don't talk like that! We're going fishing again on Lake of the Woods. Damn, that's a beautiful place. I want you to take me up there again."

"Carl, you've been a friend for a long time, but would you think less of me if you knew some of the things I've done or had to do or shouldn't have done?" Coughs and short periods of rest punctuated the sentence.

"Hey. I'm just like you. How could I think less of you? Life hands us a bunch of problems and we do our best," Carl paused as Irv coughed. "We all just do the best we can, eh?"

Irv struggled to sit up a little, and Carl helped him get more comfortable. Irv found Carl's eyes and locked on them. "I don't know. I think there were some things that weren't my best. Things I should have said no to. But the excuses were so easy, and the times were so different. I guess I knew when the boss said to help a guy disappear, it was wrong, but it wasn't so easy to say no. And my dad and Robert and I had been helpful to the boss for so long. I didn't even think much of disappearing a guy back then. It was just what happened to some people. Like catching a fish only in reverse or something. But man, doing somebody in with anchors and ropes, that just wasn't right. It just didn't sit right. I'd do that different if I could." Irv's voice faded, and Carl could feel his hand release.

He stopped at the nurse's station as he left. "Please tell Irv that I'll be back in a day or two."

"Of course, sir," the young woman replied.

1930 LAKE VERMILION

CHAPTER 38

Antonio Martinelli had told Capone about Lake Vermilion a few years back. It piqued the boss's interest, and so he added it to the spots he liked to go when the heat was on in Chicago, as he liked to say, "for a business meeting." There were several lakes in Wisconsin with resorts that were willing to close for a week or two, providing the mob with some privacy. He owned several compounds in Wisconsin, located in towns where law enforcement was either lax or easily swayed to ignore him and his entourage. Because he didn't like to be predictable, he would vary where he went when he had to hide out for a time. He had an agreement with the Saint Paul Police, too, and would often spend time in Minnesota. Lake Vermilion was one of his favorites, and Isle of Pines Lodge was very accommodating. Martinelli, Capone's accountant, liked it when the boss chose to spend time on Lake Vermilion because he got to stay in his own home on Gold Island. He even had offered Capone to stay there once, but there wasn't enough room for all his guys, so he preferred Isle of Pines.

Robert Olds, a mid-career, certified public accountant, had worked at the accounting firm of Martinelli and Shackley for the last four years. He came to the firm with excellent credentials and recommendations. Martinelli liked Olds. He was competent, quiet, and didn't seem to mind taking orders. At first, he had questioned the creative bookkeeping that Martinelli had instructed him to do, but a raise and a new car seemed to quell the man's uneasiness. He even brought some very creative ideas to Martinelli himself. So, after three years, Olds had shown he was trustworthy and was promoted.

Over the past winter, though, Martinelli had begun to have doubts. He had noticed Olds' behavior had changed ever so slightly. He was guarded and more alert, yet distracted somehow. Martinelli, ever the realist, had had Olds followed a few random times, but not by one of Capone's men. He didn't want the boss to question his choices. If something were going on with Olds, Martinelli would be the one to tell him.

Clyde Brennan, the man he had tail Olds was an old friend from school who ran a small bookkeeping service in Evanston. Several times, when Olds unexpectedly asked for an afternoon off, Martinelli would acquiesce but ask him to finish one more task before he left, which gave Brennan time to travel to Martinelli's office building and wait for Olds to leave. Each time, Brennan reported that he had followed Olds downtown; once he lost him in the crowd on Michigan Avenue, twice he lost him in the Palmer House maze of stores and hallways on the lower level, and three times he was seen with a plain woman, dressed in dull clothes and practical shoes, obviously not a babe trying to snare a husband. They didn't appear to be romantically involved, speaking only briefly before going their separate ways. However, on two occasions Brennan observed Olds pass the woman a note of some kind, which she quickly put in her pocket.

Martinelli decided to keep closer watch on Olds himself, so he invited him to the lake under the pretext of a work deadline. Capone's network of informants had reported that the Feds were being given information about the mob's financials. Someone on the inside, someone handling money or keeping the books, was working for the government, feeding them tidbits of evidence against the organization. Martinelli realized it could be someone who didn't even work for him, but because his firm kept the official books for Capone, he suspected there was a spy hidden in his ranks. He employed twenty-seven people, twenty of whom just entered numbers into ledgers and had no idea of the scope of the mob's business. The others were trusted accountants with years of experience working for Martinelli, except Olds. He had come highly recommended, but, for the life of him, Martinelli couldn't remember by whom.

The staff on Gold Island consisted of a middle-aged couple, recruited from the Chicago area where they had relatives connected to the mob in one way or another. They were paid extremely well to live on the island. The woman, Ethel, cooked and cleaned. Her husband, Roy, maintained the property, boats, and the car, and supervised any outside help they had to hire on occasion. They lived in a small house on the far side of the boathouse.

The couple went to town for supplies and groceries once a week. They would take the runabout to Shamrock Landing, where the 1928 Essex Super Six automobile was kept. Roy would ferry family and guests to and from the marina where their cars remained parked until their return. Sometimes he would go to the station in Tower if guests were arriving by train. The couple also monitored the mail that was delivered by mailboat every day for instructions from Martinelli.

When Roy reported that the rowboat was being used at night, Martinelli realized Olds was sneaking out to meet someone. He gave Roy his binoculars and asked him to watch Olds when he took the boat out to determine where he was headed when he crossed the bay. A few days later, Roy went up to the big house to return the binoculars, telling Martinelli that Olds had headed directly for Fectos Point, then disappeared because it was too far to see. The conclusion was that Olds was going to Shamrock Landing, which wasn't visible from Gold Island, to rendezvous with someone who came by car. Martinelli told Roy to keep the binoculars and continue to monitor Olds' late-night activities to see if there was a pattern.

Olds had been allotted the study on the first floor to work while he was there. It was an interior room, but French doors with glass panes covered with sheer curtains to let in light made it pleasant, and Olds worked there comfortably. On a few occasions, when Martinelli passed the room, he noticed Olds writing notes on small pieces of paper when the ledger books were closed. One time, when Martinelli went into the room, Olds quickly covered what he had been writing.

Martinelli drew the logical conclusion – Olds was hiding something. He had never dealt with a potential spy before and wrestled with how to handle the situation. It was a difficult decision because Martinelli found Olds to be an amiable guy with a lot of potential and a very competent accountant. Still, he feared that if he didn't proactively tell the boss that Olds might be an undercover agent and the boss found out some other way, Martinelli would suffer the consequences.

Yes, he would have to inform the boss of his suspicions. "I'll do it tonight at the dinner," thought Martinelli. "He was out in the boat again last night and who knows how much information he's already given his people. It's got to be done."

That evening, Roy drove Martinelli and Olds to the Isle of Pines Resort and was told to be back to pick the two men up at midnight. The gang was already in a festive mood, having drinks out on the patio overlooking the docks.

"Hey, hey! They finally arrive!" said Capone as Martinelli and Olds came up the steps. "Now we can all go in an' mange, mange!" Some of the guys greeted Olds heartily and included him in their group as they started to file up the stairs to the lodge.

Martinelli touched Capone lightly on the arm and gestured with his head to remain behind.

"Look at that beautiful lake! That's a nice boat you got, Tony," the boss said loudly and turned to face the lake, then more quietly. "What you need, Tony?"

Martinelli leaned on the railing, looking down at the water, and told his boss about his suspicions.

"How sure are you, Tony?"

"What else could it be, boss?"

"Okay, that's all I need to know."

The two men pondered their thoughts, then Capone said, "Don't feel bad, Tony. I know you liked the guy. But business is business, and we gotta do what we gotta do. You did the right thing, Tony, to tell me. Now, remember, Olds never came up here with you. He stayed in Chicago. That's how it was. You tell your people that's how it was. He's in Chicago. We'll send him back. Okay? Ya got it?"

When Martinelli nodded, the boss said, "Go up to the lodge now and tell Irv to come see me. Tell him to bring me a cigar, that I'm enjoying the quiet out here for a bit."

1950 LAKE VERMILION

CHAPTER 39

As a last get-together before the end of the summer, Elsa and Victoria arranged for the two families to meet in Tower. Tony and Carl would join them. They would have a simple lunch at the Tower Hotel, some time at the playground for the little girls, and a final stop at the library. Victoria had several boxes of books to donate, and Elsa had several books to return. It was a jovial group that enjoyed the August sun on the small-town sidewalk as they made their way to City Hall and the library.

They had stopped at their cars to pick up the books. Carl carried the bulk of them for the older man, and Elsa brought her books in a cloth bag. Chatting and corralling the little girls, they made their way up the marble stairs and into the library, never noticing someone was in the room.

"Oh!" exclaimed Elsa. "Jane! How nice to see you!" She put her bag on the table and went close to greet the new widow. "How are you?" she asked, attempting a consoling embrace.

"I'm doing fine, thank you, Elsa." Awkwardly, Jane returned

the gesture with a stiff smile and stiffer body language.

The men set the boxes on the central table and began to unload the books across the polished dark mahogany as the ladies talked about the safe subject of books. The little girls were already playing hide-and-seek among the table legs.

"Just look at all the wonderful books that Mr. Martinelli is donating," said Elsa, picking up random books off the table.

Jane ran her hand over the array, silently reading the titles, when she saw a small book of poetry similar to one she held dear in her precious memories. She picked it up, and what she saw when she opened it to the cover plate caused a gasp to escape her lips.

She rounded the end of the table in a second and slammed the book onto Martinelli's chest. "Where did you get this?" she demanded in a screech.

"I'm not sure. Here, let me take a look at it." He turned it over in his hand and looked at Victoria. "My daughter packed the boxes. She was cleaning out the guest rooms this summer. I don't remember ever owning this. It must have belonged to a guest who left it behind."

Jane snatched the book back and attacked him with it. "You killed him! You and your lousy scum mob people. He was a good man. He was…We were…You! You! I hate you!"

Carl gently took Jane by the arms, screaming curses at the old man as she sobbed, and sat her on the nearest chair as Tony and Victoria backed away from the hysterical woman. The little girls rushed to their mothers, who gathered them close and shushed them.

Martinelli, who had been stunned by the attack, began to realize the connection. He pulled a chair close to Jane, who sobbed uncontrollably. He sat for a moment before speaking.

"Jane, please. Look at me," he implored.

Jane gained control of her breath and wiped her cheeks with the backs of her hands.

"On my mother's grave, I swear I didn't kill him," the old man said. "But I think I know what happened."

Everyone in the room was silent, staring at Martinelli.

"Robert Olds worked for me. He was a talented accountant and did good work. I trusted him. Then I started to notice he would disappear for periods of time, so I had him followed. This was in Chicago. When summer approached, I decided it would be better if I kept him nearby until he finished the big project – the shadow books we called it. He was very creative in techniques to hide large transactions. But when we got up here, he again started to disappear for periods of time, taking the small boat to meet someone across the bay," he paused. His eyes bored into Jane's with immense sorrow.

"That someone was you, wasn't it?"

"Yes," she barely whispered.

"Oh, my dear. What a tragedy! What a horrible tragedy! I am so sorry!" he cried, taking her hands in his.

"When I told the Capo I thought Robert might be passing information to someone, I assumed he sent him back to Chicago. I had no idea what really happened."

"So, you did kill him! You might not have pulled a trigger, but it was your fault!" Jane raged.

"No! I never even suggested such a thing, and I certainly didn't mean for anything to happen to him." He reached for her hand again but pulled back. He ventured a glance at his daughter, feeling her unspoken disdain.

"I am an old man. Those were different times, and I did my best in so many difficult situations. I was a young widower raising a little girl on my own, barely keeping it together. I was just doing my best. I'm so sorry." He put his head in his hands.

Jane, eyes wild, began to laugh, then cry and laugh again. "And I thought Preston was to blame. Oh, of course, I knew he couldn't do such a thing himself, but I thought he paid someone to do it. But he deserved to die anyway. I'm glad he's dead. He ruined my life. Kept me from the babies I never had. His smug pats of comfort and empty smiles and disgusting habits. He lied to me – his wife. He lied, all those years! And he never, ever saw me. I was nothing to him. He was a selfish bastard with a silver tongue. I'm glad I did it. He deserved to die."

"What do you mean 'you did it'?" asked Carl quietly.

"I poisoned him. And you helped," she spat. "I'd been dosing him slowly all summer and it wasn't working so when the fishing trip came up, I decided he didn't need to come home."

"But, why? If you didn't know about Robert yet, why?" pressed Carl.

"Remember when you came to visit us at the beginning of the summer? Katy was so sweet. I wanted to pick her up and just keep her." Her thoughts drifted for a moment. She shook her head and continued.

"After you left, I told Preston I wished we had had children. And you know what my arrogant, thoughtless husband told me? That odious bastard told me that he thought I didn't want children because I had an abortion after I was raped as a young girl. And then he proceeds to tell me that he wasn't able to father a child because he had chicken pox as an adult. He tells me this after all these years! And he knew I blamed myself for our barren marriage! The guilt I carried! The sorrow! And he never told me!" She sobbed in painful anger.

"I would have run away with Robert the minute we met, but I thought he deserved children, and I thought that I was damaged and couldn't have any. It took him so long to convince me that it didn't matter and that we could adopt. We were going to go away together at the end of that summer, and then he disappeared."

Martinelli was visibly shaken and kept repeating, "Such a tragedy. I'm so sorry."

Elsa exchanged a glance with Carl as she held Katy tighter on her lap. Carl snuck behind her and out the door to go downstairs to get the Deputy Sheriff.

When Pittella entered the room, everyone was quiet and somber. Carl had given him a quick rundown of what had happened on the way back upstairs.

"Hello, everyone. I hear we have a situation." He looked from one person to the next, pausing on each face. His demeanor added to the somberness.

Carl took a seat next to Elsa and Katy. Korchenko came in unnoticed and stood, hands crossed, blocking the door.

The room was silent, except for a toddler's soft snoring. Pittella took a seat at the head of the table.

"Jane, what have you done that you want to tell me?" he asked.

She looked up from her hands and with a face as hard and unforgiving as the granite rocks on the lake shore, said, "I killed my husband. I poisoned him and tried to make him suffer. I am glad I did. The only thing I am sorry for is that I used dear Carl here to deliver the final doses. He only thought he was helping an old man remember his medicine."

The silence of confession overwhelmed the space, unwelcome and heavy. Elsa reached for Carl's hand.

As Pittella began to stand, Jane shot her arm out, pointing at Martinelli. "He killed my Robert!"

The older man spoke firmly, addressing Pittella directly. "I admit I was there that night and that I spoke to the boss about Robert and my suspicions, which, by the way, proved to be true. He was an undercover investigator for the IRS. But I had nothing to do with his death. I thought he was being sent back to Chicago."

Pittella turned to Korchenko and, with a look, directed him to restrain Martinelli. Korchenko nodded.

"I'm afraid I'm going to have to hold you until we get this all sorted out, Mr. Martinelli."

"Please, wait. There's more. Later that year, I gave Robert's shadow ledgers to the Feds and continued to work with them to prosecute Capone. I was granted immunity for all crimes related to the Mafia. You can check."

"We definitely will do that. In the meantime, since you have family here, I won't place you in a holding cell. Please stay in this room until I come back. Carl, Elsa, you two can go. Although I'll need you to come back in the morning to make your statements."

He turned to Korchenko, "I believe we can trust the Martinellis to remain in this room for a short time. I'll need you downstairs."

"We'll stay for a bit," said Carl. Elsa nodded.

Pittella stood and crossed to Jane, who was quivering like the leaves of an aspen at the end of a storm.

"I'm sorry, Jane. I have to ask you to come with me," Pittella
said gently, taking her elbow.

CHAPTER 40

Downstairs, Pittella settled Jane into the small room designated to be an interview room. It was often used for storage but had recently been cleaned out. He sat across the small table from her and began taking notes as she talked. She didn't need prompting. She hadn't spoken her thoughts out loud for so long, she purged her life's angst on the stoic Finn. He tried his best to keep her to the pertinent facts of the murder, but soon realized she had to talk it out. He asked her to pause and left the room.

He found Korchenko at his desk, and he reviewed the situation with him. He asked him to find out as much as he could about the claim that Martinelli had immunity regarding the mob. Pittella heard Korchenko start the first phone call as he closed the door.

Stopping at the electric coffee pot, he brought two cups into the interview room. It was difficult getting Jane to start talking again, and he regretted having made the interruption. But after a few sips of coffee and a few pointed questions, she started answering Pittella's specific questions.

"Do you think I could go home for a short time? I mean just to get a change of clothes and a few personal things? I would mean a lot to me."

Pittella looked at the pitiful woman and decided to allow it. "I'll have Korchenko take you out to Black Duck. You can have a half hour to gather what you need. You'll spend the night here in our holding cell and be moved to Duluth in the morning."

Jane sat straighter and, holding the book of poetry tight to her chest, said, "Thank you. And may I keep the book?"

"Sure. It's not evidence of anything."

"Oh, but it is," she replied.

A knock at the door elicited a curt, "Enter" from Pittella. Korchenko entered and reported that he had had some luck connecting with a court supervisor in Chicago. It was confirmed that court documents indicated that Martinelli had immunity.

"Good work," said Pittella. "Now, I want you to take Mrs. Bradley out to Black Duck to get some personal things and whatever she'll need for travel. See if you can get Skibo to meet you and take you over there. It will be quicker than taking the Chris Craft."

"Yes, sir."

"And don't let her out of your sight. Stay with her. I don't want any problems with this."

"Yes, sir."

Pittella went back up to the library after Korchenko left with Jane. He brought paper and a pencil for both Victoria and Martinelli to write up their statements.

"I'm afraid I'll have to ask you two to stay and write up your statements. I'll review them and ask you some follow-up questions if necessary, so please be as specific and thorough as possible. I know you want to go home, but this is very important. Is there anything I can get for you or your little one?"

"What about charges against me?" asked Martinelli.

"Your story checked out. We verified your immunity and after you've completed your statements, you'll be free to go."

"Where's Jane?" asked Elsa.

"She's in custody, but I allowed Korchenko to take her to Black Duck to gather a few things for her travel to Duluth tomorrow. She'll stay in our holding cell tonight."

"Oh, I feel so bad for her," Elsa said.

"What do you need from us?" asked Carl.

"I want you two to come in tomorrow, the earlier the better, to write up your statements."

"Certainly. We'll be here."

Carl and Elsa gathered up their things and Katy, despite protests of wanting to play longer with her little friend.

As they went down the stairs, Elsa grabbed Carl's hand, and their eyes met in sadness.

* * *

The mailboat was tied up to the back dock by the Shamrock Marina boathouse, waiting for them when they arrived. Korchenko helped Jane onto the boat and untied the ropes. No one spoke on the short trip across to the island. Korchenko had informed Skibo of the circumstances on the phone, and it was apparent he was shocked. His long-time friend had been murdered by his timid wife, a woman he had known for years. He couldn't bring himself to look at her, and Jane returned the favor.

At Black Duck, Skibo pulled up to the dock on the back side of the island. Korchenko offered Jane his hand to help her out of the boat. When she paused at the boathouse and pushed the door open to look in, she seemed to be hesitant to move. Korchenko cleared his throat. She took the hint, backed out, pulled the door closed, and moved up the path to the house.

Once inside, she moved quickly, first to find a small satchel with leather handles, then from room to room to gather a few items, a pair of shoes, some clothes, a journal, and a few photographs, which she tucked inside the book of poetry. In the kitchen and bathroom, she gathered medicines and toiletries. Korchenko kept a close watch, even when she poured a glass of water to drink.

"I'm ready. May we stop at the garden for just a minute. It's my favorite place in the world and I'm sure I'll never see it again."

"For a minute, but it's getting close to sunset so we can't stay very long."

Jane hurried down the path toward the front of the island and went directly to the bench where she had spent so many hours. Korchenko stayed back at the entrance to the garden where he could see her, but give her a little privacy.

"It's time to go, Mrs. Bradley."

When she didn't respond, he approached and repeated his statement. He covered the distance in just a few strides but knew immediately what she had done. Her jaw was slack, and her glazed eyes looked out over the water unseeing.

"Damn."

* * *

Hours later, back at the office, the two officers sat at their side-by-side desks. Pittella could tell Jane's death was weighing on the young patrolman.

"Don't be so hard on yourself, Korchenko," Pittella said.

"She must have palmed the pills when she was in the bathroom. The medicine chest door opened, so I couldn't see inside as she picked out the various items. I should have been more careful."

"You couldn't have known what was in her head. The fact that she swallowed them and made it to the bench is proof that she was one determined woman. I want you to take the rest of the day off. Tomorrow too. It's a heavy toll seeing someone die. Even if it's not your fault, which this isn't, it's hard on a person."

CHAPTER 41

With Katy tucked in and Bruno plunked down on the braided rug, Carl and Elsa sat close together on the sofa. The lights were off, but the room was brightly lit by the moon. Elsa looked at Carl and saw the tightness of his jaw.

"It's not your fault. You really didn't do anything wrong, you know that, don't you?" she said quietly.

Carl barely nodded.

"Tell me then, why do you look so guilty?"

"I gave him those pills. I made him take them. I know I didn't know what they were, but I still feel responsible."

"Carl. Jane did that. She used you. You had no reason to suspect that nice, old lady of anything. Maybe you should be upset with her. She's the guilty one. Not you."

He nodded again. They sat together in each other's arms for a long time.

Bruno stretched and boofed quietly.

"Okay, Bruno, let's go see if the moon is as bright outside,"

Carl said to the big dog.

He gave Elsa a kiss and said, "We'll be back in minute."

After a brief stop by a bush, they went down to the dock. They stood together, the dog leaning against his person, and took in the silence. It was a noisy silence filled with the sounds of small waves lapping on the shore, trembling leaves, and buzzing mosquitoes.

A wave of emotions overtook his stoicism. All the things a person should feel, standing in his shoes after all he'd been through, washed over him – relief, gratitude, survivor's guilt, love, relived fear, and self-awareness mixed with self-acceptance. *I survived. I did the best I could. I'm okay.*

When Bruno plopped down at his feet, he realized he had been standing there for a while. The moon was shimmering on the water. A loon somewhere further down the bay called out to its mate with its melodic tremolo.

"Come on, Bruno. Let's go to bed," Carl said finally.

* * *

Pittella stopped on the walk between the garage and the house. He had been hurrying to get home, slamming the car door and rushing to get inside, but something about the brightness, almost as if it was midsummer, gave him pause. He looked up at the moon and then around at all the things so familiar to him: the yard, the oak tree they planted when they had moved in years ago, the rusty swing set, the small patch of raspberries under its netting, the house just a few feet away, so welcoming.

He was glad and tired.

The house was quiet. The light over the kitchen sink was on, signaling that Minnie had left him something to eat. He sat at the table, took the pot lid off the plate, and ate the leftovers without thinking. After putting the plate and silverware in the sink, he went to the sideboard in the dining room and poured a shot of brandy into one of the good glasses. He sat on the sofa in the dark and sipped the tongue-burning, soul-soothing elixir until he dozed off.

"Come to bed," said Minnie, taking the glass from his hand and setting it aside.

"Hmm. Yah. Okay," Pittella muttered and followed her up the stairs.

As he pulled off his socks, she asked, "What will you tell me?"

"I wish I had nothing to tell you, but I know you want to hear," said Pittella as he got in bed. He pulled himself up against the headboard and told her everything he knew about Jane and Preston.

She sat next to him, slowly plaiting and unplaiting her long hair as she listened.

"You have a wound to your soul from this tragedy, I fear. Perhaps now is the time you have been avoiding. Perhaps it is time for you to step away. You have served so long and so well. Maybe you need to be just Harvey Pittella."

He looked at her for a long time. "Maybe. I know I need to think on it seriously this time, and I promise I will. I just can't believe the depth of untruthfulness there can be in seemingly good people. Don't they bear the weight of guilt like you or I would if we'd have done any of these things? You'd think after all this time, it wouldn't surprise me."

"You are a good soul, my husband. You always see the best

in people. But so many have so much to feel guilty about. Most people, like Jane, wear their guilt hidden under a stiff cloak of shame. Some people wear their guilt like a fine, beaded tunic, proud of their despicable deeds. And some people sleep in the soft doeskin nightdress of self-forgiveness, for only there can they find rest."

Pittella reached for the bedside lamp and turned it off. He kissed Minnie on the forehead and said, "And that's what I need – rest."

CHAPTER 42

The sun was shining directly in their windshield as they drove the short distance down Main Street to City Hall. They parked in the diagonal spot in front of City Hall and went up the steps and straight back to the Deputy Sheriff's offices. The door was unlocked, and no one was in the outer room.

Pittella heard them test the door knob and called from his office, "Come on in."

Bruno beat everyone in the door and was around the desk in a hurry to greet Pittella, a hopeful eye on the lower desk drawer.

"Hey. Bruno. How's it going, big guy?"

"Good morning, Harvey," Elsa said, approaching his desk. She held out a cardamom coffee bread wrapped in wax paper and set it on his desk.

"Ooh. I'll get us some coffee," said Pittella.

He returned in a few minutes with a tray holding three cups of coffee, some napkins, and a knife. After everyone was comfortable and Katy was situated in the corner with a few toys and books, Pittella put his cup down.

"I have some news I'm sorry to tell you," he said, looking from Carl to Elsa and shaking his head.

"While on Black Duck, Jane managed to take some poison without Korchenko seeing. She died almost immediately."

Elsa gasped. "No!" Carl lowered his head.

They all sat in silence for a minute, lost in the immense tragedy.

"Well, I think maybe now is a good time to take care of the statements, if you're up to it," said Pittella.

"Of course," both Carl and Elsa answered.

Pittella brought the coffee pot and refilled their coffee cups. While they wrote, he enticed Katy to sit on his lap and draw with a few crayons he kept in his desk for his grandkids if they stopped by. He stroked her head gently once as she concentrated on her drawing, the furrowed lines on his forehead melting away like the fading ripples after a bass breaks the surface of the still water.

"Now that you're done with that task. I want to thank you for all your help. But I have some other sad news for you," Pittella said straightening the papers they'd written their statements on.

"More sad news?" asked Elsa.

"I'm sorry to tell you that Irving Edgar passed away last night."

"*Herre Gud,*" said Carl, falling back on his Swedish. Elsa reached for his hand.

"We were informed by the hospital administrator who told us he died peacefully in his sleep. Pneumonia is considered cause of death. But because he was so recently involved in a fatal incident, the Sheriff's Department will request an autopsy."

"Thank goodness Ruth won't understand any of this," said Elsa.

There was a long pause. Learning of someone's death seemed to draw heavily on the oxygen needed to converse, and for Carl it felt tantamount to drowning.

"Ummh, Deputy Pittella…"

"Carl, it's just us here, it's okay to call me Harvey?"

"Uh, all right. Harvey, I have something I have to tell you. But I want you to understand I didn't mean to keep it from you, it's just…"

"You mean something about Irv?"

"Yeah, he's a friend and he was sick when he told me this, so I took it with an ounce of salt," said Carl.

Pittella rolled his eyes. "You mean a grain of salt?"

"Yeah. That's it. The grain of salt." Carl hesitated.

"Well, what did Irv tell you?" Pittella said, more amused than irritated.

"That it was his one real regret. He was talking about this fellow whose skull we found. I mean, he knew Capone and the mob killed people because some of those people were disposed of in the cremation ovens that were part of his father's funeral home business in Chicago. He was a young buck back then." He stopped and looked down to collect his racing thoughts.

"I met him completely by accident sometime around 1927. I just happened to be in the same Swedish restaurant where his mother was waiting for him to come and celebrate her birthday with her. She was a dear old lady and reminded me of my own mother, so I talked with her.

When Irv came in, his mother introduced us, and later that

evening, he took me and my friends to a speakeasy," Carl paused.

"We've been friends ever since." Carl paused again, lost on the verdant road of memories.

"And you meant to tell me something?" asked Pittella after a minute.

"Oh, uh, yes. I need to tell you what Irv said when I visited him in the hospital. He was very upset about this one incident that he had such regrets about. It was when he was directly involved in the death of someone. And I'm pretty sure it was Robert. Jane's Robert. And I was there the night the whole thing happened. I remember it so clearly because my dear friends, Werner and Gertrude, had taken me out to celebrate my becoming a new US citizen. We went to Isle of Pines Lodge. The place was closed for a private party, but Gertrude told the maître d' we were from Chicago, and when he told Capone we were Chicago people doing some celebrating, we were allowed to stay and eat at a table near the entrance. The gang had a long table with maybe twenty guys, and that was everyone in the place, except for the band.

"I saw Martinelli sitting at the table near Capone. There were a lot of guys. Some really rough looking. And I didn't notice Irv at all until at one point I looked over there and Irv was leaning down to talk to Capone who was seated at the head of the table. Then Irv stood upright and went out the door to the kitchen. I was totally surprised to see Irv there. Actually, at the time, I convinced myself it wasn't really him."

"Did you talk with Irv that evening?"

"Nope. I don't remember the next time I saw him, and we never spoke of that evening. Neither of us had a reason to bring it up, I guess," said Carl.

"Well," said Pittella. "Are you going to tell me what Irv said about his regrets?"

"He told me he regretted the death of Robert because it was so cruel. He'd seen lots of dead people and even seen a lot of people die, but it was this death that happened on his boat while he watched that bothered him. He watched as Capone's guys gagged and chained the man up and used his own boat's anchors to weigh him down, and he watched when they threw the guy overboard, and he heard his gagged scream. It's ironic, I know, that an undertaker can be so shook up by a death, but Irv really was. He was on death's door himself, and he wanted to unburden himself of those memories from long ago."

Elsa looked at Katy, who was still preoccupied. "But why? Why did Irv let that man die? I always thought he was such a nice man with a really, creepy job."

"Those were different times, honey," said Carl. "And his father was the main person involved with the mob. He never really liked what his dad was doing but it was kind of exciting for young guys to have open access to speakeasies and be known as someone on the inside. I went with him to some swinging places back then."

Elsa gave him a crooked smile.

Pittella sat, his hand clasped on his desk. Finally, he spoke. "If he was alive, I'd probably have to arrest him as an accomplice to murder. So, in a way, I guess he had time on his side."

All of a sudden, Pittella stood as if he was going to leave the room. He was visibly agitated, but after a moment he managed to regain my composure and sat back down.

"I just decided I have some other news, too," he said. "I

really wasn't ready to talk about this, but I just realized my mind is made up, so you two are the first people I'm telling."

"What is it, Harvey?" asked Elsa, sitting forward.

"I am going to retire. I just decided September will be the end of my tenure here. I've had a really good run and now I want to enjoy my grandkids," he said, glancing at Katy.

"You two helped solve the disappearance and murder of Nathan Stark, which was the first major crime I handled as a youngster on the force, and then murder of Ike Issacson, our dear friend. And now you've helped solve these two murders. And for all that I thank you. Let's hope there's no more of this." Pittella stood again. "Now, I think, I'll see you out and go on home to tell Minnie about my decision." He seemed kind of mystified that he was verbalizing the foreign concept of retirement and that it seemed so right.

"Oh, I'm sure she's already figured out that's what's on your mind," said Elsa, as Carl scooped up Katy with little kisses and headed for the door.

Pittella just smiled as he ushered them out and locked the office door behind him.

* * *

The unintended sharp intake of breath surprised even Pittella himself. Minnie laughed as she continued to hold onto her unsuspecting husband's middle. He hadn't expected Minnie to ambush him with a bear hug when he came in the front door, but when he turned to hang up his gun belt behind the door, she had grabbed him from behind. He laughed and rotated in her grasp.

"Hello, my sweet cattail! Why are you so happy to see me?"

Pittella asked.

"I am happy because you are home," replied his normally stoic wife in a sing-song voice, almost as if she was going to break into an Ojibwe ceremonial chant.

He grabbed her hand as he broke free of her bear hug and led her to the sitting room.

"Come on. What's happened? Why are you so happy?" asked the pale Finn.

Minnie sat close to him on the sofa, her long braid loose on her shoulder, and turned her body to face him. "I am happy for the future. You have been a brave and loyal servant to this community. You are right. It is time."

"But, I just decided a few hours ago. How did you know?"

"How does *makwa* know it is time to wake from the winter and come out of the cave? Time to partake in life again. Small signs. Things the same but not. An urge to shake off the dark."

"That might be true for me. But how did you know I made the decision just a little while ago?" Pittella peered into her face closely.

"I am part of you as the night is part of the day, and the sky is part of the earth."

Their embrace was as sweet as the first, so many years ago.

CHAPTER 43

"It's so dark in here. Can we turn the power back on for a few minutes?" Elsa called from the bedroom. "Never mind. I found the flashlight."

Carl hadn't heard her because he was at the back of the cabin fastening the last of the shutters on the windows. This was the major project he undertook during the summer. The idea was simple. Plywood, cut to fit each window, slid onto the permanent bolts he had inset on the corners of the window frames and held in place with wingnuts. Carl had painted the plywood a royal blue, and against the bright yellow of the window frames, they made him think of the Swedish flag.

"What? I can't hear you?" Carl answered from the ladder as he tightened a wingnut.

He had one last window to cover - the living room window that faced the woods at the far end of the cabin. He started to fold the ladder to move it around the corner when Bruno began to growl.

"What's the matter, Bruno?" Carl asked, turning to look at what Bruno was growling at. "STAY! Bruno! Stay!" he commanded quietly. Bruno remained in place, but his growl grew louder.

A large black bear had just come around the corner of the house. It raised up on its hind legs. Its trembling nose held high to find the smell of the growling threat. Carl snapped his fingers at Bruno, who went silent and sat still. Carl didn't move, and at last the bear lowered himself and ambled away into the woods. Bruno gave a single bark of good riddance.

"Well, let's get this last one done, Bruno, before our friend comes back," said Carl.

As he was putting the ladder back in the shed and locking it, Elsa came out of the cabin carrying two small cases and all their jackets draped over her arm. Katy came right behind and shouted, "Daddy! Tebby Bear! Daddy!"

Carl hurried over to help Katy down the steps with a big swing around and a hug.

"I saw him. He was big, wasn't he! I'm so glad you were inside."

"Did you see the bear? He was looking in the window on the far wall of the living room." Elsa said, loading the cases in the back of the car.

"Yep. He was a big fella," said Carl. "I'm glad you were inside."

"Me, too," she said, as she called Bruno to hop in the back. "That's it. I think we have everything. You can check inside one more time and then lock up. I left the flashlight by the door. Come on, Katy. Let's go for a ride!"

The young day was bright, a few maple trees were turning

fall colors, their leaves shimmering in the morning sun.

"We should make it home by bedtime," said Carl, setting Katy on the front seat. She stood grabbing the steering wheel to pretend she was driving.

He went back into the cabin and came out a few minutes later. "Everything looks good. Okay, move over, honey." Elsa had Katy sit down on the pillow she had placed in the middle of the big bench seat.

Carl started the engine and sat for a minute. "Even though we seem to run into some trouble now and again, I still love it here," he said.

"I was just thinking…in a few years, we won't be able to stay this late. I mean once Katy goes to school, we'll have to shorten our time up here."

"We'll just come for however long we can. You love it here as much as I do, don't you, honey?" said Carl with a quick glance at Elsa.

"You know I do, said Elsa. "It was quite a summer. I can't help but think about Jane. I mean I feel sorry for her, but…"

"And two good friends are gone, too."

Elsa put her hand on his shoulder. Her elbow bumped Katy on the head, and she laughed and gave the little head a kiss. "Sorry, sweetie."

Elsa looked out the back window to see the gravel road to the cabin disappear around a turn. She turned to look at her husband and her child and smiled. "It doesn't get any better than this," she said to herself, as Carl drove on, thinking the same.

ABOUT THE AUTHOR

Karen Engstrom writes short stories and historical fiction. *Shadowland* is book two of a trilogy set in 1950's northern Minnesota. *The Fox*, the first in the series, was published in 2024. Her short stories have been published in *Minnesota Stories, A Collection of 20 Fiction Stories about the State We Love*; *Minnesota Not So Nice, Eighteen Tales of Bad Behavior*; *WINK Magazine*; and *The Star Tribune*.

Karen has several projects on the constantly intrusive back burner, including the translation of her father's journals from Swedish to English, an illustrated cookie cookbook, and a unique family keepsake yearless calendar.

When she's not writing, Karen spends time making handcrafted fountain pen ink for a family company, Anderillium Inks. She is a native of Illinois and currently lives in Independence, MN, with her longtime partner and their ever-napping dog.

Stay tuned for *Bear Season* coming soon!